MAYNARD ALLINGTON
THE
GREY
WOLF

WARNER BOOKS

A Warner Communications Company

WARNER BOOKS EDITION

Copyright © 1986 by Maynard Allington
All rights reserved.

Warner Books, Inc.
666 Fifth Avenue
New York, N.Y. 10103

 A Warner Communications Company

Printed in the United States of America

First Printing: August, 1986

10 9 8 7 6 5 4 3 2 1

THE DEADLY HUNT BEGINS...

The crackling of the propeller filled the cabin. The pilot opened the throttle and the monoplane shuddered, rolling down the polo field. Dark woods on either side flew past and quickly fell away. The plane banked north and the landscape, bathed in moonlight, tilted and came level again.

Ryder leaned back against his kit which contained Russian clothing, a snub-nosed pistol, and the packet of two L-pills—potassium cyanide—one for Krylov, one for himself. He wondered if they would have to be used even as the black wings of the Lysander, hanging against the silver of stars, carried them toward the answer...

There were two known assassination attempts against Stalin. But what of the undocumented attempts, the power struggles, the mass exterminations of "reactionary" enemies?

Now comes a gripping thriller based on fascinating, little-known facts—The Grey Wolf. Destined to take its place as one of the most extraordinary stories of World War II.

To Savannah

Prologue

IN the dark, under the bridge, only the wet gleam of his mackintosh showed as he stared down at the black water. He preferred it that way. Dark places served his vanity.

German incendiaries, dropped early on in the blitz, hadn't left much of his face for the surgeons. The fire storm had seared away his lips and melted one ear. Above the nub on the side of his skull was a patch where no hair grew. This he covered with a hairpiece, a poor match of inferior quality—like so many things in these early months of 1942.

Across the river lay London's East End, like a silhouette childishly cut from black paper and stretched across the distant morning. Already the man recoiled from the pink glow.

Two women in laughing conversation hurried along Victoria Embankment. Government secretaries, probably, off to a six A.M. shift. They caught him turning, and at the sight of his face their laughter died. Both girls glanced away in clumsy haste. He watched as their clicking heels and whispering voices faded, and his spoiled mouth shaped into a smile—an afterthought of pain and wry anger from a man once considered attractive to women.

But he had no time for self-pity. One arrived on time for appointments with Churchill, even those called in the middle of the night. The man set off at a brisk pace past the buildings of Parliament squatting on the left, and the clock tower of Big Ben.

At a checkpoint he showed his credentials, then descended into the labyrinth of passages below Whitehall. Damp corridors took him past the flicker of lanterns and a musty silence broken by voices that were muted and sleepy at this hour. A canister in a pneumatic tube hurtled along the wall past his head. Apart from the rushing message traffic, the dungeonlike atmosphere seemed more suited to Richard III and the War of the Roses than to the scream of Stukas and the thrust of panzers across Europe.

The war room door hung open. Absorbed in charts and papers, Churchill sat alone at the conference table. The prime minister wore his one-piece boilersuit zipped to the collar. Impossible from the rumpled appearance to tell if he had risen early or been up through the night. Now he looked up over the tops of his glasses.

"Rosewall, is it? Ready to chat?"

"I came round as soon as I got your message." The man called Rosewall stepped into the room, rank with tobacco smoke and the sweaty fatigue of men only recently adjourned. He didn't sit until the prime minister motioned him to a chair.

On the table in front of the PM lay the three personnel folders Rosewall had brought to Downing Street earlier in the week. Each was the file of a professional military officer serving in SIS, the Secret Intelligence Service, and all the men shared a common skill—fluency in the Russian language.

"I've looked over the files," Churchill said. "First-rate chaps . . . all three . . ."

"Then you've decided?"

"I should think the Canadian would be right for the job."

The PM drew one folder from the stack and opened it. The identity photo inside the jacket showed a man in his early thirties. The face was tanned, the cheeks planed into flatness, one having the barbed shape of a scar indented into it. Black hair, shaggy behind the ears, badly needed cutting. It was the sort of face, Rosewall thought, that would appeal to Churchill, if only for the pale melancholy of the eyes, which suggested a grieving Achilles.

The name typed into the square was: RYDER, Antony.

"Russian parents," Churchill said, studying the file.

"The father was a cavalry officer in the White Army. He led an effort to rescue the imperial family at Ekaterinburg. After it failed, he fled the country with his wife and son."

"Family name, Rydorov?"

"Changing it to Ryder was a concession to his new Canadian citizenship, I suppose."

"According to this," Churchill said, tapping the file, "the son went back to Russia."

"In 'thirty-three," Rosewall said. "For three years."

"As an engineer?"

"The Soviet government brought in scores of them, mostly American, to construct the industrial complexes around Stalingrad. Ryder's fluency in the language made him a natural choice."

"Where is he now?"

"Beaulieu," Rosewall replied, "on loan to Special Operations. He knows a bit about demolitions, and going up and down cliffs with ropes. He works with the Poles going through the agents' course. Most of the Poles from the East understand Russian, it seems, but not English."

"I take it," Churchill said, "he's your own pick?"

"Quite so."

"Why?"

"Actually, it has to do with his wife," Rosewall said. "British girl. Only married a fortnight when he lost her. The German raid at Coventry . . ."

The PM frowned. He stripped a new cigar and lit it. The smoke, prowling upward, pulled some deep sadness from his pouched eyes.

"Coventry," he murmured.

"One has to be practical about these things," Rosewall went on. "If the choice should come down to capture or killing himself, he won't hesitate to take the L-pill. You see, he has nothing to come back to. The others do."

The PM didn't reply, but his stare seemed to say, "What a cold devil you are, Rosewall." The fine gleam of humor above the wreathing smoke of the cigar suggested an unspoken compliment.

"I understand him." Rosewall shrugged. "His wife was caught in the fire storm. She survived in hospital for two days." His mouth made the same smile as when the two secretaries had passed him on the riverbank. "In a way, we have something in common."

"All this talk of the L-pill," Churchill said, bristling. "You seem to look upon success as a doubtful outcome."

"Failure is possible, Prime Minister."

"But the risk to His Majesty's Government?"

"The only real risk would be if our man were to be taken . . . alive."

The PM rose and went to his wall maps. For a time the stooped figure remained motionless. Then a pudgy hand reached slowly across the Ukraine, blue-veined with rivers, and came to rest as a fist on Moscow. A gesture of frustration? Or of decision?

Rosewall said, "Do we proceed with Operation Grey Wolf?"

The PM turned, the printed terrain of the Soviet north hovering above his shoulders, and his manner grew brusque.

"How can we proceed with something that doesn't exist? There is no Operation Grey Wolf."

"Yes, sir." Rosewall was standing now too. He wasn't sure what to make of this odd denial. A joke? Or was the PM pointedly trying to disengage the government from any complicity in failure? Success would always be virtuous. Only in failure lay the taint of sin.

Churchill strode back to the table, away from the whorled miles of paper terrain, the inked Urals, the green of Siberian forests. He handed Rosewall the three files.

"Better take these back to MI-6."

"Very good, sir." Rosewall interpreted this as a dismissal.

He slipped the files into his attaché case, inclined his head in a respectful farewell, and started out.

"Rosewall." The growl cut at him from behind.

The SIS officer glanced around to find the plump figure back in his chair, once again peering at him over the tops of his glasses.

"Keep me advised on Grey Wolf. . . . "

Chapter
1

ANTONY Ryder left the tube at Queensway and climbed the stairs to the street. A wind sliced out of the grey afternoon, and he turned up the collar of his coat. Long strides carried him away from Bayswater Road into a drizzle as light as spiderwebs.

The signboard of the Lion's Head Inn swung above the wet pavement, and moisture fogged the casement windows. Ryder stepped into the pub filled with warmth and voices. Timbers stretched across the ceiling to the bar, and there was a smell of cheap ale and smoke. Ordering a whiskey, Ryder looked through the crowd for Rosewall. From the corner where men in working clothes threw darts, laughter erupted. It had a hollow ring. The circuits inside him for processing laughter were dead—since Coventry.

Soldiers stood around an upright piano that was badly out of tune and sang a barracks song:

She'll be there ... she'll be there
  Near the fountain in the little village square.
She'll be wearing a pretty flower

6

She'll be yours within the hour.
But the Battery sergeant major's got your wife. . . .

The barmaid brought his whiskey. Her hands were slim and white, as his wife's had been. A feeling surged through him. Anger or sorrow? Lately he couldn't distinguish between the two.

Against the dark oak of the bar the white hands counted out change for his pound note. He had a sudden desire to touch them, but at the heart of the impulse was only some posthumous resentment that the barmaid was alive and his wife dead.

"You've got to work through your grief, Tony," someone had advised him. How long ago? Fifteen months? Some grief was unworkable. He kept his, untouched, put away, like his dead wife's clothes, which still hung in the armoire.

A curtained door separated the public bar from the lounge where gentlemen drank the same whiskey at a higher price— a concession to social rank—though there could be no class distinction among kidneys, Ryder thought. He lifted the curtain and saw Rosewall warming himself before a fire. The two men looked at each other. The firelight reflecting upward into Rosewall's face made Ryder think of the Scarecrow of Oz. He let the curtain fall back, and returned to the bar where laughing conversations and the soldiers' song ran together in fragments of decimated sound: *She'll be there . . . she'll be there . . .*

In a few minutes Rosewall came out of the lounge and squeezed through the crowd. He paused beside Ryder but gave no sign of recognition and did not even look at him. Instead he leaned toward the barmaid and asked for matches. Ryder watched him in the mirror behind the bar, his image melted and distorted on the smoked glass among the reflections of polished brass. Then it withdrew, as if it had never been there. Ryder turned in time to see him leaving the pub, the leaded panes of the front door catching the light as they closed behind him.

She'll be yours within the hour....

Ryder finished his whiskey. He paused to watch one throw of the darts, then followed the other man.

Outside, the piano sounded distant, fading in and out against the creaking iron of the signboard overhead. The two men walked toward Bayswater Road and crossed into Hyde Park, which lay deserted and sodden in the drizzle.

"How are things, Tony?" Rosewall said.

"Tell me about the job," Ryder answered.

They walked out under the trees, the black winter limbs clawing at the silent grey afternoon above their heads.

"I wonder," Rosewall said, "how much you remember about the last Tsar of Russia?"

"Nicholas? I suppose he was a tragic figure."

"Or a fool?"

"It's possible to be both."

"Did you know that as a young man he had a love affair with an actress named Anna Krylova?"

"Don't all princes have affairs with actresses?"

"This one produced a son—Maxim Nikolayevich Krylov."

"Not in the history books."

"History often omits royal indiscretions," Rosewall said. "After his marriage to Alexandra of Hesse, Nicholas settled Anna Krylova and the child in Paris."

"They're alive?"

"Only the son. He's here in London. Got out just ahead of the German occupation."

They had been walking, their heads down, the turf spongy underfoot. Now Rosewall stopped, glancing around to make sure they were alone. He stared hard through the trees at a solitary figure in an overcoat, a scarf wrapped about his lower face beneath a fedora's felt brim. The man was feeding pigeons near the statue of Peter Pan. At that distance his features were indistinct, a blank of flesh.

"A few weeks ago," Rosewall went on, "Krylov was approached by a Latvian exile. The Latvian claimed to be in contact with senior military officers in Moscow plotting a coup."

"Against Stalin? That's not the healthiest way to occupy your spare time."

"We know there are officers as high as the General Staff who believe the war is lost if Stalin keeps running the show. It's what makes the Latvian's story so damned intriguing. The generals don't trust Stalin, and Stalin doesn't trust his generals."

"He shot most of them in the purge of 'thirty-seven. That doesn't inspire fanatical loyalty."

"Neither do Party commissars who countermand orders on the front line and summarily execute commanders. Every military unit has one of Stalin's political watchdogs assigned to it. It's an unholy mess and the generals know it."

"What does it have to do with Krylov?"

"The bloody generals want him in on it."

"Restore power to the crown?" Ryder couldn't believe it.

"Not quite. A crown without power. The generals aren't stupid. They'll need something to distract attention from themselves. Monarchist sentiment is stronger than ever in the Ukraine. Krylov could be a symbol for them to rally behind. On the international side there are allies to consider. Don't you suppose a military government would be easier to swallow with a figurehead tsar in the picture?"

"But why Krylov? There are still a few Romanovs around who weren't born on the wrong side of the blanket."

"For all we know the offer might have been made and refused. Krylov may be their last resort."

"How did MI-6 get into it?"

"Krylov reported the Latvian's contact to Scotland Yard. I suppose he felt obligated—as a British guest."

The cutting edge of the wind died and a cold sun beamed through the clouds. The man tossing scraps to the pigeons had shrunk in the distance but moved in the same direction, a satellite figure among the trees.

"Awkward business," Rosewall said. "The Soviet government is our ally, however reluctant the partnership. Suddenly we come into information that suggests it could be toppled. In the long view a change of leadership would clearly be in our own interest. The question is, do we have a moral obligation to warn our ally?"

"Too bad Krylov didn't keep his mouth shut."

"Unfortunately he didn't. Nor did the Latvian chap. He got word to the generals that we know about it."

"What was Krylov's reaction?"

"Krylov." The smile on Rosewall's thin mouth took a cynical twist. "They're using him, of course. But he's willing to do it."

"Then why not look the other way?"

"That might have been possible once. Now the generals want a commitment from us. Some assurance that we won't betray them. They won't move without it."

Ryder said nothing. He had a fair idea of what was coming—in the name of King and Commonwealth.

"So we've worked a compromise." Rosewall spoke as if it were a petty detail. "When Krylov goes in, one of our own men goes with him. In effect we're giving the generals a hostage to our word. A passive commitment of sorts."

Ryder knew there must be more to it. The details given him now were only the first squirt of procaine in the gum to deaden the nerve before drilling. He said, "How can they be sure we won't cross them, anyway?"

"They can't. I expect they're gambling on the anticommunist sentiments of the British prime minister. He's made no secret of them for twenty years," Rosewall said, adding quickly, "Not that the PM is aware of this, of course."

"How high does it go—in Whitehall?"

"It might be better if we didn't speak of that, don't you agree?"

"In case something goes wrong?" Ryder smiled for the first time. "I wondered why we were meeting alone in the park."

Rosewall's head was bent. Was it embarrassment or care in choosing the right words that delayed his response?

Finally he said, "If Cleopatra's nose had been a centimeter or two shorter, all history would have changed. Pascal, I believe. Of course, he was dead right. History often swings on unlikely and absurd events. The odd combination of circumstances that make this thing possible *now* may never occur again." Rosewall stopped walking and gripped Ryder's arm. "Will you do it, Tony? Will you go in with him?"

Ryder was surprised at the other man's sudden emotion.

"Can you give me one reason why I should?"

"No," Rosewall said. "I can give you a dozen why you shouldn't."

Another cold blast of wind strafed their faces. The man scattering crumbs to the pigeons had drawn closer in the trees. Ryder frowned, trying to distinguish the features above the plaid muffler that swathed the lower face, but the distance was still too great. The man suddenly crumpled the paper bag and angled away from them.

"What is it, Tony?"

"For a moment I thought I knew him." Ryder stared at the figure shrinking on the dead grey landscape. "Chap named Philby. He was at the agents' school in Hampshire until last year."

"Kim Philby?"

"Then you know him too?"

"I've seen his file. I seem to recall shaking hands with

him once. But it couldn't be Philby. He was posted to MI-5. I saw the order myself. That whole lot is at Prae Wood, now, near St. Albans."

They were walking again and Rosewall said, "I told Krylov we might be along after a bit. Care to meet him?"

"Where?"

"He's a houseguest of Lady Waring. It might give you a chance to decide for yourself."

"Decide?"

"Whether he's a tragic figure or a fool."

Chapter
2

A butler in striped trousers and tailcoat—a species nearly extinct—admitted them to the big Mayfair home. They waited among the columns in the marbled foyer until Lady Waring came to greet them. Rosewall introduced Ryder as Mr. Brown.

"Dear Max is at bridge." Lady Waring's smile played with a mole above her thin upper lip. Her bright stare seemed to say, "Oh, another of those Mr. Browns?"

"Please don't interrupt his game," Rosewall said.

"I should think it would be breaking up at any moment. Do come into the study and I'll fetch him for you."

They followed her tall figure past a drawing room lit by crystal chandeliers, and Ryder had a glimpse of the bridge players and the man he supposed must be Krylov. Perhaps it was the beard that set him apart from the others, or the way he sat, erect in his formal clothes, staring at his cards with a certain indifference, as if he had lived most of his life in drawing rooms.

Lady Waring left them in the study, which had apparently been converted into a sitting room for Krylov. A crackling fire cast its glint against the walls. Rosewall stretched out both hands to the heat and said, "He's quite good, I understand."

"At what?"

"Bridge. He played all the international tournaments before the war. Salzburg, Geneva..."

"I can think of more useful skills."

Photographs in gilded frames lined the mantelpiece. Some were of the Romanovs. Ryder stared at one of Nicholas, before his coronation, looking a bit of an impostor in his bemedaled military uniform with epaulets and braid, and a sash crossing diagonally from right shoulder to waist—too much the sad dreamer to play soldier, much less monarch. The bearded face lacked that tiny measure of ruthlessness crucial even to benevolent sovereigns.

"My father," said a quiet voice from the door, and Ryder turned to confront a striking replica of the murdered tsar. The pale eyes had the same sensitivity rounded into the pupils, and the same sadness was worn into the edge of the smile. No wonder the generals wanted him. For a people steeped in superstition the remarkable likeness would be a clever touch of theater.

"This is our Mr. Brown," Rosewall said.

Krylov extended a hand to Ryder, who grasped and shook it. Then Krylov glanced once more at the pictures on the mantelpiece. His gaze rested on one of the young tsarevitch, Aleksei, standing with three of the royal princesses in heavy dark skirts, button-down sweaters, and winter caps. The tsarevitch wore a uniform much like his father's, medals pinned to his tunic. Under the polished bill of the garrison hat, cocked at an unsoldierly angle, the boy was grinning.

"One of the last pictures," Krylov said, "taken during their internment at Tsarkoe Selo. Aleksei was no more than twelve. Too young to die for his country."

"You seem willing enough to do it," Ryder said.

"If I could exchange places." Krylov nodded, and for Ryder the words forced the pain of another memory to the surface—the hospital near Coventry and his wife lying with her hands and face bandaged. Gauze pads covered her eyes, thick salves coated patches of charred skin, and a tube and a needle infused plasma through a punctured vein. The nurse gave him a surgical mask to wear, and he sat for hours beside her unmoving figure and thought, *If I could exchange places* . . .

"But that doesn't bring anyone back, does it?" Krylov said. "Otherwise it would be too simple. Will you drink a brandy?"

Ryder watched the tall figure pouring brandy from a decanter. The whole room was linked to the past. There were the dead Romanovs in their gilded frames, French editions of Tolstoy and Turgenev crowding a bookshelf, and drawings by Corot and Daubigny on the wall. The surroundings only reinforced Ryder's impression of Krylov as a man somehow outdated, belonging to another century. The Old World manners and worn elegance had passed out of fashion; they were impractical qualities for survival.

Over the brandy Krylov said, "I wasn't able to get much out. What I do have, Lady Waring has been good enough to keep—some clothes . . . a few books . . . the pictures. . . ."

"Better than a refugee camp," Ryder said.

"Or Ekaterinburg," the other said, nodding.

"Or Russia. Why would you want to go back?"

The firelight sparkled against the brandy glass in Krylov's hands. He stared into the flames in vacant absorption.

"I've always had a comfortable life. I suppose it's lacked only one thing." He raised his head, an odd regret on the other side of his smile. "A purpose."

"Is that so important?"

"It becomes important," Krylov said, "when you find

yourself dependent upon the hospitality of others and no longer in a position to repay it."

"Fortunes of war." Ryder shrugged.

"Still," Krylov said with a smile, "I should like to believe there's more to life than holding cards at bridge."

He rose, drawn once more to the mantelpiece and its photographs, and Ryder was surprised to see the shine of tears on the man's cheeks. Or perhaps it was only some disappointed vision of himself reflected in the glass.

"They shot them in a basement," Krylov said. "Then they poured acid over the bodies, burned them, and threw the remains down a mine shaft. I never knew my brother or sisters, and I can only remember seeing my father twice. But what sort of son or brother would I be to them if I refused to do this thing?"

"Suppose it doesn't succeed?" Ryder said.

"Then I prefer to fail *with* it than have it fail without me and wonder for the rest of my life if I had been the cause."

The fire had sunk to wavering blue petals. Krylov stirred the logs with a poker until they blazed, popping sparks against the screen. The conversation turned to Paris, before the occupation. Krylov spoke wistfully of the Paris of the Boulevard St. Germain, the parlors of counts and visiting archdukes, the shops along the Avenue de l'Opéra, the gleam of cut crystal in a private dining room at Larue's. But it was a long way from Larue's, Ryder thought, to the blood and steel of the Kremlin and the mad dreams of disillusioned men.

Krylov took a sip of brandy and went on. "It was only a short walk from our apartments to the Tuileries and the Louvre, to the Paris of Monet and Renoir. That world was more alive for me, really, than the one outside. I should prefer always to remember Paris that way—a quiet moment, full of sunlight and color, in a gallery."

"And Russia?" Ryder said.

"Russia was so long ago." A frown touched the bearded face. "I think my memory of it has rather the unreal quality of a child's dream, full of terror and beauty. I've confused that vision with the reality. I suppose," he added with a smile, "that one day I shall awake into the dream, and then I'll be dead."

When they had finished their brandy, Ryder nodded to Rosewall and they stood up. Krylov went out with them to the gloomy foyer where they put on their heavy coats and said good night.

Outside, the streets sweated in the wet drizzle falling through the early darkness. Rosewall said he would walk with Ryder to the underground station at Marble Arch.

"Well, what do you think of him?"

"Not what I expected."

"Oh, he's a splendid chap. First-rate."

"Likable too."

"Quite so," Rosewall said, "though I shouldn't get too fond of him if I were you."

"Why not?"

"You may have to kill him."

Chapter
3

I N the tube Ryder turned his face to the window as the lit platform slid away.

"If things go wrong," Rosewall had said, "you can't let him be taken alive."

The lamps of the coach were strung out above his own reflected image. He stared past their glimmer at the black distances hurtling by outside the glass.

You'll be doing him a favor.

Is that what you call a bullet in the head?

Somebody has to do it.

A nerve flinched in his cheek. His mind was locked into the roaring darkness beyond the window, which flung back a scrap of piano music and soldiers singing a barracks song:

She'll be there . . . she'll be there . . .

The voices faded in and out, the creaking hinges of a signboard filled his head, and Rosewall's monotone ran itself into an echo:

Then you'll take the job?

Then you'll take the job?

That's splendid, Tony.

That's splendid, Tony.
I knew we could count on you.
I knew we could count on you.

At Holborn Station he took the lift to the street and walked to his flat. It had the convenience of a private entrance up the back stairs and in the spring a lime tree bloomed in the narrow courtyard below his window. Now he lit the gas to drive out the chill and plugged in the electric burner for tea.

The flat was a bedroom and sitting room. Three days before his wedding he had found a larger place in the West End and put up a deposit, though the apartment would not come vacant for six weeks. His wife was a Coventry girl. They'd had a week's honeymoon in the Cotswold Hills before he'd put her on a train home. She had wanted to ship her possessions on to London so they would be on hand when it came time to change apartments.

The steamer trunk—sent off from Coventry only twenty-four hours before the German air raid—arrived after her death, and Ryder had gone down to collect it. Among the contents had been linens and laces; a vanity set with matching hand mirror, hairbrush, and musical powder box; and a stuffed dog from her childhood.

He kept the dog beside her picture on the mantelpiece. Her clothes hung in the armoire next to the bed. The vanity pieces lay in a fixed arrangement on top of the dressing table. The hairbrush still had strands of her dark hair twisted in it. She might have gone down to the chemist's or out to a bookshop. As long as her personal effects remained in the flat, he could postpone some final acknowledgment within himself that she would not be coming back.

In the bedroom he switched on the lamp and started to take off his coat but stopped short, frowning. It was like staring at a forgery, trying to uncover a flaw. Surely the position of the powder box was not right. He moved closer until the glare of the lamp confirmed it—a clean, rectangular impression in the film of dust where the box had rested before someone had picked it up.

The hand mirror, too, was half a centimeter off its own dusty margins. Clothing was still folded neatly inside the drawers, yet he was sure someone had been through them. He lifted the translucent cover of the powder box and listened to the chimes. The tune had run down past the usual six turns of the key.

The teakettle sang. He went back to it and unplugged the electric ring. The sound died, like the last peal of a siren.

He went downstairs and rapped on the door of Mrs. Burgess, who owned the house. A small dog barked, and a woman's voice said, "Hush, Adele."

The door opened partially on the stout figure of Mrs. Burgess, clad in a robe of purple satin and bedroom slippers. Her face, ringed with orange curls, formed a perfect cipher, and her undersize mouth was rouged beyond its natural borders into a misshapen heart.

One sleeve was draped back on the fat, braceleted arm that cradled Adele against a mountainous breast. Adele was a Pekingese with a crushed, truculent face. Her shiny eyes bulged as if from some exophthalmic disorder, and the row of bottom teeth gleamed pugnaciously as she snapped once more at the visitor.

Behind Mrs. Burgess, in the light from a tasseled lamp, a parrot with gray, shabby plumage clung to its perch in a wire cage.

"Bastard!" the parrot squawked in perfect cockney.

"Achille," Mrs. Burgess cried. "Mind your bloody mouth, you naughty boy!"

"Awk, awk, blimy," the bird retorted, unabashed by the reprimand.

"I've no idea where he picks up such talk," she complained. "He's usually quite droll."

Mrs. Burgess, in her youth, had been a music-hall performer and still thought of herself as a trouper, though she bore no resemblance to the svelte figure in her scrapbook of clippings. Now she cocked her head and flashed her tiny teeth in a smile, and he saw that her gums had the same purple spots of gingivitis as those of Adele.

"Mrs. Burgess," he said, watching carefully to see what her expression would do beneath its theatrics, "did you happen to notice anyone at the flat today?"

"Only the dustman," she replied, "picking up ashes."

"No one else?"

She looked at him oddly.

"And you, of course," she added.

"Me?"

Once more she cocked her head, lacking only a stage mole pasted to her cheek to be the saucy showgirl of old.

"This afternoon? About teatime? Didn't I see you come down the back stairs?"

"I wasn't here."

"No? Well, I thought it must be you. He was wearing a tweed overcoat like yours, and a tartan muffler. I assumed—"

"A hat too?" Ryder said.

"I can't recall. It was raining, and the window was fogged. I didn't actually see his face, but Adele barked. She often barks, you know, when you go up and down the stairs. I have to scold her."

"He must have gone up the stairs quietly," Ryder said, "if Adele only barked when he came down."

"I expect it must have been a visitor for you," Mrs. Burgess said, "or someone looking for an address. Now and then, since the blitz, people pop in to inquire about an address that isn't there anymore."

Adele gave another impatient growl, her eyes rounded in

bright malice. From the cage the parrot stared at him impudently.

"Yes," Ryder said. "That's probably it. Good night."

As the door closed, he heard the parrot shriek, "Bastard!"

Ryder locked his flat and walked up the street to a telephone stall. He rang up Rosewall and said, "It's Tony. I'm calling from a pay phone. Better get out to one yourself and ring me back—unless you're sure the line into your place is secure."

"Yes," Rosewall agreed in a laconic voice. "Right. Give me the number."

Waiting for the call, Ryder smoked a cigarette, cupping the red tip from view. Beyond the glass of the kiosk the deserted street gleamed wetly in the blackout. In a few minutes the phone jangled and it was Rosewall.

"I thought you ought to know," Ryder said. "Someone got into my flat today."

There was a long silence on the line.

"You're quite sure, are you, Tony?"

"About the time we were at Lady Waring's, I think."

Rosewall paused again, then asked, "Nothing missing, I suppose?"

"No."

Ryder could visualize the burned face, motionless in the dark glass of another kiosk. The melted features would support no expression whatsoever. "Is there any chance," he said, "that the operation could have been compromised?"

"I don't see how," Rosewall replied without hesitation.

Once more the connection lapsed into silence until it became like a pressure on the eardrums. The stillness itself was a racing circuitry of possibilities.

"You know, Tony, it could be a blind coincidence. Chaps go about looking for digs like yours—the sort that get left unoccupied on a regular basis. He could have spotted them weeks ago and just gotten round to the job."

From his tone he might have been someone trying to rationalize a chronic cough. *It's only a chest cold, not a cancerous lung....*

"Besides," Rosewall added, "you knew nothing about it before today. How do you explain that?"

In his mind a pair of hands shifted through his dead wife's belongings. They picked up her powder box and lifted the cover.

"And if you're wrong..." Ryder said, but he didn't have to finish.

The rain was falling again. The drops clung to the glass of the kiosk like a nervous sweat.

"Why don't you get some sleep, Tony?" Rosewall spoke matter-of-factly. "I'll try to get things cracking. Don't leave your flat again until you hear from me. I'll be in touch before noon tomorrow."

Ryder walked back to the flat in the rain. Once more the kettle sang from the electric burner.

You may have to kill him.

If Cleopatra's nose...

Somebody has to do it....

He poured the tea and stood before the mantel, staring at the photograph of the girl with the shy reserve drawn into the dove-grey eyes and conventionally pretty smile. She shared the space with the stuffed dog and one other photograph—that of his father in the uniform of a White Guard cavalry officer.

At least he had that in common with Krylov—portraits on a mantelpiece. He gazed from one to the other, and part of a tune went through his mind. It was a soldier's march, and it seemed to Ryder that it had committed him to Grey Wolf long before the operation ever existed.

Chapter
4

ANTONY Ryder was eight when his father, a former colonel in the Imperial Army, fled Russia. Stepan Ivanovich Rydorov had led a detachment of White Guard cavalry in the drive against Ekaterinburg to free the tsar, but in the forests south of the city his unit had met stiff resistance. Red forces were strung along the edge of a wood where meadows cut a wide gap in the timber, and the enemy commander had set his machine guns in a crossfire. Rydorov could not advance for twenty-four hours until horse-drawn artillery pieces were brought up. Under shelling the Red troops fell back into the wood to re-form a line.

As soon as the batteries ceased fire Rydorov led a cavalry charge, the hooves of the horses thudding heavily out of the timber and into the grass, which was still bent and wet in the morning mist. There were shouts as they overtook the enemy in the trees where the smell of cordite hung in the air from the shelling, and in the first crack of pistol and rifle fire a horse went down, spilling its rider forward as both forelegs crumbled. Rydorov, mounted on a big bay, pressed the attack into the center of the line, leaning far out in the stirrups to hack and slash at the enemy with his sword.

The Red Commander fired twice at him with a pistol, and Rydorov spurred the bay into a short gallop straight toward the other man, who stood with his legs spread, and cocked the pistol to fire again. The round peasant face with a red kerchief tied in a band around the skull showed no emotion beyond a cold, murderous purpose. Only in the last second did panic roll across the whites of his eyes as Rydorov's sword flashed down, making a whipsaw sound in the air and severing ligaments and bone at the lower juncture of his neck. When Rydorov wheeled the horse into a turn, he saw the Red Commander face down with his mouth open on the leaves and his tunic drenched in blood.

But at Ekaterinburg it was already too late. In the basement room of the Ipatiev house where the tsar and his family had been slaughtered, Rydorov stared through a film of tears at the bullet-scarred wall and the smears of blood on the floorboards. On the wall, near crude drawings of the tsarina in sexual poses with Rasputin, someone had scrawled in neat, cursive German:

> *Belsatzar ward in selbiger Nacht*
> *Von seinen Knechten umgebracht*

He recognized the verse from the poet, Heinrich Heine, and the meaning, "On the same night Belsatzar was killed by his slaves."

The longer he gazed at the somber room, the more it became for him a vision of defeat, as if the mortality of Imperial Russia were fixed inexorably now in some terrible and obscene secret here in the gloomy stillness. Even as he crossed himself he was thinking that the war was lost and that he, himself, had somehow failed history.

In Canada, Rydorov settled his family among a small

group of Russian émigrés near Edmonton. His wife had managed to bring out most of her jewelry, and they used these assets to buy a boardinghouse and livery, which would provide an income.

At fifty, the former cavalry officer was still physically powerful, and his height of six-foot-six added strikingly to his aristocratic bearing. The silver of his mustache, with its upturned tips, stood out vividly against his face, which had the look of hammered bronze, but the eyes had given over their blazing dark to an odd sadness. Too many dreams were broken on the pupils, and the debris could never be absorbed.

He taught his son to ride and to shoot the dragoon's pistol that was kept locked up. Both skills were the marks of a gentleman, he told the boy, as was honor.

"Honor requires courage," he said. "Men of honor can never be disgraced, because disgrace is a form of cowardice."

When Ryder was ten, his father took him to watch a parade. On that raw November day the city was celebrating the Armistice. Long before the first marching units appeared, Rydorov cocked his head.

"Listen, don't you hear it?" he said to his son. "Soldiers' music . . ."

The boy listened intently but could hear only the wind.

"Listen," his father said.

At last he heard it, a fragment of drums and brass torn from the distance. The music came and went and came again, flung across the far-off windy silences of the day.

Now the first ranks paraded into view, flags unfurled in blowing scraps of color. The figures drew nearer and became men in faded wool uniforms, their lower legs bound in puttees and linked in motion to the beat of the drum and the blast of trumpet tunes.

His father stood, erect and rigid, while the formation of

veterans marched through his stare, each banner streaming like the flicker of a match on the dark pupils and going out on that vast emptiness that reached, in the passing moment of soldiers' music, across the steppes and beyond Moscow to the forests of Ekaterinburg.

That evening, after supper, his father seemed withdrawn and uncommunicative. The boy approached him at the lamp-lit table and said, "Are you still listening for it?"

His father, not understanding, gave him a questioning look.

"The soldiers' music," the son explained.

The nod from the creased face was barely perceptible, the eyes glazed over with some impossibly sad emotion. His father did not reply, but instead reached out and laid a hand on his head.

That night, after he was in bed, Antony Ryder heard the creak of the livery door on its iron hinges. Half asleep, he couldn't be sure of the sound that followed on the windy darkness. It might have been only a horse's hooves thudding into a boy's dream.

The police were at the boardinghouse when he came home from school the next day. His mother was weeping, her face buried in her hands. During the night his father had taken the dragoon's pistol and a horse, ridden out into the woods, and shot himself.

It was outside London, on his return in 1936 from the USSR, that he had first met Graham Rosewall. The twin-engined transport, flying out of Le Bourget, had landed at Croydon as an autumn dusk settled over the country. Ryder had stood in line in the terminal waiting for a customs inspection.

Antony Ryder was then twenty-five, just topping six feet and solidly built. The thick wrists and sturdy neck suggested an inert force, ready for use, like a wrecking machine deliberately constructed to take punishment. His olive skin was uncreased, his hair tar-black, and the smile fit loosely onto his heavy mouth as if he were always on the verge of some wry discovery. But behind that smile lay a solitary nature, a private landscape that no one entered and where he kept a few possessions—the touch of a hand, a pistol shot, a windy fragment of soldiers' music.

He had expected to pass routinely through customs. Instead he had been led upstairs to one of the airdrome offices where a lanky figure, in loose-fitting tweeds, sat with his long legs crossed. Under a sandy pompadour the neatly crafted features glowed with a ruddy vitality, the mouth rather handsome in its accumulated arrogance. The long lips had a touch of Etonian scorn for all things inferior, but they wore their smile like a prosthesis of charm to cover some cold lack of feeling. He glanced only briefly at Ryder's passport and inquired how long he would be in London.

"Two weeks."

"Sailing home to Canada?"

"If I can get through British customs."

"Have you a job waiting? Any firm plans?"

Ryder met the inquisitorial stare with a flat gaze of his own and said, "Are you a customs officer?"

"Not exactly. I belong to the military."

"You're not in uniform."

"I'm afraid I'm one of those secret types. I do intelligence work. We're supposed to be inconspicuous in mufti. It's deadly dull, by the way, not at all like the spy stories. Have you a hotel?"

"I've booked bed and breakfast in Russell Square."

"Let me take you along, then. I've a motorcar outside. Incidentally, my name's Rosewall."

Ryder glanced over his shoulder at the uniformed man who had escorted him upstairs from customs.

"Am I in some sort of official custody?"

Rosewall tipped back his head and laughed. "Nothing of the sort. I thought we might have a spot of lunch one day. I should very much like to hear about your stay in the USSR...."

At the restaurant in Soho where they dined the next afternoon, Rosewall had an eye for the women. During the conversation his gaze would stray to a passing pair of ankles or linger on the curve of a breast. All the while he spoke with an indifferent conviction about other matters.

"There's another war coming to Europe. This business in Spain is only the start. Mark you, Britain will be into it, and Canada as well. What will you do then?"

Ryder shrugged and said, "Will anyone have a choice?"

"Quite so. You'll be called up. They'll look at your background. At that point you may well find yourself on loan to British Intelligence. In fact, I can almost guarantee it."

Without the smile, Ryder thought, the features lost their mocking humor and had only a vicious purpose. A waiter came up bearing the entrée and cleared away the soup bowls.

"On the other hand," Rosewall said, using his knife to scrape peas onto his fork, "if you were to come aboard now ... You said yourself that you hadn't any firm plans."

"Except one," Ryder said. "I'm sailing for Montreal next week."

"Yes, of course you are," Rosewall said.

Two evenings later, at a pub in Bloomsbury, the subject came up again. They were in a private booth, and Ryder lowered his glass of ale and said, "You're not serious?"

"You're amused," the intelligence officer replied.

"Is this the way you people recruit to the ranks? You don't know anything about me."

Rosewall leaned back against the partition of darkly gleaming wood. He stared at Ryder, and his fingers tapped the table. He might have been contemplating the choice of a particular card in a game of gin.

"Anton Stepanovich Rydorov," he said. "Born, Kiev, 1911. Engineering degree, University of Edmonton. Your only sport, it seems, was mountain climbing. You preferred solo climbs. I understand that some of them were quite difficult. Tell me something. When you're three hundred meters up the granite face of a cliff, what happens if you lose your nerve?"

Ryder put a match to a cigarette and said, "You fall off."

"Why risk it in the first place?"

"Why not risk it?" Ryder smiled through the cigarette's wreathing smoke.

"I can think of several reasons, but they hardly matter, since I don't propose to try it. After college you joined a construction firm in Montreal. Six months later you signed a three-year contract to act as an engineering consultant for the Soviet government. Your father was a cavalry officer in the Imperial Army. He fought for the White cause after the Bolsheviks seized power. If he had one fault, I should think it was that he loved his country too much and couldn't accept the reality of defeat. In the end he dealt with it the only way that a soldier could deal with it—that is to say, an officer from the old school where honor meant something. You admired your father very much. I don't doubt for a moment that's what drew you back to Russia. You were looking for some sort of justification, perhaps even an explanation. . . . " Rosewall hesitated, gazing across the table at him for a full moment. "Did you find it?"

"Isn't that in your files too?" Ryder said.

"No," Rosewall said.

Someone had dropped a coin into the mechanical piano. Behind the cloudy glass the perforated scroll turned on its spindle, and the tinny sound of a dance tune rose above other voices. A few patrons gathered round the instrument and sang the words to the tune.

Roll out the bar-rel
We'll have a bar-rel of fun

"That's the problem," Rosewall went on. "Your file doesn't tell me anything. A chronology of events, that's all it is. I don't really know much about you at all. Nobody does. I find that rather curious. . . ."

"How?"

"Because most people leave clues behind in their relationships with other people. You appear to have had no relationships. Would it interest you to know that most of your instructors at university didn't remember you?"

"It wouldn't matter to me one way or the other."

"What does matter to you?"

"Nothing in particular."

"I rather imagined you were a bit young to be that cynical."

"It's not cynicism."

"Then what would you call it?"

"I wouldn't call it anything."

Rosewall was still leaning back against the partition and looking at him. Enough of a smile lingered on the Englishman's mouth to spoil the arrogance.

"Tell me something," he said. "When you were climbing those big bloody rocks, why did you do it by yourself?"

"I preferred to."

"That's not a very illuminating answer."

Ryder pulled the cigarette slowly from his mouth and smiled.

"Would you like to know what the appeal is? It's when you're halfway up a vertical face and the trees dangling below you suddenly have the look of a toy landscape, and it hits you that there's no way out. You're locked into the contest. Either you beat the cliff or it beats you. It's the closest you can get to death and not die. Or maybe die, anyhow, if you come off the rock, and then you take the big fall. It's quick, only a few seconds, and clean as a bullet...."

"Do you think much about dying?" Rosewall asked.

Ryder shrugged and said, "Everybody carries one free ticket."

Roll out the bar-rel
We've got the blues on the run

Rosewall said matter-of-factly, "There's a job coming up in Spain. It needs a combat engineer. Someone with first-rate climbing skills like yours and a knowledge of demolitions."

"I don't know anything about demolitions."

"We'll see you get the training. Nothing much to it, really. Question of setting off a charge properly. Have you ever been to Spain, Tony? Those Andalusian women—with flowers in their hair..."

Roll out the bar-rel...

"I should think we'd pack you off to one of the International Brigades—the Fifteenth, most probably. You see, the Soviet government has quite a large force in Spain. We're anxious to develop more information about it. With your background you shouldn't have any trouble making Russian contacts. A bit of talk here—a bit there. That's how it works."

He might have been pledging Ryder for membership in some exclusive club. An evening of cocktails at his Kensington flat brought out several pretty secretaries from MI-6 to be dangled like hidden incentives among a somewhat bland group of men distinguished from each other only by their school ties.

"One needn't lack for a social life, you know," he told Ryder, and his gaze settled on a blond girl who stood pressing an empty cocktail glass against an indecent cleavage, as if the chasm of white flesh would draw attention to her neglect. *I say, Bunny, come over here, will you? Here's a Canadian chap I want you to meet.*

But it was a dark-haired girl, too frail and thin to be part of the menagerie, who caught his attention. She stood in a loose circle of guests, holding her glass with a paper napkin wrapped around it, and only pretended to drink. The color never altogether left her cheeks, the dove-grey eyes were frequently downcast, and he saw that she would force herself to glance up through each attack of shyness when someone spoke directly to her. Even the smile on her pale mouth was full of shy reserve, as if it would dart away in alarm at the first pretext.

"Waste of time, Tony," Rosewall had said. "She's a vicar's daughter from Coventry. Properly virtuous, I'm afraid."

But he had ridden with her in the taxi to her brownstone apartment and kissed her good night at the entrance where the lamp was burned out, and her lips were tight together and inexperienced. They pressed back against his with the intensity and awkward passion of a first kiss, and afterward he watched the flash of her legs as she disappeared into the alcove.

At the end of the week he did not sail for Montreal. He could remember, instead, walking with Rosewall past the Albert Memorial and stopping in the trees near the canopied, open pavilion where a regimental band was performing. He had listened to the cymbals and brass and the beat of the drums, even as the sound had disengaged from the moment and slipped across the years where a windy fragment of soldiers' music played in a boy's mind, and Rosewall's voice had reached him there: *Then you'll take the job? That's splendid, Tony. I knew we could count on you. . . .*

Chapter
5

"I'LL be in touch before noon tomorrow," Rosewall had said from the telephone kiosk, but it was nearly three P.M. before an envelope arrived by messenger. The handwritten note contained only a number to call, and a specific time that evening when contact could be made. Darkness had settled over the district when Ryder walked to the toll phone and dialed the number. After two rings Rosewall answered. This time the conversation was brief.

"No discussions with anyone, Tony. We can't risk a leak. As far as Beaulieu is concerned, you've taken ill and gone into hospital and probably won't be coming back. By the way, I've put your flat under surveillance—on the off chance that the chap who got into it may turn up again."

"When will Krylov and I be going out?"

"The arrangements are under way. I should think we'll have something more definite for you by midweek. Don't expect to hear from me until then."

There was nothing to do but wait. To break the monotony he took walks in the park, read the papers, and listened to the news on the wireless. On the eastern front the Russian winter, not the Red Army, had stopped the German advance. In the *Daily Mail* he read that Stalin would soon mount a massive spring offensive. Did anyone believe it? Reality had to be rationed like cigarettes and butter while the people queued up for promises.

Seventy-two hours passed before he heard from Rosewall. A message came to meet him at one of the docks in London's East End, and Ryder arrived at the appointed time. It was noon of an overcast day, and Rosewall was not there. Ryder went down onto the quay past a stall selling fish and chips wrapped in newspaper. Chips were rare these days, with no lard for frying. The crisp aroma, mingled with the scent of vinegar, was oddly reassuring.

Workmen cleared rubble from a warehouse, gutted months ago in the blitz. Barriers were still thrown up around a hole where part of the dock had been blown away. Ryder smoked a cigarette and watched a tug sliding in on the current toward the wharf. Only a little froth bubbled up from the screws at slow speed. The boat drifted in until the tires lashed to the side bumped against the pier. The crew of two secured the lines. The pilot came on deck wearing a turtleneck sweater under his sea jacket. All three left the tug and walked past Ryder to the fish-and-chips stall.

He saw another figure moving inside the cockpit, and Rosewall appeared. The spoiled face once again made Ryder think of the Scarecrow of Oz. Was it a heart or a brain the Scarecrow lacked? In Rosewall's case it would most likely be the heart. Ryder frowned. It struck him that the other man had gone to considerable lengths to keep their meeting private. A concession to security? Or did someone in Whitehall want no witnesses to the operation, not even from MI-6?

Ryder went to the boat and climbed aboard. Rosewall was squinting across the quay at the pilot and crew. They had taken their fish and chips over to an empty fifty-gallon drum where a fire of scrap wood crackled.

"Fish and chips," Rosewall murmured with a fine edge of resentment. "Where do they pinch the lard, I wonder?"

"From America, probably. Everything comes from America these days, doesn't it?"

They moved into the cockpit and stood at the window by the wheel.

"You'll be going out day after tomorrow to a holding area," Rosewall said, "for orientation."

"Where?"

"Wiltshire."

"Krylov too?"

Rosewall nodded.

Ryder said, "For how long?"

"Not long, I should think."

"Then what?"

"You'll both be flown to Scotland. There's a PQ convoy forming off the Scapa Flow for Murmansk. We'll put you aboard one of the escort ships."

"Can you tell me any more about the job?"

"I'm afraid I can't give you any specifics, Tony. Not until you're at the holding area."

"Then what's the point of our meeting?"

"I thought you might want to talk about things." Rosewall looked at him. "One last time—before you and Krylov are together."

"About making sure he isn't taken alive? I expect he might consider that an indelicate topic."

"Your first priority is to protect him. In a tight spot he's the amateur. He'll need looking after."

"You don't really think the generals can pull this thing off, do you?"

"Let's suppose they fail. You still have an option, assuming the opportunity is there, of getting Krylov and yourself out."

"And if the opportunity isn't there?"

Rosewall's shrug was a masterpiece of understatement. "Then you're facing the unpleasantness we talked about before."

"We only talked about Krylov."

"I shouldn't think you'd want to be questioned by them," the other replied, skirting a direct answer neatly. "Lubyanka prison is a nasty place, I'm told. You'll carry the usual L-pill, of course."

Downriver, under the steel arms of the loading cranes, cargo ships lined the docks. The port swarmed with activity clear to the estuary, horns blared over the water, and the screeching of gulls pierced the air. A tugboat chugged upriver towing a coal barge, heavy in the water.

"Lubyanka," Ryder said. "That's a long way from Oxford Circus. How will you explain a pair of corpses so far from home?"

"You were acting on your own. Didn't your father serve in the Imperial Army? Didn't he try to rescue the tsar at Ekaterinburg? Why shouldn't you have inherited some of his monarchist sentiment?"

The smile on Ryder's mouth was hardly more than a shadow. The explanation erased any doubt as to why they were meeting alone and not in the headquarters of MI-6 off St. James Street. There would be no incriminating files— no memoranda—kept anywhere on Operation Grey Wolf. It would simply be a code name in the archives for a mission that never existed.

"And Krylov?" he said.

"Don't you imagine he would have acted on his own even if he hadn't come to us in the beginning? No, his motives are real enough. He's a bloody idealist. We'll only be telling the truth."

The waves from the passing barge slid toward them and splashed against the hull. On the cockpit windows, like a framed picture, the port rocked gently.

"We're using Krylov as much as they are," Ryder said.

Rosewall looked at him sharply, but his tone held on to its quiet calm.

"Why do you say that, Tony?"

"Because someone in His Majesty's Government obviously wants the generals to succeed—wants it badly enough to keep silent to Moscow. Krylov is the ante into the game, and I'm here to cover the bet. Isn't that how it works?"

Once more Rosewall dodged a reply.

"Idealists were meant to be used," he said.

"And thrown away after they serve a purpose?"

Rosewall picked up on the word.

"If that serves a purpose too," he replied.

Near the fish-and-chips stall, one of the tugboat crew tossed a morsel to the sea gulls who waited nearby, on the ground, like patient scavengers. A bird snatched it and rose. Others followed, shrieking.

"Is there anything you need taken care of, Tony?"

"No."

"We'll send a motorcar for you Sunday. I still believe that this business of someone getting into your digs was a bloody coincidence. But on the remote chance that you're being watched, you'd better use the tube to shake them. I'll have the car waiting for you after fifteen hundred hours at the West Ruislip station."

"All right."

The two men wandered out of the cockpit to the gunwale, and Rosewall, with a troubled frown, said, "By the way, Tony, I shouldn't speculate too deeply about things. . . . "

Ryder returned his gaze with an oddly blank expression. "I was only taking the measure," he said, "of Cleopatra's nose."

The pilot and crew sauntered back along the quay, keeping their distance. Ryder left the boat and angled away from them. He had a last glimpse of Rosewall standing aft of the cockpit, watching him. The dark figure lifted a hand—almost like a priest's blessing from the man with no heart.

Chapter
6

O N Sunday the motorcar was waiting when Ryder
climbed the stairs from the underground station to
the street. They drove out in the rain to an estate
near Ashton Keynes. The wet country drifted in and out of
low black clouds, and the driver finally turned down a
muddy road past a stone wall lined with elms. A cottage
took shape beneath the gusting rain. Smoke streamed from
the chimney above a thatched roof, and a little yellow light
glowed on the fogged panes of the casement windows.

The cottage had been the servants' quarters for the manor.
Probably the gamekeeper had occupied it, for the kennels
and stable were not far off, squatting in the downpour.

Ryder spent two days with Krylov in the cottage. In the
mornings a lance corporal came up from the stable to shovel
ashes from the fireplace and build a coal fire. The smell of
coal dust hung in the air, and later the fire threw its glint
across the pockmarked face of the intelligence officer assigned to brief them. The officer charted German positions
from the Barents Sea along a two-thousand-mile front to
the Crimea. He spoke in detail about Soviet troop concen-

trations from Demyansk, north of Moscow, to Belev in the south, and of conditions in the Russian capital. There were shortages of food and fuel, identity documents were now frequently checked, and the NKVD had stepped up its activity in the city. For all the in-depth coverage, it was clear to Ryder after one or two questions that the officer had no inkling of their mission.

By Tuesday the weather had cleared. After the noon meal they went outside to stretch their legs. Behind the cottage the land lunged toward a marbled sky. They climbed to the top of the rise and saw the Victorian manor house lifting out of the trees on the other side. The half dozen chimneys soared above the roof, a breeze blew, and a weak sun dappled the countryside.

"I would like to remember it this way," Krylov said.

"We'll have a Russian spring," Ryder said, "not an English one."

They tramped downhill past the stables and cut across the open field into a beech wood. Dead leaves covered the ground. A lark sang from a hedgerow. They walked out onto a stone footbridge over a brook and looked down at the clear water with its pale spring images.

Krylov said, "Do you think it can succeed?"

"They wouldn't try it," Ryder said, "if there weren't a chance."

He said it without believing it. Desperate men would always act recklessly. They could not distinguish between foolish hope and real possibilities.

"They'll have to kill Stalin," Krylov said.

"Caesar, beware the ides of March," Ryder said with a shrug.

Krylov snapped a dry twig and let the pieces fall into the brook. "Shall I tell you something?" he said with a reflective smile. "All my life I've wanted to be part of some noble undertaking. To find out if my having lived or died would make one bit of difference. To face some great test and see if I had the courage to meet it or not. You know, they are questions I've never been able to answer."

"If the generals fail, the answer won't matter."

"Remember Bazarov's speech?" Krylov smiled again. "Death's an old joke, but it comes fresh to everyone. . . ."

"Turgenev?"

"*Fathers and Sons*," Krylov said, nodding. "But I think we're both the sons of our fathers, you and I, in a special way. They told me about the failed rescue at Ekaterinburg. Your father tried to save mine. Now, look! Our own lives seem to be crossing under the same circumstances." He paused, and the cry of the lark fell again across the pleasant sound of the brook. "I should like you to be my friend."

Ryder had a match cupped to a cigarette. The crisp air pulled the smoke away like a fluff of magician's silk that hid a darker truth.

"Time enough for friendship when it's over," he said, following the plume of smoke with his gaze. But he was thinking that, no, it was not like Ekaterinburg. It was not like Ekaterinburg at all.

Rosewall drove out from London that afternoon with sealed orders.

"Not to be opened," he said, "until you're aboard the escort vessel. Commit the contents to memory and destroy the packet. It gives you your contact in Murmansk."

"What else?" Ryder said.

"If the generals should fail and you lose contact with the insurgent apparatus, there's not much we can do to pull you out. You're to stay together, of course." Rosewall's bright gaze held Ryder's a moment longer than necessary. "Your best chance would be to work north to Archangel on the White Sea. We've alerted the senior British naval officer at

Norway House. If you should need help, the SBNO has standing orders to give Operation Grey Wolf top priority."

"What about our cover?"

"You'll be given that by the Russians. Once we've put you into Murmansk, you're in their hands. We can't very well rehearse you for an operation we don't control and know precious little about."

They were standing outside in the drive where the low, uneven wall of Cotswold stone ran out under the elms next to the road.

Ryder said, "I suppose you could do with a spot of tea."

"I jolly well could, thank you very much," Rosewall answered.

They walked toward the house beneath the late-afternoon shadows that were flexed across the drive.

"By the way, Tony, remember that chap you thought you recognized that day in the park? The one you knew from agents' school?"

"Kim Philby, you mean?"

"Yes. Philby. I was up to St. Albans yesterday. Some business with MI-5. Damned if I didn't run into him at a cricket match on the green."

"Batting sober, I hope?"

"I expect they'd all had a pint or two. How well did you know him?"

"Only to nod hello. Why?"

"Because he inquired about you."

"Coincidence," Ryder said.

"Yes," Rosewall said with a slight frown. "That's what I thought too."

Just after dark they heard the drone of an aircraft, and then the distant sputter of its engine as it touched down.

They loaded their kits into the boot of the motorcar that had brought Rosewall from London and drove down the road in the dark. The driver stopped in front of the manor house and left the motor running while Rosewall went in to the operations room of the Special Duties Squadron. He came out, and the car turned down an overgrown lane along a hedgerow that led to a polo field.

The plane waited beside a refueling truck at the edge of the cropped turf. It was a high-wing single-engine Lysander with a fixed undercarriage. The wing struts angled down against the cabin, which looked to Ryder as if it would be cramped and noisy. Painted black, the aircraft had no markings.

"Good luck, Tony," Rosewall said. "We'll have a drink at the Lion's Head when you're back."

From the cabin of the Lysander, Ryder had a last glimpse of Rosewall standing, hands in his pockets, the collar of his overcoat turned up. The lower half of his face had the look of wax that had tracked down a candle and hardened again.

The crackling of the propeller filled the cabin. The pilot opened the throttle, and the monoplane shuddered, rolling down the polo field. Dark woods on either side flew past and quickly fell away. The plane banked north, and the landscape, bathed in moonlight, tilted and came level again.

Ryder leaned back against his kit, which contained Russian clothing, a snub-nosed pistol, and the packet of two L-pills—potassium cyanide—one for Krylov, one for himself. He wondered if they would have to be used even as the black wings of the Lysander, hanging against the silver of the stars, carried them toward the answer.

Chapter
7

IN Moscow, two weeks later, Lieutenant Colonel Valery Vasilyevich Balov left his office above Dzerzhinsky Square and went down to a waiting limousine. The boulevard, black under an icy crust, trailed away in the rear glass as the driver put the car into motion.

En route to the Kremlin, the NKVD officer opened a file containing an intelligence report, notes, and a photograph. It was a photograph of Antony Ryder taken on a windy day on Mamayev Hill in Stalingrad, the city spreading out to the horizon behind him.

How long ago? Seven years? The Canadian was one of half a dozen foreign engineers for whom Balov, then a case officer for State Security, had been assigned surveillance. Balov's own cover as a Soviet engineer had given him a legitimate access to their activities. In Ryder's case a friendship had been easy to develop. The two were not far apart in age, and Ryder was fluent in the language. Both men were quartered in the same apartment building in the sprawling workers' complex south of the factory site.

Balov had a clear recollection of the park across the street, with its shade trees and stone fountain. On warm evenings in summer the two had played chess at a lighted table under the leaves, and he could remember the Canadian studying his moves behind the slow plume of cigarette smoke rising past the concentration on his tanned face. The park lamp had shone up against the undersides of the leaves, the fountain had misted the air, and sometimes young people had danced to an accordion.

At the center of a garden, where flowers were planted in the shape of a red star, an oversize sculpture of Lenin petting two stone lions loomed on a pedestal. Lenin the visionary— guarding his revolution, perhaps—though no one could assert positively what the monument signified.

"Anton Stepanovich," Balov had said, "can you guess the meaning of the lions?"

The Canadian had remained silent, staring up at the immense mane carved across the blazing astronomy of the night as if the notched stone would conceal its riddle among the secrets of the universe.

"I only know what Achilles said," he had answered finally. "That between men and lions there can be no covenant."

"What do you think he meant?"

"He was talking about the death of an enemy," the other man had replied, turning his gaze from the monument. "Maybe it's better if the lions have no meaning."

"Good," Balov had said with a grin. "Let them walk across the stars with Lenin."

At that time there had been no reason to suspect that Antony Ryder had any ties to the British Secret Intelligence Service. Probably the first contact had taken place after his return home. A Russian-speaking engineer, back from three years in the Soviet Union, would have been an irresistible target for recruitment.

The NKVD officer settled back in the sedan. At thirty-five, his blond good looks were starting to go, but this did not diminish the excess of vitality or restless intelligence in the face. The columns of muscle sloping down from the oversized neck exaggerated the impression of latent power concentrated into his six-foot five-inch frame. For all of his great size he remained still narrow at the waist and well proportioned.

He gave the photograph of Antony Ryder another glance that mixed relief and regret—relief at this positive identification of the British agent assigned to Operation Grey Wolf, and regret that events must now break a friendship formed so long ago and make them adversaries. It seemed, almost, to follow the pattern of all friendships in his life, though he was not a man easily given to regret.

Red Square flowed past the window as the sedan slowed for the checkpoint at Spassky Gate. Then, in low gear, the car ground slowly down a narrow lane of the Kremlin among the churches and chapels and palaces of the past.

A short while later an aide led Balov into the office of General N. S. Vlasik, chief of Stalin's personal guard force of some four hundred men. Without looking up from his desk the general waved the aide from the room. Photographs of Lenin and Stalin on the wall seemed out of place in the imperial setting of gilded cornices and the spaciously high ceiling. So did Vlasik, whose face was all brows and flat Slavic planes where each pore in the rough skin stood out prominently.

"Well, Balov, I don't have much time. What is it you want?"

"Your advice, Comrade General—on an important matter." Balov remained standing.

"Everything is important these days."

"Which is why the wisdom of a few experienced people, like yourself, is so valuable."

"Well, all right, then." Vlasik's manner lost its sharp

edge. He glanced up but did not set his papers aside. "Let's get on with it."

Balov found it hard to hold back a smile. Flattery always worked with these old Bolsheviks. Vlasik was a crony of Stalin's from the civil war. He owed his position solely to that circumstance. Otherwise he was strictly a *kolkhoznik*—an uneducated peasant with hair bristling from his ears and nose. His manner was crude and his sexual excesses well known, but because of his favored position, people feared him.

"I've brought a file," Balov said.

"Never mind." Vlasik scowled. "Just tell me what's in it."

Probably the Comrade Bastard had difficulty reading, Balov thought. A small detail, but one to remember.

"A few days ago," Balov said, "a Royal Navy ship on convoy escort put two men ashore in Murmansk. One of them we know definitely to be an agent of British Intelligence. The other we haven't been able to identify yet."

"Why don't you pick them up and find out?"

"An arrest now would be premature."

"Well, that's your affair," Vlasik said, picking his bad teeth with a match whittled to a sharp point. "How did you get wind of this business?"

"We have a source—highly placed—in British Intelligence."

"Who?"

"I have no idea," Balov lied. He wondered if Vlasik was aware of Kim Philby's operation at St. Albans, outside London. If not, it was better to keep Philby's identity secure. For Soviet Intelligence the Englishman represented an impossible stroke of luck. Recruited out of Cambridge, he had managed to infiltrate SIS, working initially in a nonsensitive position in Section D. A year after the outbreak of the war he had been transferred to the SOE agents' school at Beaulieu in Hampshire. But last summer a post had come open in the headquarters of MI-5 at Prae Wood near St. Albans, and Philby had been moved into it, opening a sieve of sensitive information.

"What information did he pass?" Vlasik said.

"Three things. The identity of the agent bringing the second man in. Their contact in Murmansk. And a code name—Grey Wolf."

Vlasik frowned and said, "Couldn't he get more details?"

"He's at MI-5 in St. Albans. Evidently the operation was initially conceived there, but our source was never directly involved in it. He had one stroke of luck, though. He got access to a cipher originating from the senior British naval officer in Polyarnoe and confirming a contact for Grey Wolf in Murmansk. Just a cover name, Vera, and a telephone listing. Then, according to our source, the operation was suddenly removed from MI-5 to London. Security was tightened. There was no more cipher traffic. It was almost as if Grey Wolf had ceased to exist and they were doing their best to erase every trace of it. The operation hasn't gone through the usual channels, which means it has to be sensitive."

"Or something they'll deny any connection with." Vlasik's little pig eyes were suddenly shrewd.

"There are a lot of unanswered questions, Comrade General. Did the senior British naval officer initiate contact with someone here in the Soviet Union? Or did someone *here* initiate contact with him? Our source at St. Albans thought it might involve some internal plot in Moscow. Maybe a reactionary cell within the Party. He doesn't know how or why British Intelligence got involved, but it may have something to do with the second man."

The matchstick stopped moving. For the first time the general seemed interested, his thick brows clamped together.

"While the convoy was at sea," Balov went on, "we traced the contact in Murmansk. Vera turned out to be a young woman named Katerina Serova. But it seems she was only a courier. Her job was to bring them to Moscow. I made a decision to replace her with one of our own people."

"So you have someone with them, after all?"

"Yes," Balov said.

"Then it should be a simple matter to arrest them when they get here."

The stupid *kolkhoznik*! But no, his ignorance made him worse. The general was surely *krestyanin*—a peasant of the old days. Couldn't he even recognize the problem when it was laid out before him?

"It's a question of what we're going to find out from all this," Balov said. "What's really going on? Why are the British concerned enough to commit one of their own people? Why would they risk putting him illegally on Soviet soil without a legitimate cover? You see how it is, Comrade General? We know what's going on. But what's behind it?"

At last Balov could see a glimmer of comprehension in the other man's eyes.

"It might involve anyone," he added. "The Army, or even a plot against Comrade Stalin himself."

Now the interest on the flat Slavic face passed into genuine concern. The guard chief abandoned the match and said quickly, "Have you proof?"

"Just speculation," Balov said, "but I suppose we can't be too careful. It's why I thought you ought to be brought in on it."

"You did the right thing," Vlasik said, nodding.

Balov smiled. It was Postychev, his own superior, who had ordered him to brief Vlasik, Stalin's chief guard. Postychev—silver-haired, dignified, with indecision and worry creased into his face—how he feared the general! But Postychev wouldn't last much longer. Balov fully expected to take his boss's job soon.

"While this thing is developing," Balov said, "I thought we should coordinate our activities. It would help if I knew more details of Comrade Stalin's schedule."

The grainy seams in the general's face would not let go of their scowl. Nor could his mind process two pieces of information at the same time.

"You wanted advice," he said, his gaze finally coming back to Balov.

"I would like to know," Balov said, "if you think it wise to brief the secretariat chief?"

The head of Stalin's personal secretariat was A. N. Poskrebyshev—a short potbellied man with a crooked back, a head too large for his body, and dark, carnivorous eyes. The hunched back and piercing stare were less sinister than his daily proximity to Stalin.

Vlasik shook his head.

"Don't worry," he said. "I'll mention it to Poskrebyshev."

Balov knew he wouldn't. The jealousy and suspicion that existed between the two directorate heads would block any communication. It was just as well. At this stage of the investigation Balov wanted no interference. If Stalin got word of it now, the whole operation would be paralyzed. On the other hand, if Balov's own effort failed, he could shift some of the blame to General Vlasik for failing to inform Poskrebyshev.

"Thank you, Comrade General."

"*Nyeh zah shto*," Vlasik said. "Just keep me advised."

Balov sent his sedan on without him. He preferred to walk, so he could use the time to think. He walked out past the red brick of the Spasskaya tower, stopping once to look up at the big clock where the tallest spire lifted above a frieze of figures.

Outside the wall, he turned toward St. Basil's and the bronze statues of Minin and Pozharsky, the heroes of 1612, and walked down to the river. The trees along the bank were still bare, the river frozen, but dark, slushy bruises had formed under the ice where the sluggish water strained toward the surface.

A crust of snow covered the ground under the trees. The branches were etched against the sky. He stood under them, a solitary figure in an overcoat too tight for his shoulders, the flaps of his fur hat turned up, the powerful hands thrust into heavy pockets.

For a long time he stared out across the frozen whiteness as if some important secret were lost among the gleam of ice crystals. The intervening years since Stalingrad had changed him. He was mentally much tougher, more cynical about people, even himself, yet confident of his own ability to make the system work *for* him, not against him. You were safe in the State security network only as long as you remained indispensable to it. He would never become a victim of it. For destruction it chose incompetent fools like Vlasik, or frightened ones like Postychev.

He wondered, now, to what extent the years had changed Antony Ryder. He was like Ryder only in that there was a corner in both men's souls that was Russian. From there each viewed the landscape differently, one through a dream of the past, the other through a vision of the future, and so their expectations diverged. Balov's own were clear-cut: to reach the top of the apparatus by the shortest route. It formed the basis of his commitment. Revolutions were conceived by fanatics, fought by fools, and preserved by the fittest out of self-interest, not ideology. Marx was boring. Did anyone believe his drivel? It provided a moral excuse to shoot a Romanov or two and seize power, that was all. Balov much preferred a woman's naked body, or a good joke, to some half-baked economic theory of history.

And as for Ryder, who could really say what his expectations were? If they existed at all, he kept them in some private place, out of view. Until now Balov had imagined he knew as much about the Canadian as anyone. The more he thought about it, the more he realized he didn't know him at all.

Then there was the second man, for whom British Intelligence would risk one of its agents. And Grey Wolf! The operation had to be linked to some activity in Moscow that involved the British. Balov frowned. He was sure the identity of the second man would provide the connection. Finding the answer was the next logical move in the game. Moves and countermoves were already taking shape in his mind.

He glanced toward the spires and cupolas of the Kremlin in the spring light. In the game of foxes, he thought, someone had to lose. But losing at anything had never been a part of Balov's nature, not even as a youth in the slums of Simferopol in the Crimea.

Chapter
8

IN Simferopol, before the revolution, Balov's father had worked as a mill hand, but drinking and Marxist zeal had kept him from holding any job for long.

His mother had been a servant on the Yanov estate. She was devoutly religious, and two possessions she brought to her marriage were an icon case with several holy relics, and a tallow-burning icon lamp. Balov could remember its crimson flicker, at night, on the stained-glass cover of the case.

Drunk, his father scoffed at religion. Once, storming out of the house, he had knocked over the icon case. Balov could remember his mother on her hands and knees picking up broken glass, and that night he had prayed that his father would die.

The house consisted of two rooms. Water had to be drawn from a communal pump outside, and several families shared an outbuilding where a pit served as a toilet. Balov slept on a straw mat near the dark iron of the wood-burning stove.

His father had formed a close friendship with one Viktor Pavlovich Antonov, an ex-schoolmaster and Bolshevist. Antonov was then in his late thirties, stocky and balding.

Wire-rimmed glasses exaggerated the cold intelligence in his face, the strength of the features lessened only a little by a weak chin that he concealed under a goatee, brown and trimmed to a point.

One night during a driving rainstorm, Antonov had turned up at the house. The door shook under his pounding fist, and moments later he stood, dripping, in the glow of the kerosene lamp. He was on the run from tsarist police for his political activities.

"It won't be safe for you here, Viktor Pavlovich," Balov's father had said. "But I know a place across the river—a deserted barn where they used to cure tobacco. The boy can bring you food."

The barn lay deep in the woods. High and narrow, it sagged on rotting timbers, and the floor planks of the loft still had the faint redolence of tobacco bales once stored there to mellow.

The first afternoon, Balov had taken bread and cheese and a goatskin of Massandra wine to Antonov. He had slipped into the shed, dim and hot in the August sun, and stood barefooted in the dust. He called out softly and heard a scraping overhead as Antonov dropped the ladder down from the loft.

The former schoolmaster was dressed impeccably, but now his white shirt was soiled where the sleeves billowed from the tight vest. A ring of dirt and sweat had soaked through the collar. He had eaten ravenously, washing down the bread and cheese with gulps of wine.

"Did the police come to your house?"

"Yes."

"What did your father tell them?"

"That he hadn't seen you."

"Valery Vasilyevich, listen. The police may come back. They might even take it into their heads to question you separately. You'll have to tell them you know nothing about me. Can you do that?"

Balov had nodded, giving his promise.

"Good. We'll make a Bolshevist out of you yet."

He could remember the cart with grain sacks over a false bottom. His father had used it to sneak Antonov out of the city. Antonov had political friends in Sevastopol. They would get him out of the country. It was the last time Balov saw his father. Word had come later from the police in Sevastopol that he had been fatally stabbed in a drunken argument over a prostitute.

His mother still had friends among the servants on the Yanov estate, and he had gone with her several times to beg for scraps at the kitchen. Once, while they waited outside, he had seen a troika, with the Countess Yanova and her daughter, Darya Alekseyevna in it, wheel onto the grounds. It flew toward them, the three white horses swelling quickly to size in the thudding of hooves and flashes of silver from the studs hammered into the black harness. The driver on the high seat had worn a stiff cap and polished boots, his long Cossack shirt belted with a red sash. When he drew the leather of the reins in toward his body, the animals slowed, their manes no longer streaming in the wind. Finally they stopped.

Darya Alekseyevna was ten, the same age as Balov. She had worn a dress of white taffeta tied at the waist so that the skirt billowed out, white stockings, and a hat banded at the crown with colored ribbon that trailed down over the brim against the coppery sheen of her hair.

The driver had removed his cap and bowed low at the waist as the two stepped down from the carriage. Balov had stared at the girl and could remember the look of resentful annoyance passing over the pretty features when she caught sight of him. She had whispered something to her mother, and he had grown suddenly conscious of his uncut hair and the dust caking his bare feet and the wretched state of his own clothing.

Not long after this, word had reached his mother through one of the servants that no more scraps would be given out from the kitchen.

That was the year of the revolution in Petrograd, ending the war against Germany. But it was a false peace, the fighting itself like a game that only adjourned while the players regrouped into Red and White. Later there were reports that Antonov, the ex-schoolmaster, had returned to the Crimea and was commanding Bolshevik partisans in the mountains to the south.

During the final winter of civil war, typhus and smallpox had ravaged the district. In the end Balov could remember refugees streaming past on the frozen road, strips of burlap tied about their lower legs for warmth, their heads bent into the icy winds blowing down from the mountain passes. Then came the remnants of the White Army retreating south toward the coast to escape by sea. For two nights soldiers had tramped by in the dark, the road jammed with trucks and wagons and mules with machine guns lashed across their saddles and ammunition tins bulging in canvas packs that swung against their sides. But on the morning of the third day the road had been empty, running out to the horizon in a hard-packed crust of ice blackened by oil and axle grease and the dung and urine of the pack animals.

In the first grey light Balov had gone out, hoping to find something to eat in the frozen refuse heaps. Near an abandoned field kitchen he had stumbled upon a dead cavalryman in the snow. The horse was dead, too, and several figures were crouched around the stiff-legged carcass, butchering it for meat. The soldier looked to have been shot with a rifle. Someone had stripped the corpse of boots and trousers. Only the blood-soaked tunic remained, frozen to the skin. Balov had managed to claw and tear loose a piece of the hindquarter. He could remember his final glimpse of the slain man facedown in the snow, buttocks exposed and fists clenched, like a child in a tantrum. The scavengers hadn't spoken, but moved methodically in their dark clothes, looking like a circle of vultures. He had wondered if they would chop up the corpse, too, after the horse was gone.

The day after Red forces marched into Simferopol, a military staff car had appeared in the slum. Balov soon found himself in the headquarters of the former White commander where a Red general sat alone at a desk signing papers. It had taken him a moment to recognize Antonov. The goatee had gone to grey, and the face was heavily creased. The ex-schoolmaster had come around the desk and gripped Balov by the shoulders.

"Well, Valery Vasilyevich, you've grown to be a man since we last met. How long—seven years? You must be almost fourteen now, eh? I had hoped your father would be here to see this day, but never mind. I haven't forgotten the boy who brought me food. You'll see what I mean soon enough."

Antonov had been appointed chairman of the Revolutionary Military Committee for the district. He had seen to it that Balov and his mother were moved into quarters with a toilet and cold-water line and that they had food through the months of famine after the war. In time he had used his influence to secure a position of leadership for Balov in the Komsomol—the Young Communist League.

By the time he had turned eighteen, Balov had reached his full height. In the fields he could lift heavier loads and cut more grain than any of the other workers without tiring.

The Revolutionary Military Committee had converted the Yanov estate into a sanitarium. Count Yanov was dead, murdered by Bolshevik peasants as he had attempted to flee by motorcar with his wife and daughter to Yalta. In an ironic twist of fate, Darya Alekseyevna, on becoming eighteen, had been assigned work as a nurse on the estate where she had once lived. Balov had first become aware of this one afternoon when Komsomol volunteers had taken books to the sanitarium to read to the older patients. He could remember his first glimpse of her, slim and fetching despite a certain arrogance bred into the straight nose and pink mouth and high cheekbones, and the eyes that were cold and hard in their spoiled vanity. He had waited in the warm shade of the garden and met her coming down the steps and said, "You shouldn't be walking alone in these woods, Darya Alekseyevna."

"I have nothing left to steal. The State took it all."

"Aren't you forgetting your virtue?"

"And you? What are you stealing these days?"

"Nothing more than a kiss."

"I thought it must be food from a kitchen."

"See?" Balov had laughed. "You *do* remember me."

"You needn't walk with me. I know the way."

"I don't mind making the sacrifice."

He could remember the patterns of leafy shadow flowing across her moving figure, and how the spring sunlight gave her waist-length hair the dazzling shine of copper. By the time they had reached the river, his bantering remarks were drawing smiles from the pink mouth.

"You're smiling. It can only mean one thing. I'm no longer the object of your vicious snobbery. Try to remember this bit of wisdom, Darya Alekseyevna. Beautiful lips like yours were created to smile, not to pout."

Later he had called on her, bringing flowers for her mother, and had observed the same genetic codes of glacial superiority engineered into the older woman's face, reminding him of the day on the Yanov estate when she had stepped down from the carriage and stared blankly through him as if he were not permitted to exist in her world.

But she could no longer dismiss him. His position in the

Komsomol gave him power of rank over ex-countesses. When he mentioned that he might be sent on to university in Moscow, he saw her lips repeat the word *Moscow*, and some obscure glitter of self-interest passed across her stare.

It had become clear to him, after several visits, that she perceived an opportunity for her daughter. Wasn't he an important young man in the Komsomol? He would undoubtedly be invited to join the Party and might well rise to a position of influence.

As for Darya—the first time he had slipped his fingers into the gleaming thickness of her hair and kissed her, the pink, desirable mouth had clung ardently to his. Soon after this he had been intimate with her one night on the knoll behind the padlocked church. He could clearly remember the fence of wooden pickets, sagging and overgrown with honeysuckle that streamed down in thick clumps, and Darya lying back among the trumpet-shaped flowers and looking up at him, and her quickening excitement when he brushed her throat with a kiss. Then he had slipped his hand under her dress. She didn't pull it away, and he had slid it higher up along her thigh to that dampening nest that had left its honey-thick sweetness on his fingers.

Six weeks later Darya's mother had gone to Antonov complaining that her daughter had been made pregnant.

"It's young Balov! He took advantage of her, and she hasn't seen him since!"

"I'll look into it," Antonov had said, giving her a cold stare of dismissal. Later he had sent for Balov.

"Well, Valery Vasilyevich, what do you have to say for yourself? These are serious charges." The officer had winked to reassure him that the charges were not really serious but that the two men must maintain the fiction of a formal hearing. "Did you take advantage of this girl?"

"She was willing enough the night it happened."

"Very well." The officer had struggled to keep an air of

official gravity, and Balov had listened from the next room when the mother returned. Antonov's words of comfort to the incensed parent had been: "You shouldn't be so careless with your accusations. Balov has given me his word as a young communist, and I don't doubt that what he says is true. My advice to you is not to make any more trouble. There are places for troublemakers who give their tongues to slanderous lies, and these places are not widely acclaimed for their comfort or balmy climate."

Not long afterward Antonov had called Balov aside and said, "Have you heard the news? The Yanova bitch aborted her baby. It was the mother's doing. The old witch squirted a lye solution into her daughter's womb. The doctor reported it because the girl almost died."

An image had immediately taken shape in Balov's mind— a woman and young girl stepping down from a carriage. The scornful rebuke on their faces as they stared at him across the years implied that it had been presumptuous and impertinent of him to have thought of fathering a child by Darya Alekseyevna. For a while the two had simply stood there, in Balov's mind, holding their parasols in the sunlit brilliance of memory. Then the girl had murmured something to her mother. The stern reproach on their faces had vanished, and they had both smiled at him with a jeering superiority until he had blinked, the scene going to pieces on his pupils.

A few days later Darya had hurried to him in the street, putting a hand on his arm.

"Valery Vasilyevich! Please, I must speak with you. They've arrested my mother."

"Who?"

"The *chekists*! Someone denounced her for counter-revolutionary activity. She may be sent off."

"Why come to me?"

"Your friend Antonov. He has influence with the secret police. He could help."

He could remember staring down dispassionately into the tense, upturned face, wondering if she had ever been compelled to plead for a favor. A tremor of sympathy had shot through him. But on the other side of it a new sense of power worked in a different direction. Hadn't she killed his child in her womb? For that she would have to bear some consequences.

He had drawn his arm out of her grasp and said, "You see, Darya Alekseyevna? People don't always beg at kitchens."

That was the year his mother had contracted pneumonia and died, and Antonov had insisted on taking him into his own home.

"Remember when I was on the run and you brought me food? Your father risked his freedom for me. He was a good communist, and I owe him this. Besides, if I'd had a son, I would have wanted him to be like you."

Antonov's wife, Lidiya Andreyevna, was then a full-breasted woman of forty with thick brown braids looped on either side of a round face. Her waist was thickening, though a few opulent curves still showed under the dark winter clothing. An air of suppressed nervous energy clung to her laughter, and she had made a motherly fuss over Balov.

"You must think of this as your own home, Valery Vasilyevich, and try to get over your sorrow. Your poor dead mother wouldn't want you to go on grieving forever, would she?"

Lidiya Andreyevna had seemed to find pleasure in taking care of him, washing his clothes, darning his socks by hand, mending his shirts on the treadle-operated sewing machine. She would chide him for not eating as heartily as he should, and sometimes she teased him about girls.

Then Antonov had been called away to Moscow for a

few days. Snow had blanketed Simferopol the evening Balov hitched the horse to the sleigh for the ride to the railway station. They had waited on the platform by the tracks in the crisp cold as snow began to fall again, flakes shining in the headlamp of the approaching engine where the beam cut through the driving splinters. Lidiya Andreyevna had given her husband a cheek to kiss before Balov handed up his bag. In his seat Antonov had stripped off his gloves and waved them from the lit window of the coach as the train pulled out.

Balov could remember the drive back to the house, the sleigh bells flinging their sound into the racing darkness beyond the brass lamps of the carriage, and the runners lifting a cloud of powdery snow that slowly sank behind them. Under the lap rug, Lidiya Andreyevna had pressed close to him, gripping his arm with both her hands. The night air cutting their faces had left a flush on her cheeks under the fur hat where ice crystals gleamed. Once, when a ski skimmed a snowbank, her fingers had tightened on his arm while she laughed with the exuberance of a young girl.

At the house Balov had carried in an armload of wood for the fire, stamping the caked snow from his boots on the doorstep. He could remember Lidiya Andreyevna, still flushed from the ride, heating water in the samovar for tea and later sitting with him before the blazing birch logs and saying little.

During the night he had awakened to a figure leaning over him in the dark. A warm hand caressed his cheek. He started to cry out, and immediately a passionate mouth sank down on his. A woman's bare breasts were crushed against his chest. Fingers seized possession of his sex, which hardened insubordinately even as it was thrust into a wet female opening. There it remained, scissored between two of her fingers, while muscular vaginal contractions drove him helplessly to climax. The mouth with its ardent hunger had grown finally less aggressive, the tongue tracing a pattern slowly inside his own lips—a soft exploration—before it withdrew like a tide seeping out.

"Lidiya," he had protested in a strangled whisper.

"Be still," she had cried, clamping her fingers over his mouth. "Don't speak."

He had remained lying on his back in an agony of sexual guilt and stunned confusion.

"Go to sleep," she had whispered in a scolding tone.

When he'd awakened, she was gone. He had shut his eyes, trying to squeeze out the memory. The whole episode remained for him like some sinful ejaculatory dream, made all the worse by the scalding rush of pleasurable feeling. Antonov—his friend. How could he face him ever again? But, no—his future was tied to Antonov's patronage and goodwill. Why throw away such an opportunity? The more he considered his situation, the more trapped he felt.

At first light he had heard Lidiya Andreyevna moving in the kitchen. Finally she had called out to him, "Valery Vasilyevich! Time for you to be off to school."

He had found his breakfast waiting on the table, and Lidiya Andreyevna bustling back and forth between stove and pantry, making her usual matronly fuss. It was enough to make a man cynical forever about women!

On the third night she had come to his bed again. He had thrust her away. She had begun to cry in the dark, sobs wrenching her body. Amid these convulsions of breathless anguish she blurted out that she would kill herself. No sooner had he let her under the coverlet than she began to kiss his face with hot salty lips. He could feel the splash of feverish tears on his skin, and she whimpered that she loved him. Her hand groped down his bare chest to his groin. He tried to hold her off, but she giggled and grasped him, anyway. The fingers seemed to have a concupiscence all their own. Almost at once his will melted, as if a paralyzing agent had been introduced into his conscience to deaden his fierce loyalty to Antonov, and once more he had surrendered to the pleasure of those mounting contractions and to the seminal release which was the ultimate betrayal. In the spent fluids there had been only disgust and flat hatred for her, and remorse for his own sexual hyprocrisy.

Could Antonov have known? Even as the older man had stepped down from the train there had seemed to be some unspoken accusation on each flashing glint of his spectacles.

On the drive home along the snow-packed streets he had hardly spoken at all. No sooner had they gotten inside, among the panels of darkly polished wood in the dining room, than he had held out his hand and said, "Give me your Komsomol badge."

So he knew! Balov had surrendered the card imprinted with the letters K.I.M. and Lenin's picture, and watched while Antonov tore it to pieces. But then the officer had opened the flap of his portfolio and drawn out a second card.

"Your Party card."

Balov had only shaken his head, unable to speak.

"Don't look so surprised, Valery Vasilyevich. Why do you think I went to Moscow personally?"

"But I don't deserve it."

"Nonsense. Besides, it wasn't so difficult. After all, your father died a hero's death in the cause of Bolshevism."

Balov had felt his mouth trying to twist away from a smile. By what dialectic of Marx did one equate a stabbing death, over a prostitute, with revolutionary sacrifice? He was his father's son, all right, breathing new life into the tradition of sexual misconduct—and for this sterling cuckoldry, a Party card!

"I have arranged for you to enter the State Security

School," Antonov had said. "It's a splendid opportunity for a young man. I know you won't disappoint me."

Lidiya Andreyevna had stepped forward to squeeze his hand.

"*Valya*, I am so happy for you!"

"Yes, you unfaithful cow," Balov had answered silently with his own stare.

"And now," Antonov had said, "I should like some wine to toast the event. Let's make it Massandra, eh?" He had winked at Balov. "For the boy who brought me the wineskin that day."

They had raised their glasses. Antonov's face, in the ruby sparkle, had remained shrewd and sad behind a smile. If Balov had owned a pistol, he would have shot himself.

Before leaving for Moscow that spring, he had ridden a bus out to the village where his mother had been born and later buried. He had walked down the dirt lane to the church cemetery and laid a bouquet on the plot, kneeling in the sun to touch the stone cross.

"Excuse me, God," he had prayed. "I don't believe in your divine autocracy anymore, but *she* did, and exalted You, and so the prayer is for her. If You really do exist by some cosmic accident, I hope You take better care of her now than You did in life, and please don't waste your forgiveness on me, because I can't forgive You for the pain You gave her."

The words had come, not as blasphemy, but rather as a confession of his feelings, stripped of rancor. Afterward, out of some conditioned reflex of religious habit from his boyhood, he had crossed himself and stood up.

Immediately the years had begun spinning backward in his mind, and images had floated up across his stare as if disengaged from that centrifugal vortex of memory: the nude corpse of the cavalryman in his posture of childish outrage; the frozen garbage heaps where he and his mother had rooted for food that winter; the countess and her daughter alighting from the carriage to mock them; his mother picking up the broken shards from the icon case and smiling tearfully as he had tried to comfort her with a hug. That was the only image he wanted to keep, but it was already drifting away with the others into some weightless region of his mind, as distant and dim as the glimmer of a candle on stained glass.

Better to be a realist about such things. Not even the bouquet would bring pleasure to the woman who slept now in the rotting flesh and satin beneath the stone cross where maggots devoured dreams. Over a lifetime her death had been paid for in small installments of disillusionment. As for himself, he intended to project a different mortality.

Chapter
9

AN air raid delayed the train six hours in the rail yards at Murmansk. While they waited, Ryder, Krylov, and the woman, Katerina Serova, huddled close on the floor of the boxcar to keep warm. All around them other figures sat jammed together in the pitch-black silence.

Convicts and political prisoners had worked through the night loading freight cars with supplies for the Moscow front. In the light of acetylene flares, crews repaired track torn up in the raid. Ryder could hear the scrape of shovels on cinder beds and the ringing clang of spikes being driven to secure the fishplates. The guards cursed the cold and shouted at the convicts to move faster.

An hour before daybreak the train slid out of the rail yards. The whistle shrilled as they picked up speed.

Now, as first light seeped through the cracks in the sliding door, Ryder saw that about forty others were packed into the boxcar. There was a stove but no wood to burn, and he could feel the draft from the hole chopped into the floor for a latrine. The cold sliced through his padded clothing. He wanted to get up and stamp his frozen feet, but there wasn't

room. Krylov dozed, his head on his arms. Ryder wasn't
sure whether Serova was asleep or not. Already something
about her manner troubled him. But it was too vague even
to formulate into a reason.

Two days earlier they had followed her through the snowy
dusk of the port to a room behind a fishery. The plant was
shut down. She lit a kerosene lamp, straightened, and the
scarf fell back from her head. In the light her skin had the
glow of honey, and her hair was swept back in a shining
knot at the nape of her neck. Winter wheat was that color,
and her eyes had the grey distances of winter in them, too,
the emotions icebound and inaccessible.

"There are blankets in the back," she said. "Smoked fish
and bread, too, if you're hungry. No more tea, I'm afraid.
I'll bring you some hot food tomorrow."

"How long will we be here?" Ryder said.

"Not long. I'll know more tomorrow. Did you bring a
pistol from the boat?"

Ryder stood near the lamp, which flung their shadows
across the bare wall spotted with fish-oil stains, and gazed
back at Serova.

"Does it matter?" he said.

"You'll probably be searched before they let you on the
train," she said, "especially if it's carrying munitions and
armament. You'd better give me your pistol now, if you
have one. I'll get rid of it."

Ryder shook his head. The smile on his mouth was carelessly evasive.

"No pistol," he said.

Her stare pressed the interrogation for perhaps a second.
Then the glint of the lamp fell away from her face as she
turned.

"Good," she said, and was gone.

In the morning she brought cabbage soup and a loaf of

black bread. This time she took off her coat, and Ryder had a glimpse of long legs and heavy breasts swelling into the bulky sweater as she stretched on her toes to hang the garment over a peg.

While the men ate, Serova sat across from them on a stool at the high table, which was only a thick block of wood where fish were gutted. There was a tin sink in the center with a cold-water spout and a drain for the offal, and the surface of the slab was scored and nicked from the cleaning knives, as well as stained from the blood and milt of slit fish. Sawdust covered the floor, and the walls were bare except for a trawler net slung from a peg. Krylov broke bread to dip into his soup and asked Serova if she lived in Murmansk.

"Yes, but I know Moscow. I was educated there."

Her father, she told them, had been a staff officer to Marshal Tukhachevsky, Stalin's top commander. But Tukhachevsky had fallen in the purge of 1937. The NKVD had arrested him out of the blue and shot him just as suddenly.

"They kept my father in Lubyanka for six months and sent him off to a labor camp. After his arrest we had to come back here. Now I work in the fishery when it's operating. And you?" Her grey stare held fast to Krylov's face. "What about you? Where do you come from?"

Ryder answered for him, "Didn't they tell you?"

"I only know where I'm supposed to take you."

"Then it shouldn't matter where we came from. Only where we're going."

"You're right." A self-deprecating smile curled into her mouth. "We shouldn't ask questions. Better if we don't know these things."

Before the two men were finished eating, Serova got up to leave. She put on her coat and asked for their papers.

"Why do you need them?" Ryder said. Once more, something in her manner bothered him. It was hardly more than an imperative lilt in her tone.

"We're preparing travel documents. They have to be checked against your identity papers—the ones you were given aboard the British escort ship."

"What makes you think we came into Murmansk on a British escort ship?"

"Didn't you?" she said.

Ryder smiled but did not answer. Staring at her, he reached inside his coat and handed over his papers. Krylov did the same.

Serova took the papers and said, "I'll be back."

From a crack in the boarded window Ryder watched her go away from the fishery, a tall figure, once more shapeless in the thick coat that came down to the tops of her boots. The scarf wrapped about her head and throat snapped in the wind. He watched until she passed beyond the snowdrifts at the end of the street.

"A pretty girl," Krylov murmured.

"The weather's clearing," Ryder said. But he wasn't thinking about the weather. He was thinking that Serova asked for too many details.

That afternoon Soviet batteries on the Sredny Peninsula, a few kilometers north of the harbor, opened up a bombardment. Both men lay back on their blankets, and Ryder laced his hands behind his head and smoked one of his Russian cigarettes.

"What do you think they're shelling?" Krylov said.

"Maybe Petsamo. German shipping."

"I wonder how close the Germans are?"

"Close enough."

Before dusk, enemy bombers came in low over the barren Arctic hills crimped to the north. The window shook with the thump of bombs falling on the rail yards. Shortly afterward Serova returned with their papers. Ryder looked at the documents in the lamplight and saw that both men were identified as production engineers.

"En route to Omsk," Serova said, "by way of Moscow."

"What's in Omsk?"

"The tractor works. They've converted the assembly line to tank production."

Ryder nodded.

"It's a decent cover," he said.

"It gives us a high travel priority," Serova said. "We're less likely to be put off along the way to make space for some Party official."

The glimmer of the kerosene wick touched out the shadows on their faces from underneath. Above the clear glass of the lamp Serova gazed at them and said, "We'd better go to the yards now. The raid will change the schedules. We could lose our place on the train."

They reached the yards after dark. A few fires still pitched in the night wind. A sentry checked their papers with a flashlight. The papers blew wildly in his hand. He shone the light in their faces, handed the papers back, and told them to go ahead. At the train a second guard waved them past. It was too cold to bother with papers.

What was it that troubled him about Serova? Now, in the roaring darkness of the boxcar, he tried to pinpoint the source of his feeling. First the business of the pistol . . . then the questions. It seemed to him that the questions went beyond simple curiosity or any operational requirement for information. But perhaps he was overreacting. For a long time the doubts lay shallowly entrenched in a frown above the hammering grind of the undercarriage.

Other faces took shape as the first daylight spilled into the overcrowded car. Ryder pushed to his feet, climbed over two figures on the floor, and stared through the crack of the sliding door at the country streaming past. The tundra sprawled out to the horizon and gleamed, unbroken except for a few stunted birches, dark against the snow. Two reindeer grazed among the trees. They were grazing for lichen. Their heads jerked up as the train approached. They stood, rigid, antlers lifted high.

Ryder motioned to Krylov, who came over and looked out. Krylov grinned and nodded. The reindeer were closer now, still rooted in their tracks. The train whistle shrilled, piercing the clear dry air, and the animals bolted. Both men watched them plunging across the icy crust, glazed in the morning light.

Later Ryder had a glimpse of ski troops in hooded white cloaks, rifles slung across their backs. The detachment moved beneath a low ridge more than a kilometer away, their supplies lashed to a sled pulled by a team of dogs.

Serova said, "They patrol the railroad line south to the White Sea."

"Was there much fighting this winter?"

"Some," she nodded. "Mostly with German mountain troops along the Finnish border. Now they're waiting for the spring."

At noon they were stopped on a siding near a village north of Kirovsk. A guard pounded on the door and said the train would be sidetracked for several hours. All but a few passengers climbed down.

From the village a woman and her two daughters tramped downhill in the snow toward the train. The three were bent under bundles of firewood and twigs. The mother bartered with a circle of passengers, arguing over a few kopecks. The girls, in scarves and long black skirts, sat on the bundles of wood.

Nearby the soldiers riding the train as guards stood together, smoking and talking while they watched the girls. The older girl raised her head shyly in their direction. The color burned into her cheeks, and she looked down again.

As soon as the sale was completed, the girls followed their mother back to the village. The soldiers joked and laughed as the girls went by. The older girl glanced back, and Ryder heard the mother scolding her.

"At least we'll have a fire in the stove tonight," Serova said.

"Were you cold last night?" Krylov asked her.

"Cold enough," she said.

"But you must be used to it"—Ryder looked at her—"in Murmansk."

"Yes, of course. It's very cold there."

The train pulled away from the siding at dusk. Ryder watched the lights of the village receding on the dark sky-line. He went back to the others. They sat cross-legged on the floor and unwrapped the last of the smoked fish Serova had carried from Murmansk.

The stove was poorly vented. Acrid smoke escaped into the freight car, and people close to the glowing metal skin covered their faces. A sick infant began to wail. Someone opened the stove grate to pitch more wood into the fire. In the moving, half-lit shadows Ryder had a glimpse of Serova's face, expressionless, her grey eyes looking straight into his. Then the grate clanged shut, pulling them back into dark-ness. Perhaps she didn't trust him, either.

During the night there were many stops. The train would give a jerk, move slowly for a while, and stop again until the next wrench of steel couplings. Ryder slept only once. When he woke, he was thirsty from the smoked fish.

At daybreak they were stopped again between Belomorsk and Onega near the White Sea. They had come south during the night into timber. Patches of forest were dark against the snow blanketing the landscape, and the morning light shone through the trees in long avenues.

The passengers left the freight car and went off to relieve themselves. Ryder and Krylov wandered down through a thin neck of woods beside the tracks. From the edge of the trees they watched the sun coming across the frozen marshes along the White Sea.

Krylov said, "It reminds me of the country outside St. Petersburg."

"Leningrad, you mean."

"We lived in a fine country house with servants. My father came twice that I can remember. What splendid occasions they were! A great stir among the servants—and my mother wore a long dress of white brocade, with her hair bound on top of her head with pearls. I think she loved him very much."

"How old were you?" Ryder looked closely at the bearded face staring across the marshes with a reflective smile.

"I'm not sure," Krylov said. "Both visits were in winter. My father came on horseback. I remember how the hooves sounded in the snow, and how the animal was winded, and how the yellow froth around its mouth near the bit was starting to freeze. My father handed the bridle to old Misha, and the horse kept stamping around in the snow until Misha led him away. Then we went inside to the fire."

"Did you spend much time with him?" Ryder said, thinking of another tall figure holding a boy's hand and the first fragments of soldiers' music flung across the windy silences: *Listen, don't you hear it*?

"Actually," Krylov replied, "we didn't have that much time to spend. The next day he took me out on the horse. Misha walked beside us with two hunting guns slung over his shoulder and cartridges bulging in his pocket. I think they were looking for wild birds. We stopped near a frozen pond, and my father lifted me down. Misha was pointing. I saw a wolf in the trees across the ice. A grey wolf. Alone, not in a pack. It just stood watching us from the woods, more curious than afraid, the snow glistening like powder on its silver coat.

"My father had the gun to his shoulder. I cried out. It must have spoiled his aim. The blast of the gun filled the woods, and the wolf was gone.

"We circled the pond. My father ran ahead. His boots sank into the drifts, and when we reached the far side, there was blood in the snow. I started to cry. The tsar handed the gun back to Misha and lifted me up. He kept insisting the wolf was all right. We rode back to the dacha, but he left Misha to track the wolf and finish it."

Ryder gazed at the other man and thought, *Will I have to do the same thing to you?* He said, "Was that the last time you ever saw the tsar?"

"No," Krylov said. "I was with him one more time, just before we left the country for Paris. It was still winter. The thaw hadn't set in, but the sky was blue and the air crisp. This time we walked down to the pond, my father and I, alone. We were looking across the ice at the trees where the wolf had been. I asked him if the wolf was still all right, and he told me it was dead. It seemed important to him to tell the truth. I remember his words quite well. 'Some living things have to be killed,' he told me, 'because they are a danger to the rest.'

"He was kneeling down with his hands on my shoulders, and tears had formed in his eyes. I didn't understand then. I thought he was sad about the wolf. But he was saying good-bye."

Serova came down out of the trees.

"Everyone back on the train," she said.

Krylov turned for a last look at the marshes, locked fast in frost and sheet ice and the pale, posthumous gleam of winter.

"Are you glad to be back?" Ryder said.

"There's a proverb," Krylov replied, smiling, "which says that any Russian may leave his country to live somewhere else, but those who are truly Russian will always come back to die."

No, not all of them, Ryder thought, and could remember the creak of a rusty hinge on a livery door, and thudding hooves torn out of a dream on the windy darkness, and an unheard pistol shot in a forest.

Chapter
10

ABOVE Plesetsk, a bridge was out. The train slid into a rail yard south of Onega. They walked back to the station on snow that lay hard-packed and dirty between the sets of tracks.

The station was an old tsarist relic with a high ceiling and thick walls covered by lesions of flaking plaster. People crowded together on benches or curled up on the stone floor, and the air was rank with tobacco smoke and the smell of unwashed bodies. There were many wounded soldiers, some with limbs missing, others wearing filthy dressings. One infantryman sat by himself, the smoke from a sweet caporal lifting past the grimy shine of his face. His abdomen was bandaged under the slit tunic, the dressing darkly suppurated where the abscessed wound drained through the adhesive. Ryder thought the wounded must be going south to Vologda. From there they could be shipped east to rehabilitation clinics.

There was hardtack for sale but no bread. An old woman bundled in rags squatted over a steaming samovar brewing tea to be sold for a few kopecks.

They drank a glass, black and bitter. An officer came in to check papers. He had a wide Armenian face and a chipped front tooth. The soldier who accompanied him had a rifle slung over his shoulder. The officer took a long time with their travel documents. He handed Serova's back to her but held on to the papers of the two men.

"Engineers?" he said.

"Yes," Ryder said, thinking that it would not do to be caught by an overzealous captain so early in the game. What could be wrong with their papers?

"Traveling to Moscow," the officer said, "then on to Omsk?"

"To the tractor works," Krylov said.

"They've moved the plant from Stalingrad," Ryder said. "All production has been converted to tanks. Do you know anything about the new T-34 tank, Comrade Captain? You'll be seeing plenty of them in the field soon enough."

The officer ignored the question.

"What business have you in Moscow?" he said.

"Coordinating production goals with *Stavka*," Ryder said.

The captain folded their papers but still did not return them.

"You'll have to come along with me," he said.

"With you?" Ryder frowned. "For what reason?"

"Some questions to be answered."

"About what?" Ryder said, his tone soft and flat with a calm intransigence.

"Discrepancies in these." The captain waved the papers.

"Why can't we answer questions here, Comrade Captain? What are the discrepancies?"

"You'll have to talk with someone else about that."

Ryder could feel the weight of the automatic pistol strapped to his calf. Behind the easy patience of his smile, he was conscious that the whole thing could be lost here in a rail yard eight hundred kilometers from Moscow.

"Who is someone else?" Ryder said.

"Never mind. Just come along."

Serova grasped Krylov's arm and said to the officer, "This man is my father. You saw our papers. We're on our way to Omsk. I'll only be working on the assembly line. Not half as important as his job and you're detaining him? If my papers are in order, then his must be too."

"We're looking for two deserters," the captain replied, "with forged travel papers. They deserted under fire. A very serious charge."

"But these two have never been in the army," Serova insisted. "They're doing important, patriotic work critical to the war effort."

"Then they have nothing to worry about, do they?"

Serova said angrily, "I demand to know where you're taking my father."

The officer's neck swelled red above the collar of his tunic.

"Be quiet," he said, "if you don't want to make trouble for yourself."

Krylov smiled at her and said, "Don't worry. We'll go and find out what he wants. After all, we're not deserters. It shouldn't take long to clear up the misunderstanding."

Ryder watched Serova. The worried concern on her face seemed genuine enough. Either she had no idea what was taking place, or it was a splendid performance.

"At least tell me how long they'll be gone," Serova pleaded.

"If you wait here," the officer said, "you'll find out in due time."

"But suppose our train leaves?" she protested.

"Nothing will be moving for a while. When they open the line again, the troop trains will have priority."

Outside, on the platform, Ryder hesitated. Once more his reflexes waited in some restrained and careful expectation beyond the pistol secured to his leg inside the fur-lined boot. The captain might telephone the unit from which the men had deserted and speak to the political officer. The political officer would be able to describe the deserters, and that would end it. But suppose the captain were to telephone Omsk? The factory would know nothing about two production engineers. That would start them digging. Well, Ryder thought, it was surely a piece of bad luck. He would have to deal with it. Killing the captain and the soldier had to be the last option. He didn't want to do it. Not if it could be avoided. Perhaps the officer could be frightened.

"Listen," Ryder said to him, "we have appointments to keep in Moscow. The deputy chief for war production isn't used to waiting, especially if the delay is caused by some stupid error with travel documents. If there's a mistake in our papers, you may wish you hadn't questioned it before we're finished."

"Why should there be a mistake?" The officer looked at him.

Some of the crowd inside the station watched them through the window. He could see Serova's face, slightly distorted by the frozen beads of moisture on the glass.

"Then I want to know by whose authority you're detaining us," Ryder said. "Or we're not going with you."

The officer looked past him at the faces in the window. The cords in his neck were swollen and angry, his thick brows jammed together in a frown. He opened the flap of his holster and lifted the pistol halfway out.

"Here is my authority," he said.

Chapter
11

THEY followed the main rail line out of the switching yards. The country was rolling and spread out before them. It had the look of a miniature painting done with a tiny fine brush, with patches of forests and villages flung across the white terrain. The stacks of an iron foundry, sunk on the horizon, left a smudge no larger than a childish scribble of charcoal low on the sky.

Ahead, a drainage ditch angled away from a log trestle, and the officer signaled with his hand.

"This way."

Tramping along the high embankment, they kept in single file. The soldier brought up the rear, the thumb of his mitten hooked into the rifle sling. Ryder heard the crunch of the felt boots in the snow behind him and knew there would be no chance to bolt. What could Serova do? Probably nothing.

The odds of talking their way out of the situation seemed to Ryder dead even, one chance out of two. The percentages, if he chose the other option, struck him as being about the same. There was no doubt in his mind that he could take the rifle from the soldier. It would still leave Krylov vulnerable—between himself and the captain. Would Krylov have the sense to dive out of the line of fire? The whole equation came down to Ryder's own quickness in handling the rifle, balanced against an X factor of wasted seconds while the officer jerked open the holster flap, drew and cocked the pistol, and fired. The shots might attract attention—another risk to weigh. All of these details raced through Ryder's mind in a clear flash, hardly more than an instinctive reflex of thought.

But the soldier never drew close enough to turn the possibility into a reality. They crossed the frozen canal and climbed the opposite bank into a stand of trees. The ground sloped down through the bare branches to the roof of a barn. The captain called to the soldier and sent him ahead. There was a moment when the officer, watching the soldier slip downhill, had his back to them. Ryder could have lunged for him, but this time an altogether different instinct checked him from it.

The captain faced around, smiling with his chipped tooth.

"I know who you are and why you're here. Don't worry, you're with friends. I'm Captain Avalov, aide to General Vlasov. He's waiting to talk with you."

In his head Ryder ticked through the alphabet of Soviet generals whose names had been mentally imprinted, for one reason or another, during the intelligence briefings at Ashton Keynes.

Vlasov—a lieutenant general—was one of the few career officers with military talent who had survived the great purges. He had fought with sufficient distinction at Przemysl early in the war, and at Kiev in the Ukraine, to be given command of the Twentieth Army defending Moscow.

Ryder said, "I thought General Vlasov was commanding troops on the Moscow front."

"Yes," Avalov said, "but now he's being moved to take

command of the Second Shock Army, trying to relieve Leningrad."

Krylov said, "Is General Vlasov—"

"Part of it?" Avalov interrupted. The cocked eyebrow seemed to say, "You'll know the answer soon enough."

"Where is he?" Ryder said.

"Not far. A few kilometers. Can you ride?"

Both men nodded.

"Good," Avalov said. "I sent the soldier to bring the horses. The roads are impassable where we're going. We want to stay clear of them, in any case."

Once the soldier brought the horses, Avalov told him to wait at the barn until they returned. The three men set out on horseback, going east on a course parallel to the river. The low, rolling plain swelled and lifted into timber that spilled darkly over the country. Ahead, in the saddle, Avalov leaned from side to side to avoid branches as he picked his way through the trees. The sun was overcast and dull like a pearl, and sometimes a fine powder of snow sifted down from the wet black limbs overhead.

Andrei Andreyevich Vlasov . . . hero of Kiev and Moscow. . . . The more Ryder thought about him, the more convinced he grew that his own cynicism about the operation might have been premature. Vlasov was known for his courage and calculated risks in the field, and it struck Ryder that the general was exercising both traits now by revealing himself as one of the anti-Stalinists. His rank, alone, must put him close to the top of the conspiracy. If enough officers of Vlasov's caliber were involved, there had to be a chance of success.

"What about Serova?" Ryder said to Avalov. "The woman we left in the station—does she know about our meeting now with your general?"

"She's only a courier," Avalov said. "Her knowledge is

limited to the details of her job. Better for her and all of us if we keep it that way."

About twenty minutes later they dropped down through another tract of heavy timber in the snow to a farmhouse. The smell of wood smoke drifted up into the trees. The horses—two bays and a sorrel—were winded, and the breath blowing from their flared nostrils froze into white plumes.

They tethered the animals behind the house under a lean-to. Nearby a stake fence encircled several graves. Only a few wooden pickets stuck up above the snow; the rest were buried under a drift. Krylov glanced at the stone markers and made the sign of the cross.

Inside, an officer warmed himself before the fire. His boots shone in the flames, and his overcoat was draped over his shoulders like a cape. He turned, a man in his early forties, hollow-cheeked, the eyes intense and searching behind horn-rimmed glasses.

"I am Vlasov."

"Yes, I know of you, Andrei Andreyevich," Krylov said. Ryder watched the two men embrace in the Russian tradition of an older time.

"Maxim Nikolaycvich," Vlasov said, "I'm pleased you had the courage to join us before the fact. I can promise you it won't be forgotten."

Krylov only shook his head to indicate that it didn't matter.

"Have you eaten?" the general said. "There are food stores here. Vodka. *Braga*, if you prefer. Avalov will see to it. We can talk while you eat. I was afraid we'd missed you. I haven't much time, but I'll try to answer your questions."

The bare room had only a few sticks of furniture. The yellow blaze from the fireplace cast its moving glint across the floorboards, planed from Siberian larch, the logs chinked with moss, and the shutters intricately carved with their gingerbread patterns. They sat on benches at a table made from hand-hewn planks and ate tinned meat and dark bread and drank vodka. Ryder heard the scrape of boots upstairs— more than one pair—but no one else came down to join them.

Vlasov said, "This may be the only chance for us to talk. I'd planned to meet with you in Moscow, but I've been given the Second Shock Army to command."

"Leningrad?" Krylov said. "Your aide told us."

"The Second Army is pinned down in the Volkov swamp to the south. No air support. No reserves. I'm supposed to break through the German encirclement and relieve the city. Militarily it's hopeless. Stalin won't listen. He knows more than his generals, of course."

"Are things that bad?" Krylov said.

"I'll tell you how bad. On the second day of the war we lost our Air Force, thanks to his meddling. Then he went off to his villa in Kuntsevo to sulk. The country didn't hear from him for ten days! No message to the people. Just silence. Better for us if he'd stayed there, brooding. But the master tactician came back. Surely you know about his campaigns. Minsk? Smolensk? Kiev? A million dead and wounded because he wouldn't listen. He shifts armies around like toys. Shall I tell you what our losses have been in his so-called winter offensive? And for what? What did it accomplish? Tell me the strategic purpose if you can."

While the general spoke, Ryder gazed at him quietly. The pain and disgust, backed up behind the frustration, were obviously genuine. How many of his men had paid for Stalin's mistakes with their blood? How many more would pay? The half-formed questions seemed a permanent part of his expression, buried in sorrow and fury and a decisive purpose.

"Andrei Andreyevich," Krylov said, "do the other generals feel the same?"

"The good ones," Vlasov said, nodding. "They can't issue

an order unless it's countersigned by their political commissar. If a commissar doesn't agree with a decision, he changes it. The commissars are afraid of Stalin, so they do what he wants, not what the situation in the field requires. I tell you frankly—Russia is lost if we can't bring him down."

Ryder said, "How will you do it?"

The crackling fire filled the silence.

"Kill him." Vlasov stared hard at them.

"It's been tried before," Ryder said.

"By mad fools and amateurs," Vlasov said.

"Everyone who fails goes into that category," Ryder said. "Even generals and tsars."

"British Intelligence too?" Vlasov's thin mouth made the only smile Ryder would ever see on the general's face.

"Especially British Intelligence," Ryder replied.

"Better, then, if we don't fail," Vlasov said.

"When will you try it?" Ryder said.

"Soon." Vlasov looked at him. "You ask me when. I say it will happen before the rivers run again. Stalin's eyes won't see the last winter ice melting in the streams of Russia."

"Then what?" Ryder pressed him.

"You should understand," Vlasov said, "that I can't go into military details for reasons of security. When it becomes necessary for you to know, you'll get all the specifics you need from your contact in Moscow. His code name is 'Uncle Vanya.' I can tell you this much: There'll be a coordinated strike. The targets have already been assigned. People. Communications. Key facilities."

"And the NKVD?" Ryder said.

"Beria and his deputies will be arrested. The NKVD will cease to exist as an independent arm of State Security. Beria will issue the necessary orders—at gunpoint if necessary."

"Don't they have armed units at all the fronts?"

"Yes." Vlasov nodded. "Shooting anyone who tries to

retreat. Even an orderly retreat isn't permitted. Don't worry, there'll be no sympathy for the NKVD."

On the wall an icon held the glitter of the fire on its dark wood. The figure of the Virgin seemed to be reaching, through the shuttered gloom, into the past.

Krylov said, "I think I have only one more question. I ask it out of respect to the memory of my father, the tsar. I ask you to answer it, Andrei Andreyevich, out of respect to his memory. If your operation succeeds, what part will I play afterward?"

Vlasov slowly pulled off his glasses and laid them down on the rough boards of the table. He rubbed the bridge of his nose with his thumb and middle finger. Some of the hardness came away from his face, which looked tired, creased, old beyond its years. For all his reputation as a cool and intelligent field commander, he struck Ryder as a man consumed by a reckless hatred. Some terrible fatigue lay on the other side of the bloodshot eyes, but it could not get past the blind purpose there.

He said to Krylov, "We view the monarchy as a symbol. I tell you frankly, Maxim Nikolayevich, a major concern to us now is how the Germans will exploit the thing we do. The Ukrainian masses, thanks to Stalin and his gangsters, are disillusioned with the Party. They don't trust it, and why should they? On the other hand, the imperial tradition embodies all the greatness and grandeur of the Russian past. If we can apply the will and spirit of the people to that idea, it may be possible to consolidate power without any major conflict."

"And the Party?" Krylov said.

"For the present the new government will operate through the Party apparatus. But the power structure will be changed. Instead of Party bosses, a joint military command will exercise authority." Vlasov replaced his glasses. They pulled the hard symmetry back into his face. Ryder stared at the features in the moving firelight. Did the cold resolve come out of some noble purpose? Or did it pass beyond that into blind ambition and a larger vision of himself? The general went on, "After the war we see a socialist state and a monarchy—preserved along British lines but Russian in its soul."

They heard the hollow clump of boots on the stairs. Avalov appeared, looking worried about the time. Vlasov nodded and stood up.

"There's a plane waiting for me. I'm supposed to be making an air reconnaissance of the German salient below Lake Ladoga. You see, Maxim Nikolayevich, we had to improvise this meeting rather hastily. My transfer from Moscow was quite unexpected. But I wanted to meet with you face-to-face—so we might have a look at each other, eh? And talk like this. I thought we owed you that, in case..."

Vlasov shrugged. The unfinished remark drew a faint smile to Ryder's mouth. In case it failed, the general meant.

"Will we see you again," Krylov said, "before the operation moves?"

"Maybe. Who knows anything these days? The operation will go with me or without me. Avalov will take you back to the train."

"Then God keep you, Andrei Andreyevich," Krylov said.

"Yes, God. I remember Him." Vlasov adjusted his fur hat and pulled on his gloves. "But God won't cast out our devils for us. We have to do it ourselves."

Chapter
12

B ALOV stood in the street before the address General Vlasik had given him, one of the newer apartment buildings overlooking the Moskva River. In rooms on the third floor Vlasik kept half a dozen girls to entertain friends and important Party officials. Balov knew all about this arrangement. So did the militia of city police who didn't interfere.

On the boulevard, with its electric tram lines strung tensely above the streetcar tracks, the air no longer knifed into the lungs. Winter was cracking away from the city, leaving behind burst water pipes, buildings without heat or sanitation, shortages of oil and coal, and a half-starved population.

At least Vlasik's building had heat, though the elevators didn't work and the ceiling bulbs had been unscrewed from all the corridors. Balov climbed the stairs to the third floor. Even in darkness he had no trouble finding the apartment. Voices and laughter drifted into the hall, the sort of laughter that was rare these days, and it didn't stop under the heavy rap of his knuckles.

A tall girl clad only in a silk chemise with a lace ruffle above the knees opened the door a crack and giggled. Balov had a glimpse of red hair and crooked teeth and freckled cleavage before someone dragged her aside. Thick fingers gripped the edge of the door, and a shaved head appeared.

"Well?"

"I'm Balov. General Vlasik asked me to meet him here."

"Balov. Yes." Some of the truculence went out of the curled underlip. "The general's been delayed. He left word. You're to stay until he gets here. Come in and relax."

Almost a dozen men and half as many women crowded the small apartment with its cheap, plain furniture distinguished only by the multitude of cigarette burns in the fabric and wood, the battle scars of too many parties. Most of the men were in uniform, older headquarters types. Probably people to whom Vlasik owed a favor or who were here to be indentured for one. Laughter, loosened by alcohol, drowned the sound of a radio that kept trying to unscramble balalaika music from static.

Balov at once found a glass of vodka thrust into his hand. The man with the wrestler's body and shaved head seemed to have charge in Vlasik's absence.

"If you want a woman, take one," he said. "Except her— over there."

The girl in question stood at the window looking out. The spring light shone on her black hair, which curved across her cheek to a bun at the nape of her neck. She looked shy, but he decided this was only an impression created by the pink bloom, which was not altogether faded out of the white cheeks, and the overripe mouth, with its look of crushed innocence. Her body, beautifully curved, took the drabness away from the dark dress. It became instead a garment made erotically chic by the upward tilt of her breasts and the swelling of her hips into the clinging fabric. She stood quite straight, with an air of self-possession that interested him.

"Who is she?"

"Kozlova. Vlasik's girl. Pretty, eh?"

"I haven't seen her before."

"No? Her father has a shop off Arbat Street in the Old Quarter."

Balov smiled. To imagine her enduring the attentions of a dull, stinking brute like Vlasik was beyond human comprehension. A sin against nature. Yet, immediately, because Balov couldn't have her, she became the only woman in the room he wanted.

He took a swallow of the vodka, staring at her over the rim of the glass. The man with the shaved head was now across the room talking to someone else. Balov slipped over to the girl.

"Why do you look so sad?" he asked.

It seemed a long while before her eyes turned from the window. They were nearly as black as her hair, and they regarded him for an equally long period before she replied.

"Not a time to be happy, is it?" Her voice was low and honey-smooth, as if it had been created for sexual intrigue.

"But why be miserable in the bargain?"

Across the river the city stretched toward the blue distances. People were shadows moving in the dirty slush of the streets.

"Ask those people down there why. Some of them won't last through another winter."

"Maybe the Germans won't, either."

"What's to stop them?"

"*Devushka.*" He smiled at her. "Better take care. Defeatist talk can get you into trouble."

"Not if you have friends."

"Like Vlasik?"

"Who told you that?" The cool tone smothered nicely any emotional reaction.

"Someone."

"The man who let you in. Golikov. From the Central Committee. He knows everybody's business except his own."

"All departments have their share of incompetent fools. How did you meet Vlasik?"

"I should think that's none of your business."

"Exactly." Balov smiled. "That's why I asked."

"Who are you? Have we met before?" Her dark gaze interrogated him. In the black reserve of her eyes it seemed to Balov that there was at least a psychological chastity. Perhaps she withheld that during intercourse. It could always be kept intact behind a faked orgasm, the oldest and easiest form of sexual trickery.

"No," he replied, shaking his head. "I'm Balov. Valery Vasilyevich. And you?"

"Natasha Ivanovna."

"Your father is Kozlov," he said. "He has a shop off Arbat Street."

"Should I be impressed?"

"If you want to be."

"I suppose you're NKVD?" She glanced across the room. "Like the others not in uniform."

"Yes," he said, "but not like the others."

"How are you different?"

"I'm not afraid of Vlasik."

The remark dragged a smile, faintly speculative, into one corner of her mouth.

"Maybe I should tell him you said that."

"You could." Balov shrugged. "But you won't."

"What makes you suppose so?"

"Because he wouldn't be happy if he knew you had an intimate talk with a stranger in his apartment. *You* have to please him. I don't. Besides, I can do something for you he can't."

"What?"

"Make you smile."

Below, a sedan pulled up to the curb. From the window Balov saw Vlasik and another officer climb out. The wind sent Vlasik's hat cartwheeling over the icy pavement. The aide scrambled after it and came back, wiping the bill on his sleeve. The general took it from him and disappeared into the building, leaving the aide alone in the street.

By the time Vlasik entered the apartment, Natasha Ivanovna had joined a circle of people in conversation across the room. Balov remained at the window. There were shouts of hello as heads turned. Several figures, including those of Golikov and the red-haired girl in the silk shift, crowded close to the general. The girl struck Balov as decidedly tipsy. She seized the general's hat and thrust it on her own head with the bill cocked sideways. Vlasik retaliated by flicking one strap of the chemise off her freckled shoulder, exposing a snowy margin of breast. Even as the girl clutched protectively at the garment, the general pinched her high up on the buttock. The girl gave a squeal of outraged innocence and bounded out of range.

Natasha brought Vlasik a glass of vodka and stood beside him. Reaffirming her territorial dominance, no doubt, Balov thought. The general looked sallow under the stress of the day but managed a smile for her. He downed the vodka in a gulp and wiped a sleeve across his mouth. His other hand slipped from Natasha's waist and came to rest just above her backside in that no-man's-land of semiprivate terrain that made the gesture seem more respectfully intimate than crudely provocative, as he had been with the red-haired girl. My God, Balov roared inwardly. Was it possible that the stupid ox had fallen in love with her?

Natasha whispered something in Vlasik's ear. Her gaze

settled on Balov even as she went on smiling and whispering. It was her way of demonstrating, for his benefit, the extent of her prestige and influence. The curve of her backside, so enticingly near the general's hand, reinforced the priorities of power. The whole exercise filled Balov with suppressed amusement. Now Vlasik looked at him, too, and made a motion with his head that meant "Come on."

Balov followed the stocky figure into the dining room. Vlasik waved the others out and drew the sliding doors together on the windowless room. The light from the tasseled lampshade shone upward into the general's face, leaving its glint on the pitted skin.

"Well, Balov, let's hear the rest of it. They've reached Moscow, have they?"

"Forty-eight hours ago," Balov said, nodding. "They've gone to an address near Sokolniki Park."

"Who lives there?"

"The apartment is assigned to a family named Kishkin. The father was killed at Demyansk. The wife and one child were to relocate next month to the steel works in Magnitogorsk. They left early, but the apartment is still listed as occupied."

"Quite a few cleared out during the panic without telling anyone. Maybe it was just a mistake."

"I don't think so. We found a link. The woman's brother. A colonel named Shevchenko."

"Shevchenko?" Vlasik frowned. "The name sounds familiar. Don't I know him?"

"He commands a tank battalion. This winter it was detached from the Twentieth Army and put under General Sinilov for the defense of Moscow."

"Then Shevchenko's here? In the city?"

"Yes."

"Concealing enemies in the apartment of a relative," Vlasik concluded, thumping the table with his fist hard enough to jar the lamp, which sent a hemorrhage of light across the wallpaper.

The dull, stupid ox! But, no. Why insult the intelligence of oxen? The general would be several rungs farther down on the evolutionary ladder, and uncastrated in the bargain.

"We'll know soon enough if he's concealing enemies," Balov said, "the first time he goes near the place. He's under twenty-four-hour surveillance."

"What about the two in the apartment?"

"They can't do any harm, and we know where they are. It's their trip down from Murmansk that bothers me. An army captain pulled them off the train near Onega. They disappeared for about three hours."

"What reason did they give?"

"They said it was the NKVD checking on a mistake in their travel documents. We know that isn't true."

"Did you identify the captain?"

"All we have is a description. He had a chipped tooth."

"Then you don't know what was discussed?"

"No," Balov said, "but we may have identified the second man."

"Well?" Vlasik scowled.

"Comrade General," Balov said, smiling, "if I hesitate, it's because I don't quite believe it myself. We think his name is Krylov, and he may be the natural son of Nicholas Romanov and a woman named Anna Krylova, an actress who worked in Leningrad fifty years ago. If the story's true, she and the boy were sent off to Paris before the turn of the century. We're trying to verify it through old Cheka documents. In any case, the age and description seem to fit. The physical resemblance is quite remarkable."

"What would a Romanov bastard be doing in the Soviet Union that would interest British Intelligence?"

"And why would they disappear for three hours with a

Soviet officer? Maybe both questions have the same answer."

"Is your courier still with them?"

"Our best stroke of luck," Balov said. "Evidently the woman, Serova, wasn't known by sight in Moscow. We'll keep her in place as long as possible. The problem is, the real Serova wasn't involved in whatever they're up to. Her job was only to escort them to Moscow and look after their needs once they arrived."

"When will you arrest them?"

"Not until we have an idea of what's going on and who's involved."

"That could be awhile." Vlasik frowned. "Better not wait too long."

"One other thing," Balov said. "Rather curious too. Serova overheard part of a conversation. Something about a grey wolf and St. Petersburg and blood in the snow."

"Leningrad?"

"What could Operation Grey Wolf have to do with Leningrad?"

"Who knows?" Vlasik shrugged. "The city's probably lost. The Boss turned over the Second Shock Army to Vlasov. Nobody really believes Vlasov can break through."

"Vlasov?"

"Of course, he's a proven field commander. One of the best. But the Luftwaffe has control of the air. So what possible connection could you make between Grey Wolf and Leningrad?"

"*Nichevo.*" Balov shrugged and smiled at the same time. "We'll find out."

Chapter
13

THE next afternoon Balov found the secondhand shop run by Natasha's father. It was in a lane off Arbat Street where Pushkin and Scriabin had once lived. He stood before the shop window looking at the display. The items would be sold for a merchant's commission: a balalaika, a faded shirt, scuffed leather shoes, a straight razor, a brush, and a shaving mug. Busts of Caesar and Lenin ignored each other. There was no price card under the bronze of Lenin. Perhaps his presence was only meant to sanction this semicapitalist enterprise. The shoes had a price of five thousand rubles—more valuable than Caesar's garlanded head.

The unkindest cut of all, Balov thought. But in desperate times grandeur went cheaply. One only paid for necessities.

The door, opening, tripped a bell. It took his pupils several moments to adjust from the street's cold sunlight to the dark interior. An edict curtailed use of electric lights during the daylight hours. Racks of used clothing, smelling musty, came out of the gloom. More statuary took shape on the shelves.

Balov heard a click of beaded curtains and raised his head. Natasha Ivanovna stared at him from the shadows. A dusting cap and apron were white against the dark of her hair and clothing.

She said, "Why are you here?"

"To cheer you up."

"I don't need your help for that," she said, but the cold impatience in her face struck him as contrived.

"Are you so full of proletarian joy?"

"Now who's talking heresy?" she said.

"Heresy in small doses is good for the soul."

Someone coughed behind the beaded curtains.

"Did you come in to buy something?" Natasha said.

"The balalaika in the window."

She looked at him sharply. Some of the combativeness went out of her attitude, but still she remained cool.

"The balalaika has a string missing. You can't replace it anywhere."

"Then why keep it in the window?"

She gave a shrug and replied, "A reminder."

"Of what?"

"Pleasant things. Better times."

"Well, then. The bust of Caesar. How much?"

"Nine hundred rubles."

He smiled and said, "You don't put much value on dead civilizations."

"Sooner or later we all become relics of one, don't we?"

"I'll give you a thousand for it," Balov said, "on condition . . . ?"

"What condition?"

"That you come for a walk with me."

Someone coughed again from the other side of the beaded curtains. A man stepped through. Under a grey stubble of beard, the face remained sallow and stern.

"My father," Natasha said. "Ivan Nikolayevich."

The older man looked in ill health. His eyes watered, and each rattling cough drew a grimace of pain. But apart from the physical distress, Balov sensed a larger resentment. Not difficult to guess the reason. General Vlasik was taking care of them. Natasha was the General's whore. Clearly her father didn't wish to see the arrangement jeopardized.

On the other hand, Balov's own NKVD status made him someone to respect. The father wavered between two anxieties. Then, too, one had to consider the bust of Caesar— a potential sale. A merchant's instinct for easy profit could override the other conflicts.

"Excuse us, will you?" Natasha said. "Please."

The girl and her father disappeared behind the beaded curtains. Balov heard low voices, then silence. In a few minutes Natasha stepped out. She no longer wore the dusting cap or apron. Now she carried a coat over her arm.

"I can go with you for fifteen minutes but no longer. My father's not well, and I have to get back to the shop."

Balov refrained from smiling and held the door for her. They walked up the street to a square, lit by a weak sun. The air streaming into their faces carried the scent of *rasputitsa*—the spring thaw. Soon the bare branches of the trees would bud into leaf. The slush in the streets had turned soft, too, and hardened only at night.

They sat on a bench. The cloth coat was too short for her, though it revealed nicely curved legs. Probably they would turn plump later in life. But that was a deferred consolation, for at the present time they were quite desirable in their contours.

"Tell me about yourself," Balov said.

"I thought you knew everything about me."

"Not yet."

"I was a biology student at the university before it closed last fall."

"Planning to be a scientist?"

"I would have preferred to go into music."

"Why didn't you?"

"I couldn't pass the examination for the conservatory. I had the desire but not the ability." Her smile had just enough self-derision to be suddenly open and appealing. "Anyway, biology is more practical."

"You keep up with your studies?"

"I work one day a week at the Institute for Herpetologic Research. Metlin is the curator. Do you know him?"

"Metlin? I don't think so."

"The Institute stayed open. They let Metlin keep his collection of exotic snakes. I've heard it was because someone had a plan."

"A plan?"

"If Moscow had to be abandoned, they were going to leave poisonous reptiles behind in the Kremlin. For the psychological effect. You can't stop a mamba when it's stirred to anger. They come at you too fast."

"You handle them?"

"I was afraid at first. You have to force yourself. It's the only way to overcome your fear."

Balov lit a cigarette, the smoke crinkling his stare. Nerve was a virtue he could admire. Natasha had both hands in the pockets of her coat, and she stretched out her legs, with the ankles together, into the sun's cold gleam and glanced down at them. Balov looked at them, too, and smiled. She noticed his interest and immediately withdrew her legs from view, crossing them in a manner that signaled some firm impregnability. Crossed, they became even more provocative, for it was not in his nature to be put off by obstacles.

He said, "What did you do after the university closed?"

"I joined the volunteers digging tank traps outside the city. Then I worked on a timber brigade cutting wood for fuel—until the river froze and the timber barges couldn't get into the city."

"Patriotic work."

"It'll be more difficult now."

"Why?"

"My father's sick. At the clinic they told him it was a cancer. I can't leave him alone anymore."

Balov blew a stream of smoke that twisted away in the chilly breeze. He felt like an interrogator, dragging information from her in pieces, to be used against her in a sexual pursuit.

"How did you meet Vlasik?" he said.

Natasha turned her face idly toward the sun and closed her eyes.

"Why do you want to know?"

"Just the curiosity," he said, smiling, "of a high-principled fellow looking out for your welfare."

He thought she wouldn't answer, but she surprised him.

"I met him on the street while I was queuing for a copy of *Pravda*. He stopped his car and called me over. It was an official car, and I was afraid. There he was in the backseat, in his general's uniform, smoking a cigarette, and he told me I was under arrest."

"Arrested? For what?"

The memory drew a smile into her mouth.

"He said pretty girls weren't allowed in queues. Then he sent the driver to the kiosk, ahead of everyone else, to bring back a paper."

Balov found to his surprise that he was annoyed. Not to any observable degree, only the faintest prick of displeasure on the other threshold of his emotions.

"Are you such a faithful reader?" he said.

"It's paper, isn't it? There were a hundred uses for it last winter. You could stuff it in your clothing to keep warm in daytime or spread it underneath the mattress at night."

"So Vlasik developed an interest in your . . . welfare?"

"He was nice to me. After I met him, things changed for

us. He saw that we got a wood stove. The plumbing was fixed too. He even sent food, things you can't buy at the cooperatives—butter and fresh fruit and sometimes meat. We might not have lived through the winter without his help."

"Yes." Balov smiled. "The general's known far and wide for his touching generosity to citizens in need."

Some cool antagonism came back into her stare. A defensive mechanism, Balov decided. He wondered how often they slept together. Or perhaps Vlasik hadn't yet exacted payment. But that would surely come. Gratitude was the cheapest aphrodisiac of all.

"It's time for me to go," Natasha said. "You needn't walk back with me."

"I have to pick up Caesar."

"No," she said. "You don't have to buy it."

"But I want it."

"Why? It's not very practical."

Balov laughed and said, "But that's the best reason of all."

Two evenings later Balov returned to Arbat Street in the Old Quarter. The shop was dark. He knocked on the glass panels and rattled the door. It seemed to him that sexual desire in a man for a woman was the least biodegradable of all emotions. By satisfying it, you ran the risk of intensifying it and took a step closer to the trap of a permanent relationship. So far, in life, he had avoided that outcome deftly.

On the other side of the furled lace at the window, a shadow approached, and he heard Natasha's voice.

"The shop is closed."

"Open up. It's me. Balov. I haven't come to buy anything this time."

The key turned in the lock and the door opened.

"Why are you here after curfew?" The irritation in her voice did not sound wholly convincing. Perhaps she had been thinking about him a little bit too.

"I've come to pay my respects." He inclined his head in a courtly way. "To you and your father. Why are you always so suspicious of my honorable intentions? Look, I've brought a surprise. Here's vodka. Butter. Two fresh eggs for your breakfast. How can you resist anyone with such an extravagant nature?"

"I don't know what to think about you." The girl shook her head but stepped back to let him in.

Balov followed her through the dark shop. In the empty space behind the beaded curtains she said, "Careful, the ceiling slants low here. Do you carry matches? We haven't one to spare."

Balov ransacked his pockets, found a match, and snapped the head with his thumbnail. The walls flared out of the dark. Natasha lit a piece of tallow. Shielding the flame with her hand, she mounted a flight of wooden stairs. Balov climbed behind her, watching the candle flicker off the wall against the backs of her legs.

Upstairs, in the cramped apartment, he heard water running in the bathroom and the sound of someone clearing phlegm. Kozlov came out. A regulation sixteen-watt bulb burned under the paper shade of a solitary lamp. The dim light exaggerated the dark circles under the old man's eyes. The sallow skin, tight over the cheekbones, gave his face the look of a death's-head. Balov said, "Hello, Ivan Nikolayevich," and caught the same glitter of contempt in the other man's stare as in their first meeting.

But the sight of the vodka and other rationed items appeared to soften his intolerant feelings. He motioned Balov to a chair and told Natasha to bring glasses.

At the kitchen table the two men talked and drank vodka. Natasha had both hands in a dishpan, her back arched. The sleeves of her bulky sweater were pushed up to her elbows. Balov watched the glint of candlelight on her bare arms. He liked the bloom of color in her face and the way her skirt was tightly belted at the waist and flared over her full hips. Her vitality made a stark contrast to the man across the table. The vodka affected Kozlov quickly.

"We drank this often in the old days." He stared into the candle flame, which danced its own shadow, like a memory, across his face. "Only the best, you understand. It was so long ago. . . ."

"How long?"

"Before the revolution."

"Were you *dvoryane*?" Balov asked. Under the tsars, *dvoryane* were landed gentry, the top social class. Balov knew they weren't *dvoryane*, but he thought it would flatter the old man to hear it.

"No." Kozlov shook his head. "We've always been *kuptsy*. Merchants. Successful enough, mind you, and cultured too. That's the real mark of success, isn't it? What I mean is, to be educated in this world and appreciate the finer things."

"Of course. That's what matters."

"We lost everything in the revolution," Kozlov said. "Our property and our business were taken from us. I remember how it was—families packed together and rats everywhere. You couldn't leave an infant alone because it might be bitten. Did you know that the old people made their own coffins? You think it's bad today, well, it's no worse than the winter of 'nineteen." The thin mouth twisted down in a smile of resentful anger. "But, of course, heroic sacrifices had to be made. We were constructing the socialist state."

Natasha poured hot water from a kettle into the dishpan. She glanced from her father to Balov and frowned.

"Why talk about it at all?" she said.

The older man had drunk too much. It made him careless. He seemed to forget he was speaking to an NKVD officer.

Or perhaps he no longer cared. Pain and sickness consumed other anxieties and left only the smell of death.

Balov said, "Maybe things will get better for you, Ivan Nikolayevich."

Kozlov didn't answer, his chin on his chest. The thick brows lifted slightly, as if he were beyond caring. He was full of an old man's anger. The revolution had confiscated all his possessions but left him his life. Now that would be appropriated too. A fleck of spittle shone at one corner of his mouth, and his button-down sweater reeked with oil of camphor.

Balov thought, *He's an enemy of the people. I should report him.* But he was an enemy who posed no threat. Broken. Too sick to wipe the trickle of saliva from his own mouth. Cancer would purge him from the system. Besides, Balov had other worries at the moment, in the forms of Antony Ryder and British Intelligence. He smiled. It was, after all, a question of addressing the correct priorities. Defending the socialist state and depriving Vlasik of his mistress took precedence over one dying old man. Let him keep his counterrevolutionary heresy if it helped to kill the advancing pain.

"I'll bring you more vodka next time," Balov said to him.

"Can you get matches?" Natasha said. "We've been making them from glycerin and manganese dioxide, but they've run out at the chemist's."

"I'll try."

Balov said good night to the older man, who nodded from his chair but did not get up. Natasha had the candle. At the foot of the stairs she pinched out the flame.

"There aren't any blackout curtains. Give me your hand. I'll lead you out."

Her hand felt slightly moist in his. At the front of the shop a patch of moonlight spilled through the window. Her face was upturned in it, pale, full of confused desires. Impulsively Balov kissed her. Her mouth, impossibly soft, didn't return the kiss or resist it, either.

"Come out with me tomorrow," Balov said.

"I can't."

"To the ballet. Bogulubskaya's dancing. I can get tickets for the performance."

"No." She shook her head firmly.

"I thought you liked music?"

"I do."

"Then come."

"No, it's impossible."

"Afraid Vlasik will find out? Is that it?"

She didn't reply, but he knew it was true.

"Don't worry," he said. "You won't bump into Vlasik or his kind at the Bolshoi. Besides, I can handle him. Let me take care of things."

"I've never seen Bogulubskaya dance. They say she's lovely."

"Yes." He touched her cheek. "But not as lovely as you."

"Tomorrow's my day with Metlin." Natasha shrugged. "I suppose you could come by the Institute. I could leave early."

"Good. Two o'clock, then. It's settled."

He wanted to kiss her again but decided not to press his luck. Better to leave before she changed her mind. Outside, the night wind put its icy respirations into his face. He sensed Natasha watching him from the curtain as he crossed the street, but he didn't turn to wave.

Chapter
14

THE Institute for Herpetologic Research lay a few blocks off Sverdlov Square. The building had served as a private bank before the revolution. Balov arrived a bit before two and found Natasha upstairs on the gallery above the main hall. She wore a laboratory smock and rubber gloves and carried a small cage. A furry shape moved inside the wire mesh, and Balov caught the swirl of a pink tail.

"One of the snakes has to be fed before I leave."

"Shall I come with you?"

"If you like, but it's not a very pretty sight."

"I'm not squeamish."

What had been the main floor of the bank was now an exhibit hall. The snakes inhabited a dozen large enclosures, glassed-in for viewing, each set in the decor of a natural habitat. Vivid hues of jungle foliage gave way abruptly to sand and desert rock, dead limbs bleached and twisted like driftwood, and the prickly spines of counterfeit cactus. A brass rail encircled the pens to keep spectators back, and a printed card identified each species.

"That's a tic polanga from India," Natasha said, pointing to one as they passed along the rail and moved on to the next enclosure. "And here's our only surviving mamba."

"Where?" Balov stared through the thick glass of the pen into an African setting.

"In the tree."

Now he spotted it, easily three meters long and as thin as a coach whip, in the limbs of an artificial tree. Dead still, the mamba blended treacherously into the slender branches and arbors of green leaf. All at once it moved. The green form melted out of the tree and was gone in a single quick slither into a rock crevice.

They stopped before the last of the pens. The card read: GABOON VIPER—*BITIS GABONICA*.

The serpent lay stretched in an *S* shape over a rocky shelf. Not quite two meters long, with vivid markings, it presented a far more fearsome appearance than the mamba. The flat, triangular head was as wide across as the back of Balov's hand. The slender neck swelled almost at once to a repulsively stout body, thick as a python's at the center and shrinking abruptly to a stubby tail. A blunt horn protruded above the snout, and the eyes were like two silver scales.

"Ugly devil," Balov said.

"One of the most dangerous too," Natasha said. "Quite powerful and very unpredictable. I don't like to handle it."

"Don't you keep serum on hand in case of a bite?"

"For some species, yes. But there's no specific antivenin for a Gaboon viper. You just have to be very cautious."

Natasha unlocked a sliding panel in the wooden frame beneath the thick glass of the pen. She pressed one end of the feeding cage to the opening, lifted the wire door, and ejected the rat into the rocky enclosure. Immediately she closed and locked the sliding panel.

It was a large rat, a resident of the sewers from the look of its scruffy coat, and the eyes flashed like watermelon seeds. The tail jerked apprehensively. Balov had a glimpse of two sharp incisors as the whiskered muzzle nervously sniffed the air.

At first the snake didn't move. Then Balov saw a glimmer of life in the silvery eyes. The heat-seeking tongue flicked out. Flicked again. The flat head lifted slowly and dropped back. The thick body eased over the rocks in a slow glide.

The rat made a growling sound, more a reflex of fear than aggression. It knew instinctively the danger of the snake. Its body trembled. It seemed unable to react, over-taken by a paralyzing inertia.

The coiled neck of the snake hovered off the ground. The tongue flicked once more—a vanishing filament.

The rat tried to spring out of range, but the striking head was too fast. A blur of movement and the inch-long fangs were embedded in the animal's neck, the glands ejecting venom.

The rat lay on its side, pink feet jerking outward, its belly inflating and deflating rapidly. In seconds the convulsions ceased. The panic stayed frozen on the black, seedlike eyes.

The heart-shaped head of the snake remained next to its dead prey, the tongue still dancing out in lightning-quick thrusts from the scaly snout.

At the Bolshoi, Balov and Natasha sat alone in a theater box that looked down on the stage. Bogulubskaya danced the role of Juliet in the Prokofiev ballet. The high-waisted costume billowed out in a swirl of taffeta, she wore flowers in her hair and a silk ribbon at her throat, and the footlights gave her skin a warm glow of color.

From time to time Balov watched Natasha, profiled against the velvet drapes of the box, her downturned face alive to the beauty of the dance. She was totally absorbed in the performance, unaware of his attention.

But during an intermission, with the theater lit once more,

she seemed mildly anxious. The audience consisted largely of military officers in uniform. Below, on the main floor, was a section of ambulatory wounded and a row of nurses from the hospital. Natasha's attention strayed from them to the faces peering from the tiered galleries.

"Still worried about Vlasik?" Balov said.

"I don't want to complicate things."

He smiled, and his eyes looked straight into hers.

"But it might be interesting to complicate things." His tone challenged her with a soft insistence.

"They're complicated enough already." She looked at him gravely.

"There's no chance you'll see him here," Balov said, laughing. "He wouldn't know Prokofiev from Pushkin. Or either one from a breaded pork chop."

Her manner grew more relaxed when the massive chandeliers dimmed to a glimmer of crystal high up in the darkness. A hush swept over the crowd. In the orchestra pit the conductor tapped the podium with his baton and raised both arms. Again Natasha became lost in the performance.

At the end of the ballet the applause went on for several minutes. Most of the audience stood. From the section of wounded two soldiers went forward to the footlights and handed flowers to Marianne Bogulubskaya.

"She's enchanting," Natasha said.

It was the first time Balov could remember seeing her face lit with pleasure. The emotion, unguarded and close to the surface, had a charming innocence. When she turned to look at him, the radiant sparkle in her stare touched some unfamiliar chemistry of feeling in him, dangerously high-principled and noncarnal.

"All women are enchanting," he said.

"Some more than others?"

"Naturally."

Outside, the sky still held a little light after the matinee performance. They drifted down the wide stone steps, away from the soaring columns of the Bolshoi, into Sverdlov Square.

"I have vodka for Ivan Nikolayevich," Balov said. "Some packets of matches too. We can stop by my apartment for them if you like. It's not out of the way."

She didn't protest, and he interpreted the lack of a response as agreement.

They took a streetcar to Balov's district. The tram ground slowly down the tracks in the dusk. The coach was crowded at this hour, and they stood pressed together in the crush of people. Balov caught the scent of perfume in her hair and wondered if Vlasik had given her that too. The lashes were black against her cheeks, and when their hands touched on the support bar, Natasha looked up at him but did not move her fingers away.

Balov was sure they would go to bed in his apartment. He was, after all, experienced at breaking down resistance in women. He know how to appeal to their romantic instincts and how to give them pleasure. Preliminary advances were psychological, not physical.

Then why the second thoughts? That damned look on her face in the Bolshoi. It was enough to confuse a man. Sexual activity was nothing more than a healthy biological practice. Love, on the other hand, was a toxic emotion. Once it invaded the system, it lingered like malaria.

By the time they climbed the stairs to his apartment, Balov was less certain of his ground. Natasha's feelings seemed once more well concealed behind the now familiar surface of icy control. Gone altogether was that sense of intimacy from the tram when their fingers had touched and remained in contact. Now he couldn't decide what thoughts about him were flashing through her mind.

The apartment was only two small rooms, but it had the luxury of a private bath and toilet, and a fine view of the district. A matching sofa and upholstered chair faced each other across a Turkish rug intricately patterned in vivid gold and crimson like a coat of arms. On a low wooden table were several pewter pieces of miniature artillery, an ivory chess set, and the bust of Caesar. Natasha paused to touch the garlanded head and remarked, "You've hardly room for him here."

"Everyone has to make sacrifices these days," Balov said. "Even dead emperors."

Natasha moved on to the window and looked out at the charcoal smudge of the evening that hung above the rooftops. Balov glanced at Caesar and smiled. *We all have our Rubicons*, he thought. *What else to do but cross them?*

He approached Natasha from behind, immediately put his arms around her waist, and softly kissed her neck. A shiver of pleasure passed through her. He moved his hands to her breasts and held them and went on caressing the side of her neck with his lips.

He heard a tiny moan, hardly more than a gasp. Natasha turned toward him, her head thrown back, and this time the overripe mouth was explicit in its own need. Her lips stirred heatedly under his; she was sexually aroused, and the intensity of her desire passed all the way into the fingers trembling at the back of his neck.

Just as suddenly, Balov felt a barrier rising in her. Her hands slid down to his chest, and he could sense the passive resistance in them even as her mouth broke off the kiss.

Her reaction puzzled him. He knew she was attracted to him. Whatever psychological conflicts operated in her now, Balov was sure she desired the physical intimacy. Probably he could force it, but he didn't want her that way.

He touched her cheek with his fingers so she would look at him. She might have been one of those classical players behind a Greek mask with the emotions painted onto it.

"What is it, Natasha Ivanovna? Tell me."

"No." Her gaze slid away from his. She shook her head. "I would like so many things to be different. My whole life, in fact. But wishing it so doesn't change it."

"Different? What things?"

"We all have obligations," she replied vaguely. "They come first, before personal feelings."

Balov thought she must be talking about Vlasik. But after he had taken her home and left, he turned the phrase over in his mind and wondered if it had another meaning.

Chapter
15

DURING the night Tony Ryder dreamed about his dead wife. German planes hung above the searchlight probes on the sky over Coventry. Ryder began to panic. His wife . . . Where was Fighter Command? Why weren't the raiders being intercepted?

Bombs screamed down, exploding in tiny eruptions of light. The silhouettes of buildings took shape in the flames. A rosy glimmer enveloped the city.

Suddenly, in the dream, he was in the burning district where his wife lived. He kept shouting her name. *Cathy!* All around him flames soared above the gutted shells of buildings. He raised a hand to ward off the intense heat. Then he saw his wife wandering toward him. He shouted again, but the roar of the fire storm deadened the cry. A wall collapsed in blazing rubble. A billowing sheet of fire swept into the street. She covered her face and screamed, turning back and forth in it. Her clothing and hair ignited as she ran blindly from the conflagration. Ryder was running, too, but couldn't overtake her. The whole nightmare was one of intense desperation in which he found himself powerless to change events.

He woke with the debris of the dream on his eyes. Nearby Krylov slept soundlessly. Ryder got up from the pallet. In the dark he went out into the front room, opened the blackout curtains, and checked the street.

The apartment was on the second floor above the boulevard and consisted of three rooms, cramped and small, with thin walls like a hutch. A threadbare rug covered the floor only partially, the brown wallpaper was flaking in spots, and the few furnishings were rickety and old with stuffing herniated from rips in the worn upholstery.

It was now six days since their arrival in Moscow, and they still waited for the man Vlasov had called Uncle Vanya. Perhaps the conspiracy would turn out to be a Chekhov plot after all, one in which the characters could never see past their own vanities and conceits into the failures of their lives. Ryder didn't care. The angry pain over his wife's loss made him indifferent to the catastrophes of others.

He looked out at the rooftops, dark against the skyline—a long way from Coventry. Now a different image superimposed itself on the glass pane over the memory of his wife. He turned and saw Serova in the doorway. In the dark he couldn't distinguish her face, only the figure in the cloth robe, the white hands tying the cord at her waist. His wife's hands . . .

"I heard a noise." She came to the window. "I thought someone cried out."

"Only a dream," Ryder said.

"Can't you sleep?"

"No."

"I can't sleep, either."

Her breasts were lifted together, round and high in the cheap cloth, and two banded sheaves of hair fell down either side of her face.

What was it about her that tripped the silent alarm in his nerves? Behind a frown his mind groped with the problem.

It wasn't the first time her manner struck him as overtly sexual and deliberately provocative. Clearing dishes from the table, she seemed to make a point of leaning close. The heavy breasts spilled forward, loose and unconfined in the bulky sweater, and, once, the tip of one grazed his cheek. Another time her thigh pressed against him. Always he was aware of some careless sexuality in these physical contacts but kept just out of reach behind a smile, or a stare held a moment longer than necessary.

"Are you worried about Uncle Vanya?" she said.

"He'll come when he's ready."

"Suppose he's been caught and questioned?"

"It's possible."

"What will you do?"

Ryder shrugged and said, "What can I do?"

"I don't know. But you must have thought about it."

"I think about quite a few things."

"Your wife?" Serova smiled at him. "You're married, aren't you?"

"Yes."

"Don't you think about her?"

"When I can."

"Where is she?"

"Waiting for me."

"Do you love each other?"

"Why do you ask so many questions?"

"Shouldn't I be curious about you? Shouldn't you be curious about me?"

Ryder said, "We loved each other."

"Then it must be difficult for you," Serova said, "to be without a woman."

She stood directly in front of him, an attitude of passive confrontation in the nearness of her body. In the moon's pale radiance he was aware only of the persistent, questioning smile on her mouth and the deep line of cleaving flesh the robe exposed.

Ryder's own shirt was open down the front. Serova put her hand lightly against the matting of hair on his chest.

"You have black hair," she murmured, and ran her fingers through it. "Very thick. Mine is thick too. But it's blond."

The fingers continued to caress his chest. They sent a pleasurable excitement all the way through him to some white-hot seminal core of compressed feeling. The smile was tight on her mouth, and all the undeciphered meaning of the last week was suddenly clear, impatient, no longer encoded in the stare that held his.

"Shall I show you how thick?" she said, and drew his hand into the folds of the robe and pressed his fingers to the flowering of hair already damp with sexual heat.

Later, in his own room, Ryder stared up into the dark. Krylov still slept soundly on the other pallet. The episode with Serova had been swift, explosive. He had a memory of hot, bare breasts, a sliding wetness enfolding his erection, straining vaginal movement, and his own hardness breaking in her. Pain and pleasure flooded out of him. He withdrew roughly from her and heard a faint whimper. He couldn't see her face in the moonlit shadows, only the inside of her parted legs and the wetness of his ejaculation shining on them.

Now he lay with his forearm across his eyes, trying to forget. A sense of infidelity mounted in him. Remorseful shame burned out of his cheeks. He thought of his wife's picture in the flat, and her stuffed dog on the mantelpiece, and for a long time the only reaction left in him was a crushing sadness.

In the morning Serova gave no indication that anything was different. She went about her usual routine with her familiar, quiet efficiency. Nothing in her manner suggested they had been lovers the night before. Her glances contained not even a trace of cool lust. The absence of any residual emotion, even a negative one, puzzled him.

At ten-thirty A.M. she went out as usual to the telephone kiosk in the park to await the call—if it should come—from their Moscow contact. From the window Ryder watched her cross the boulevard into the park, a scarf tied over her head, a string shopping bag looped about her arm. If the telephone call did not come, she would go on to join the queue outside the food cooperative.

A streetcar clanged past on the tracks below the window. The sides had been stripped from the coach for loading and unloading cargo. Sacks of cement, piled high, were being hauled to the outskirts of the city to harden fortifications. Now, with the spring thaw, there was fear that fighting would soon resume in the capital.

In the park Serova passed out of sight behind the mounds of firewood that had been cut and stacked by the timber brigades in the fall. Most of the neat piles were collapsed now in a tangle of logs where children played "Partisan," using sticks for rifles.

Krylov came in and stood in the sunlight at the window and listened to their shouts.

"Even the children play war," he said.

"The game may not stop for some of them."

"If I could only change one thing," Krylov said, "it would be that."

"Maybe you'll get your chance."

"It would be nice to think so. But I'm afraid events shape men, not the other way around."

"If you really believe it, Maxim Nikolayevich, why did you come here?"

"Because I'm a victim of events like anyone else—the same events that touched my father and sisters and brother."

"Is that the only reason?"

"Because I believe in honor," Krylov added, "still."

"Enough to die for it?"

"Yes, if it comes down to that."

The remark touched a memory: Honor requires courage. . . . Men of honor can never be disgraced. . . .

Ryder said, "Better not confuse honor with nerve."

Krylov hesitated and replied, "I think it may be possible to have courage without honor, but not honor without courage. I believe that when they murdered my father, he faced down his executioners in those few seconds before the shots rang out. I know he wouldn't have turned from them. He was too proud. That's the only inheritance I collected from him. Until now I've never had to spend any of it."

"Maybe you won't have to."

"I wonder what you believe in," Krylov said.

"I don't have time to think about principles. Sometimes they only get in the way."

"What do you think about?"

"The job."

"I know what your job is," Krylov said.

Ryder stared quietly at the other man and did not reply.

"Don't look so surprised." Krylov smiled sadly. "British Intelligence sent you along in case something goes wrong. You're supposed to kill me. It's true, isn't it?"

"My job is to keep you alive."

"I know you can't admit it." Krylov shrugged. "Don't worry. You won't have to do it. I'll use the pill—if the time ever comes. They say it's very quick. It's one thing to face your executioners, as my father did, when they are murderers and cowards. But how do you face your friend?"

Another tram went by in the street, and Ryder frowned. On the other side of the park Serova came out of the telephone kiosk. She did not turn in the direction of the market cooperative but hurried back, under the bare trees, toward the apartment building.

"It's Serova," Ryder murmured.

"Did she hear something, finally?"

"She's coming back."

"She looks in a hurry."

"Be careful of her," Ryder said.

"Serova? Don't you trust her?"

"We're too close to things now to take any chances," Ryder said.

Chapter
16

"HE'S coming after dark," Serova said.

"Tonight?" Ryder said.

She nodded.

Krylov said, "Was it the same man you talked to six days ago?"

"The voice sounded the same."

"What else?" Ryder said.

"He'll knock twice, wait, and knock twice again."

Ryder looked at the time. It was not quite eleven. Still the long afternoon ahead, but at least events were moving.

Serova left once more for the cooperative. Ryder and Krylov played chess at the dining table with its cracked oilcloth cover, but they were too preoccupied to concentrate on the game.

"I wonder who he is," Krylov said.

"One of Vlasov's people, I suppose."

"I wish Vlasov were here in Moscow."

"If it succeeds," Ryder said, "he probably will be."

Across the table the bearded face glanced up from the

inert conflict on the chessboard with a sad, questioning smile.

"And if it fails?"

Ryder lit a cigarette and squinted through the smoke at the board where only a few pawns remained in the decimated ranks.

"Then it won't matter," he said.

Serova came back at two P.M. They heard her at the door, and Krylov went to unlatch it. The string bag contained sausage and black bread but no fruits or vegetables. At the electric burner she boiled water and brewed tea from pumpkin rind sliced into tiny flakes and left to dry.

Ryder took his cup to the window. Komsomol youths, shouting patriotic slogans, dragged carts of scrap metal down the street. Customers went in and out of the shoe repair shop on the corner. In the park children once again played war games. An old man used his spectacles to magnify the sun and light a cigarette held under one lens.

Later the park fell silent. Evening hung in the bare limbs. The shoe repair shop was locked. The sound of a distant tram faded away. A man sat alone in the park. Uncle Vanya? Waiting for darkness? Ryder watched him. But a little while later the man got up and walked down the boulevard.

The red evening slipped off the horizon, leaving dark lesions of shadow behind in the park. Ryder heard a sound in the hallway, followed by two knocks. His hand slipped inside his coat to the pistol in his waistband.

The door carried the second rap of knuckles into his nerves.

"Who is it?" Serova called.

It seemed interminable seconds before the muffled voice came back.

"Uncle Vanya."

Serova glanced over her shoulder at Ryder, who nodded. She unlatched the door.

A Soviet officer stepped quickly into the room. He had a chunky figure, short and wide, with an oversized neck and a dockworker's muscles corded into the shoulders. Hard to tell where the neck ended and the shoulders began. The low, sloping forehead, thickened ridge of a brow, and cave-like sockets belonged more properly on an ape, or on one of those links to prehistoric man where the features had been reconstructed over skull fragments.

"I am Shevchenko." The voice was surprisingly articulate. He glanced from Ryder to Krylov and said, "Maxim Nikolayevich?"

"Yes," Krylov said.

"We have many things to talk about, I think, and not much time."

The Soviet colonel sent Serova down into the park. Then he took off his greatcoat and sat at the table where a candle, stuffed into the neck of a bottle, threw its flickering gleam back across his face.

"What I have to say is only for the two of you." He unfolded a map of Moscow and smoothed out the creased landscape with a square, blunt fist.

"When will the operation go?" Ryder said.

"Seventy-two hours from now," Shevchenko said. "On the fourteenth of April."

Krylov said, "Will it be confined to Moscow?"

"The main thrust is centered here—in thirteen of the twenty-five military districts. We have two rifle brigades supported by a tank battalion. Armored units will be prepositioned at various locations, the greatest number concentrated just outside Red Square. These will move on targets inside the Kremlin."

Ryder said, "What about Stalin's Guard Directorate?"

"The commander will be absent," Shevchenko said. "Owing to his passion for a certain young woman. We've arranged that he should consummate it at a villa near Kuntsevo on the fourteenth of April. One of our own officers will assume command. He will divert guard units from the Spassky Gate and war room, then surrender the force once our tanks are inside the Kremlin."

"Suppose they ignore the order?" Ryder said.

"How do you ignore 76.2-mm cannons on T-34 tanks?" Shevchenko replied.

Krylov said, "What can I do to help?"

"Once we've occupied the Kremlin and secured communications, a representative of the Provisional Military Government will make a radio address. You'll follow him with a message to the nation. I've brought the speech so you can read it now. If you disagree with anything, we can discuss changes."

While Krylov studied the text in the other room, Shevchenko drew a cigarette packet from his tunic. Only four and a half cigarettes remained, and he laid them side by side on the table.

"Smoke?" he said to Ryder, and took one himself.

The loosely packed tobacco burned quickly. Ryder squinted through the streaming plume and said, "How much of the army is committed?"

Shevchenko frowned, taking time to reply carefully.

"Here is what you have to understand about the army. Numbers mean nothing. It's not a question of how many are committed but, rather, how many will oppose us. The whole issue of success or failure swings on one event...."

"One event?" Ryder smiled and could remember Krylov saying, "Events shape men, not the other way around."

"Yes, and it is central to everything else. If we fail to kill Stalin, no one will support us. If we succeed, no one will oppose us. Of course, there are a few loyal Stalinists—Timoshenko, Voroshilov, Budenny. But the best field commanders will side with us once they know Stalin's death is a fait accompli. Why should they resist? They have everything to gain. The commissar system in the army will be summarily abolished. If a gun were pointed at your head and you had a chance to turn it away, wouldn't you seize the opportunity?"

"What about NKVD troops?" Ryder said. "They don't take orders from the army."

"Next to Stalin, the NKVD is our major concern. Beria heads the list of key figures who will be arrested. Armored units are committed to key targets. The NKVD barracks, here," he said, tapping the map with a heavy forefinger, "and over here"—another tap—"the headquarters at Lubyanka prison. They are priority objectives. Once we've broken the back of the NKVD in Moscow, the rest of it will crack easily."

Ryder said, "How will you kill Stalin?"

The tough features of the Soviet officer grew contemplative in the candle's wavering glow. The thick fingers, blunt and flat across the nails, teased one of the cigarettes that lay on the frayed oilcloth.

"Poison," he said.

"Not always reliable," Ryder said, shaking his head.

"It will be done by someone close to him," Shevchenko said, "an individual he would never suspect. That's all I can tell you. Even if the rest of this business should fail, *that* has to succeed. He's a sick, dangerous fool. His madness comes and goes unpredictably. For the sake of Russia . . ."

Krylov came back and stood in the candlelight with the papers.

"I see no reason to change anything," he said. The familiar melancholy in his gaze fastened on Shevchenko. "I would like to believe that the men who wrote these words aspire to the same decency."

"They're faithful to Russia," Shevchenko said.

"Will General Vlasov take power?" Krylov said.

"As soon as the situation has stabilized, Andrei Andreyevich will fly back to Moscow from the Leningrad front. Whether he'll assume a role in the military triumvirate or not, I can't say."

Shevchenko reached for another cigarette. He took the one that had been cut in half, leaned close to the candle, and lit the tip. Even in this his movements were decisive and direct.

"Anyway," he said, smiling, "we don't always end up doing the things we planned to do in this life, do we? I wanted to study architecture. Here I am, instead, a soldier. You can't change events."

No, Ryder thought. Not a firestorm at Coventry or a bloody cellar at Ekaterinburg.

The Soviet colonel rose to put on his greatcoat. He stood for a moment with his back to them. Above the collar the overdeveloped neck looked more suited to a circus strongman, for bending iron bars, than an architect.

Ryder said, "How well do you know the woman who brought us here?"

"She's only a courier." The other turned, buttoning his greatcoat. "I don't know her at all."

"How did she get involved?"

"She was recruited."

"Who recruited her? Is he here in Moscow?"

"Killed." Shevchenko shook his head. "In the fighting for Kholm."

"Doesn't anyone else know her by sight?"

"She's from Murmansk."

"But she went to school, once, in Moscow. She told us her father was a staff officer for Marshal Tukhachevsky."

"It's true. They all fell in the purge of 'thirty-seven. There's a photograph of Serova with her father. I've seen it."

Ryder moved to the window, drew the blackout curtain

away from the glass, and looked down at the street. Serova sat on a bench at the entrance to the park, her figure partially obscured by night shadows.

"A picture of the woman sitting down there?"

Shevchenko came over and stood beside him.

"It was an early photograph of very poor quality. The girl in it looked about fourteen."

"Is it the same person?"

"How can I be sure? The face was fuller somehow."

"But that's understandable," Krylov said from the table. "The difference between a girl and a woman."

"What color was her hair?" Ryder said.

"Blond, as I recall," Shevchenko said, "and very light." A loose smile curled around the stub of the cigarette dangling from the heavy mouth. "Like the woman in the park."

Before he went out, the Soviet officer turned for a last word.

"Be ready to leave here at nineteen hundred hours on the evening of the fourteenth. We'll send a car. The driver will use the same signal. Two knocks and the code—Uncle Vanya. You'll be driven to a holding area near the radio station. Good luck."

A few minutes after Shevchenko's departure Serova came up from the street. The cool evening had brought the blood to her cheeks. She took off her coat, brewed tea, and served it at the table.

"But it's real tea!" Krylov exclaimed.

"I've been saving it," she said, "for a special occasion."

They were silent, savoring the tea. Krylov caught sight of a pendant on a chain around her neck and remarked on it.

"It belonged to my mother. It was a gift to her from my father." She held the gold shape toward him on the end of the chain, but her gaze shifted to Ryder. "See? It has my mother's name engraved on the back."

"You've never worn it before," Ryder said.

"You haven't noticed, that's all."

When she had finished her own tea, Serova overturned the dregs into her saucer and reflected over the arrangement.

Krylov smiled and said, "What do you see in the leaves, Katerina Alekseyevna?"

"It seems we won't be together much longer. . . ."

"Three more days," Krylov said.

"The fourteenth? Am I supposed to take you somewhere?"

"They're sending a car."

Ryder looked at her sharply. The familiar mistrust cut a little more deeply into his nerves.

"Don't worry," he said to her. "You'll get your instructions."

Chapter
17

ON the twelfth of April, Balov and Serova met in a room above the shoe repair shop on the corner.

Balov arrived first, entering from the rear of the building away from the street. The old cobbler in his leather apron, shirtsleeves rolled above his elbows, nodded from his bench and went on working. Balov went upstairs and waited by the window of the narrow room where the cobbler lived. The cot was unmade, and the pillow, soiled and rank from old perspiration, had no case. A bare bulb dangled from a ceiling cord over a cluttered table. The chamber pot hadn't been emptied, and there was a smell of ammonia from standing urine.

Balov lifted a pair of opera glasses and screwed them into focus until the park jumped, sharp and clear, into the lenses. The trees and boulevard raced through the glasses as he swung them to the left and held steady on the window of the apartment occupied by Ryder and Krylov. No sign of activity. He lowered the binoculars, settled down in a chair, and watched the boulevard.

In a short while Serova came out of the apartment building, tying a scarf, and glanced up at the dark clouds massing over the city. She crossed the street and started through the park, both hands thrust into the pockets of a raincoat belted tightly at her waist.

Balov picked her up in the opera glasses. The long legs were a marvel of engineering, and the glasses drew into detail her breasts heavily steeped against the raincoat. He had a vivid memory of the tips, flushed and swollen hard with erotic feeling, during a weekend in bed with her in his apartment. The experience convinced him that her sexuality passed beyond normal limits into some clinical range of nymphomania.

Pity the Hitlerites if they ever occupied Moscow. She would surely send an aging field marshal or two into cardiac spasms during one of those sexual Götterdämmerungs. Smiling, he lowered the binoculars.

A few minutes later Serova climbed the stairs.

"Shevchenko came to the apartment last night," she said as Balov helped her out of the raincoat.

He nodded and said, "I saw the surveillance report this morning."

"I had to leave while they talked."

"I know that too."

"But it doesn't matter. I have the date. Whatever they're planning to do is going to happen on the fourteenth."

Balov stared at her.

"The fourteenth? You're sure?"

"They're sending a car to pick up both men."

"Two days," Balov said, frowning.

"Now you know why I had to see you."

Sounds drifted up from the shop: the cobbler pounding nails into a shoe, the grinding hum of a belt-driven machine.

Balov gazed out the window at the apartment. Two days. Not much time. The surveillance of Shevchenko had produced nothing important. The officer was either too wary or too clever to make the kind of mistake Balov had counted on. Now, suddenly, the advantage had shifted out from under him.

"If it's a military move to take power," Balov said, "it would have to involve significant numbers of people. Senior officers . . . units . . ."

"Why do you say *if*? How can you believe it's anything else?"

"Because," he said, shaking his head, "I find it inconceivable that any operation of that size could have been kept secret this long."

"Not exactly a triumph for State Security, is it?"

Balov smiled and said, "In the old days you could have been denounced and sent off for a remark like that."

"Then who would do your dirty work for you?" she replied with suppressed amusement. "Anyway, Balov, what else could it be except a militarist plot?"

"Yes," he said. "What else?"

"Face it," Serova said. "You've run out of time. You'll have to make your arrests now."

"So the ones at the top can slip away?" he said. "To try it again?"

"Shevchenko must know the details," she insisted. "He's the key."

Again Balov fell silent. He found it maddening to be this near, yet unable to close the net. He had, after all, manipulated things to keep control of this investigation, even withheld information from his superiors. The success had to be his own, not a collaboration. Failure, on the other hand, would also be his responsibility. He found a certain grim humor in the prospect of a bullet behind the ear. Two days. Forty-eight hours. Clearly the narrowed time frame reduced his options.

He said, "You're right. There isn't any other way. We'll pick up Shevchenko tonight."

"The others too?"

"Not until the fourteenth. You mentioned a car coming for them. . . ."

She nodded.

"Yes. At nineteen hundred hours."

"We'll wait until then."

"Suppose they find out Shevchenko's in custody?"

"Shevchenko's arrest will have to be kept secret."

"How?"

"He's under the command of General Sinilov. We'll say he was called out to Sinilov's headquarters on secret business. It's a matter of covering his absence for . . . how long? Thirty-six hours?"

"What if Sinilov is involved?"

"We'll arrange something for him. Maybe a meeting. I don't know. In any case, I'll have a commissar with him even when he wipes his behind."

Thunder rolled across the distance. The smell of rain drifted through the open window.

"If I could be alone with Krylov . . ." Serova said, then shook her head. "But it's impossible."

"What sort of man is he?"

"A fool," she said. "It's the Canadian you'd better worry about, not Krylov."

"Why?"

Serova frowned and replied, "It's just a feeling I have when I'm around him. He'll be dangerous, Balov, if you give him the chance."

"I don't intend to give him the chance."

The first drops of rain spattered like grapeshot against the window. Balov closed it. Then he held up the raincoat for her and said, "Weren't you able to seduce him?"

"What do you suppose?" She slipped into the raincoat, tying the belt.

His hands smoothed the collar of the garment. It didn't

take much to arouse her—just the caress of her shoulders. He could feel the voltage come back from her body into his fingers. She was a clockwork of springs, too tightly wound. Maybe when this business was finished...

An afterthought worked to the surface, dragging a troublesome curiosity behind it.

He called after her, "What kind of a lover was he?"

Serova turned on the stairs, the railing dark and still under her hand. The tiniest smile, wry and arrogant, pulled at the edge of her mouth. Even before the railing began to slide under her hand again, he knew it was the only answer he would get.

Chapter
18

THE man chosen to kill Stalin was Major V. I. Chernov. At daybreak on April thirteenth he was fencing with General Zhukov at a barracks not far from the Kremlin. It was an old cavalry barracks from tsarist days, and many staff officers, including Chernov, were quartered in the redbrick billets.

The indoor arena, where the two officers fenced, had once been used during long winter months to train cadets in the skills of horsemanship. Now the first morning light shone through the windows in the arched dome, high overhead, and a few falling rays touched the earthen floor, which still held the faint improvisation of hooves on its hard-packed surface.

The foils rang across the silence. The two figures drew apart. They faced each other in their protective wire masks, padded jackets, and leather gloves, foils extended, legs flexed, left arms upraised.

Zhukov, the heavier of the two, attacked. Always the general relied on brute strength to force the issue. Chernov had the more graceful movement, superior quickness, and supple wrist action. Zhukov feinted to a *quarte* thrust. Chernov parried it and scored his own riposte, which drew a grunt of surprise from the senior officer.

Both men stepped back, saluting with their blades. Zhukov lifted his protective mask and stripped off his gloves.

Sweat poured down his face onto the quilted jacket, already drenched. His competitive nature drove him to try to win at any physical cost, though he respected ability in an opponent and did not hold silly grudges over losing.

Chernov raised his own wire mask. The features had only a light glaze of perspiration. The heavy mouth, full as that of an African idol, gave an impression of sensuality.

A staff intelligence officer, Chernov was known for his mental quickness, mastery of detail, and scholarly pursuit of military history. He had a background in classical literature and philosophy, a self-acquired knowledge of opera, and had authored several papers on the Napoleonic campaigns.

Zhukov said, "Will you ride this morning, Chernov?"

The vitality of Stalin's best general seemed indefatigable. He would fence with subordinates, then gallop a horse until the animal collapsed—all before breakfast.

"Thank you, Comrade General. But I have an early briefing. My charts need work."

"Tomorrow, then." Zhukov shrugged. He added with jocular sarcasm, "Unless you have important plans on the fourteenth too."

"The fourteenth? No, it's just another day."

After Zhukov had departed, Chernov walked to his own quarters, bathed at the tin basin, dried his face and arms, and put on his tunic. He ran a brush through the thinning strands of sandy hair, then hooked on his glasses. They changed his appearance, emphasizing a cold intelligence, more intense than restless, in the thirty-five-year-old features.

He drew an American phonograph record from its jacket, fitted it on the Victrola, and lowered the coiled neck of the needle. Caruso came off the disc—the quartet from *Rigoletto*.

From his briefcase Chernov took two segments of a pointer. He joined them together, then examined the tiny hole, nearly invisible to the naked eye, at the rubber tip. Gripping the lower end of the rod, he twisted the upper section two full turns in a counterclockwise direction. Now a twenty-two-gauge hollow needle projected two and a half centimeters from the tip. Inside the tube the needle joined a balloon sack. The contents could be swiftly discharged by the action of a compressed plunger.

It was the device that would assassinate Stalin. A clockwise twist retracted the needle. Chernov broke down the pointer and hummed with Caruso. He wondered if it were possible for such a voice to occur more than once in a century.

Chernov came from a Leningrad family that had been well-to-do before the revolution. His father, an agricultural engineer, managed one of the royal estates on the banks of the Neva outside the city.

The mother, Lizaveta Mihalovna, had been born into the gentry. At the conservatory, where she studied the piano, she had passed her examinations with honors. Friends whispered that she had married beneath herself, though her husband held a position that paid handsomely.

In those days Chernov saw little of his father, whose duties tied him to the estate. The boy spent most of his time with his mother. He had a clear recollection of her seated at the Austrian-made Bosendorfer grand where the darkly polished piano wood reflected the whiteness of her brocaded dress with its long sleeves and flowering cuffs. She would play Brahms intermezzi and romantic works of Schumann, her eyes cast downward at the keyboard, and the brown hair luxuriantly piled atop her head seemed to the boy as soft as mist.

The doctors had warned Lizaveta Mihalovna after the birth of her son that she should bear no more children, and so she lavished attention on her only child. Each July they left their apartments in the city for a summer house where the high windows seemed always to melt sunlight into the rooms, and there was a fine view of the white birch wood slanting down to the marsh grass of the lake. They gathered wild berries, and his mother read stories to him, taught him songs, and dressed him in a sailor's suit with a square collar and nautical tie and round cloth cap. Whenever his father came, the three of them went out on the lake in a small boat after the heat of the day and rowed along the shore while the long twilight extinguished itself on the water. There were white nights, too, when the sun hardly sank over the horizon, and the sky and lake turned to mother-of-pearl and filled the rooms with a soft, radiant glaze.

The boy grew up indulged and spoiled. In school he excelled easily, an accident of brain chemistry, for he could process and retain information at a glance with almost a photographic clarity. His mother hoped her son would turn to music, but early on he developed a fascination for military history and a passion for chess. At age fourteen he played to a draw with a grand master of the game, and one foreign newspaper called him a chess prodigy.

By this time, however, the family's circumstances had undergone a radical change. The revolution had deprived them of their properties and livelihood. Only the fact that both parents had been openly sympathetic to the need for social change kept them outside the stern vengeance of the new government. Even so, their bourgeois past proved a hindrance at every turn. Because of his connection with the former royal estate, the father could find no work. Chernov could remember his mother, soon after this, watching in tears from the window as the Bösendorfer piano was carted off.

The family subsisted on buckwheat groats and dried codfish. The father attempted to join the Communist Party so that he might secure rations for his family, but his application was rejected. He was now in ill health and did not survive an attack of pneumonia the following winter.

Lizaveta Mihalovna managed at last to obtain work teaching school. She stubbornly persisted in efforts to have her son enrolled in the Komsomol. At home she permitted no mockery of the new regime, insisting that the collapse of the old system had been inevitable.

"You must deal with things as they are," she told him in a firm tone, "not with things as they might have been."

But sometimes in the drab apartment on a long winter night, when a fire blazed in the glowing iron belly of the stove, she would stare into the flicker of shadowy impressions and speak of the old life: of splendid balls in the palaces of St. Petersburg, the swirling whisper of high-waisted gowns as girls danced with young men across their own reflected movement on gleaming marble floors, and the music of Strauss drifting up, to be lost finally among the crystal tears of chandeliers as if, from above, they wept at some passing vision.

Chernov listened to his mother and found himself torn between his loyalty to the Komsomol and the privileged life that the revolution had arbitrarily confiscated from him.

Lizaveta Mihalovna had taken care to cultivate contacts who might prove useful. She tutored students privately in piano, and among her pupils were the children of the district Party boss. It was enough to tip the balance and secure for her son admission into a military school for officer training.

Chernov was now nineteen, just under six feet, his slim frame strung to a wiry tension. Smooth, fair skin gave him a boyish look, notwithstanding the early retreat of the sandy hair at his temples. He wore spectacles for reading, and the lenses fit nicely the icy glint of intelligence in his eyes. His mouth was molded to an exaggerated fullness, as if some arrogance had been deliberately shaped into it. His manner reflected an abrasive superiority made all the worse by a quick, acerbic wit.

In the classroom, during a discussion of Kutuzov's campaigns against Napoleon, he startled his instructor by saying, "Kutuzov was a fool. He could have beaten Bonaparte at Austerlitz, and there was no excuse to lose the field at Borodino, either."

The audacity of the remark produced a stunned silence.

"Are you such a tactical expert?" the instructor said. "Perhaps you would like to point out Marshal Kutuzov's mistakes. I'm sure your fellow cadets would appreciate the benefit of your genius."

Chernov strode forward, took the chalk, and diagrammed from memory the disposition of troops and artillery. His remarks had a clipped assurance as he proceeded to make his point.

The instructor nodded grudgingly after the boy had returned to his seat. "Possibly you have a point, but remember this. History is like a scorned lover. She reveals her secrets after the fact, not before."

In the class of officer trainees was an NCO who had fought under Budenny against Wrangel in the Crimea. The sergeant's name was A. N. Gritsky, and he had applied for officer training twice before but could not pass the written examinations. Now, under the strong endorsement of his battalion commander, an exception had been made to admit him as a cadet.

Gritsky was of medium height but sturdily built. He had grown up swinging a pick twelve hours a day in the coal fields of Silesia and he had a roughneck's sloping shoulders and big callused hands. His eyes were little more than flashing beads above a broken nose, and craters of extinct acne spoiled his lower face. Slumped low at his desk, his cheek resting in one hand, he listened to Chernov's comments.

That evening in the barracks, where the tiered cots were set up along an even row in the open bay, Gritsky came up to Chernov, who was polishing his boots.

"They want you down at the stables," he said.

"Why?" Chernov asked.

"In the Army you don't ask questions," Gritsky said. "You just obey orders. Come on, I'll show you where to go."

But when they reached the stables, the low-slung sheds were dark. The odor of manure and fodder hung on the air. Gritsky tipped one shoulder against a cornerpost, his arms dangling at his sides. The tight grin might have been wired into his thin mouth.

"I've been watching you," he said. "You're too smart for anybody's good. It makes the rest of us look stupid."

Chernov stared past the other man at the lights of the barracks uphill in the trees. The windows glimmered from a great distance. He would have started back, but Gritsky pushed away from the cornerpost, blocking his way.

"You need a lesson," he said, "in discipline. That's how it's done in the army. Now I'll show you a few tricks that Napoleon didn't know—or Kutuzov, either."

Chernov knew nothing about fighting with his fists, but that hardly mattered. He slipped out of his tunic, draping it across a bale of hay. If he had to take a beating, there was no point in ruining a uniform. He took off his glasses, folded them, and laid them on top of the garment.

The smirking pleasure never left Gritsky's mouth as the two men circled each other. Chernov held his fists low. Gritsky dropped his left shoulder in a feint and hit Chernov twice. When Chernov swung back, the other man blocked it and dug a fist into Chernov's midsection. Chernov doubled over, the wind knocked out of him. Another splat of fists drove him backward, and the plank boards of the stable shook as he slammed into them. He was down on his hands and knees. He spat a mouthful of blood and grabbed the other man's trouser leg, trying to get up. Once more the pounding fists left him gasping for breath in the thick dust. This time he had no legs to get up on.

"From now on," the ex-sergeant said, "there'll be no more showing off in front of the officers. I give the orders around here. Keep that in mind, or next time I'll break some teeth for you."

Chernov watched the stocky figure moving uphill toward the lights of the barracks. He struggled to his feet and staggered over to the trough. The water shone blackly in the tin gutter. He dipped a handkerchief into it and made a compress for his eyes. Both were swollen and sore. Already his mind was at work on a strategy of retaliation.

Next day, in the classroom, the instructor noticed Chernov's eyes, blackened and puffed. He did not comment but seemed faintly amused. Gritsky, too, regarded him with a satisfied sneer. Chernov was starting to understand how the system worked.

At the first opportunity he went out of his way to be helpful to the ex-sergeant. During examinations he would feed him answers to difficult questions. In a group he found subtle ways to acknowledge Gritsky's authority. By making himself gradually indispensable, Chernov assured his own position. Gritsky now became his protector instead of his antagonist.

The ex-sergeant fancied himself a man with the ladies. In the final months of training he began to see one girl exclusively and bragged that they were sleeping together. He had devised a way of getting out at night after the evening parade. This depended upon who was assigned as officer of the guard, for certain individuals were known to be conscientious in making required bed checks, while others went to sleep themselves in the guardroom where the rifles of the company were locked in racks. Gritsky would stuff his overcoat under the blankets of his cot and leave his polished boots displayed beside his footlocker. The cadet sentinels posted outside the barracks knew better than to report him. He would reappear before dawn, climbing in through a window that Chernov unlatched for him.

Two nights before graduation, a senior lieutenant named Orlov drew duty as officer of the Guard. Orlov had a reputation for laxity and sleeping through his tour. An hour after lights out Gritsky slipped away from the barracks. But this time, when he returned, the window was locked. He circled the billet to the entrance and tried to sneak past the guardroom. Lieutenant Orlov sat, wide-awake and vigilant, at the wooden table where the lamp threw its glare across the corridor. At morning parade Gritsky was absent from ranks.

That afternoon, the graduating cadets were given an off-post privilege until 2100 hours to take care of personal business. A group, including Chernov, went out to a party at a brothel. It was Chernov who left word where they would be. Before departing, he stopped by the armory and asked for six brass cartridge cases that had been fired from Nagant revolvers.

"What good are empty brass casings?" the armorer said.

"It's a joke we're playing," Chernov said.

In an upper room of the brothel they danced with half-clad prostitutes to music from a Victrola, and there was much drinking and loud laughter, and the cigar smoke hung in the light of paper-shaded lamps.

Chernov sat at a round table playing cards. The high collar of his tunic was open at the throat, and the lamp left a glint on his cheeks. Suddenly the voices around him broke off, the laughter fell silent, and Chernov glanced up from his cards to see Gritsky standing in the open doorway across the room. Gritsky was in uniform but no longer wore the shoulder boards of a cadet. One hand was clamped high up on the doorjamb, as if he were barring anyone's departure. Finally the hand dropped, and he advanced slowly to the table. The other players lowered their heads. Only Chernov met his stare.

"They've decided to deny my commission," Gritsky said. "I'm being sent off to a disciplinary battalion. Someone informed on me. I think it was you."

"Of course it was," Chernov said.

"Then you admit it? In front of these others?"

"It's for the good of the corps," Chernov said. "You're unfit to command troops in the field. For one thing, you're too stupid. For another, you're a coward."

Gritsky leaned forward in the light, resting his fists on the table. A look of blind incomprehension worked across his face, and he shook his head. One hand swept away a pile of chips that fell, clattering, across the floor.

"I'm going to show you who's a coward," he said.

"No," Chernov said crisply. "I'm going to show you. It's simple enough to demonstrate. Pasha!" he called out to the big Ukrainian whose job was to protect the girls in the brothel. "Bring us your revolver."

No one moved. Chernov glanced sharply at the Ukrainian. His tone had acquired a peremptory air of command, as if he were naturally in charge.

"Well? Didn't you hear me? Bring it here and be quick. I'll take responsibility. There'll be no trouble."

Pasha cast about for some countermanding instruction, but the faces remained blank. Finally he shuffled over. Chair legs scraped uneasily on the floor as the other players left the table.

"Sit down," Chernov said to Gritsky as he took the revolver matter-of-factly from Pasha. It was, as he knew from previous visits to the brothel, a single-action gas-check 7.62-mm Nagant. He opened the loading gate on the right side of the frame and pumped the extractor rod to eject the seven live rounds. Then he drew the six empty brass casings from the pocket of his tunic and reloaded them into the weapon. Finally he picked up one live round, which was indistinguishable from the six inert ones, for the 108-grain bullet was seated entirely in the brass cartridge case with its powder load of 12.3 grains of smokeless powder. This he inserted into the final empty pocket of the cylinder, rotating it several twists before he closed the gate. "Six cartridges on the table," he said, "and one live round left in the cylinder. Look, I'll take the first chance."

Chernov cocked the Nagant, pointed it at his temple, and pulled the trigger. The hammer snapped on an inert round in the chamber.

"Now you have a turn," he said. "Six chances out of seven to stay alive. Of course, they're diminished slightly by the law of averages. You'll have to figure that variable for yourself. I can't slip you the answer this time. Go ahead, pick up the revolver."

Gritsky stared at him for a long time. It was the night behind the stables all over again, but now the positions were reversed.

The others in the room remained silent, as much in rapt fascination as in fear. The needle of the phonograph made a scratching sound in the groove at the end of the record, but no one made a move to lift it. Gritsky's face had turned sallow. He opened the lever of the loading gate and gave the rotating breech several twists. After what seemed an interminable time he put the muzzle to his head and squeezed the trigger. The snick of metal on metal as the hammer dropped harmlessly seemed to pass all the way through his nerves, releasing the tension that surfaced into a weak smile on his mouth.

Chernov immediately picked up the Nagant, pressed the barrel to his temple, and pulled the trigger. He had not bothered to spin the cylinder. Once more the hammer clicked benignly. The whole sequence had taken no more than two seconds, just long enough to cock the piece.

"It's a matter of luck," Chernov said, "and luck is largely a question of knowing the mathematical probabilities. I would say the odds are now slightly weighted that the next shot will blow your brains out through your skull."

A lock of hair hung down over Gritsky's forehead. Though the room was not especially warm, perspiration shone on the ex-sergeant's face.

Gritsky stared at the Nagant. Long moments passed before he gripped it. He seemed lost in thought, perplexed, as he raised the piece to his temple. His finger tightened on the trigger, taking up the slack, but then it appeared to meet some terrible resistance. The revolver trembled under the physics of an altogether different force. The muzzle crept downward, as if moving by its own volition, for now Gritsky was like a man in a dream. The cocked revolver came to a stop, pointing at Chernov. A gasp broke across the tense silence in the room. One of the prostitutes screamed. Several cadets started forward, shouting at Gritsky to stop. Chernov only stared at the other man, the corner of his mouth curled down in acerbic contempt.

"You see?" he said. "Either way you're a coward."

Something cracked in Gritsky. The revolver became an enormous weight in his hand, sinking, until the barrel rested on the table. One of the cadets took the weapon gently out of his unresisting grip. Not looking to either side, Gritsky walked slowly out of the room.

Chernov raised the cocked revolver, put it to his temple,

and squeezed the trigger. Again the hammer dropped with a dull click. The faint smile on his mouth remained unchanged in its contempt, even as his friends crowded around him, everyone shouting at once.

Chapter
19

O N the morning of April thirteenth, while Chernov
worked on his briefing charts, Ryder and Krylov
were once more alone in the Kishkin apartment near
Sokolniki Park. Serova had left early to join the queue in
front of the cooperative.

Ryder heated water on the electric ring for shaving.
Stripped to the waist, he used a lump of hand soap in a cup
to build a lather, then scraped at the black stubble with a
straight razor. He had no strop or whetstone, and the blade,
cutting with a gritty sound, made the task impossibly slow.
But everything had slowed in this week of waiting.

Krylov sat near the window on the narrow sofa with its
flattened coil springs and ruptured stuffing. A copy of
Tolstoy's *Resurrection* was open in his hands, but his mind
seemed elsewhere. Ryder saw him close the volume and
get up from the sofa. He took a chair near the basin, holding
the book on his lap, and said, "I wonder who will do it?"

"Do what?" Ryder murmured.

"Kill Stalin."

The razor stopped moving halfway through its track. Ryder straightened, wiping the soap from the blade onto a strip of paper.

"What's the difference as long as he succeeds?"

"Somehow I wish it could begin without murder."

"Murder didn't bother them at Ekaterinburg."

"Still . . ."

Ryder turned from the glass and gazed down at the other man.

"Maxim Nikolayevich," he said. "Don't worry about things you can't change."

"I suppose you're right."

Ryder went back to the slow scraping. Behind his frown lay a different concern. It had to do with Vlasov's sudden reassignment from Moscow to the Volkhov front at Leningrad. The timing seemed too much a coincidence. Perhaps the whole affair had been compromised from the start. But if that was the case, why hadn't the NKVD moved to crush the conspiracy? Was it because they hadn't identified the assassin, either?

"I wonder who the other generals are?" Krylov said. "Zhukov, perhaps? They say he has easy access to Stalin."

"It won't matter." Ryder talked into the mirror. "If he goes along with it after the fact. Anyway, why shouldn't he? Vlasov was right. They have everything to gain now, and nothing to lose."

The other generals . . . Suppose there weren't any? Only Vlasov . . .

And Krylov? They would use him, Ryder thought, as long as he suited their convenience—a symbol of their noble intentions. Did the meek really inherit the earth? No, they were the disinherited. What little they had would be taken from them.

From the chair the bearded figure stared at him, as if he knew his train of thought.

"You don't believe their promises, do you?" Krylov said. "You think nothing will change, after all?"

Ryder shrugged and said, "Something always changes, Maxim Nikolayevich."

They fell silent. Ryder dipped a cloth in water and wiped the patches of lather from his face. A nick had drawn blood along his jaw, and he held the cloth against the cut to stop the flow.

Krylov said, "I've often wondered what my father could have done for Russia if the rescue had succeeded. I believe he came to an understanding of history too late. You can see it in his face at Tsarkoe Selo when the last photographs were taken—the resignation and dignity in his expression. They say he worked alongside his own guards, tilling the ground in the vegetable garden. Shall I tell you what I believe? If the monarchy had been restored, he would have transferred significant powers of State to the Duma. I think his murderers knew it too. They were afraid of that, most of all. . . ."

"You can't be your father," Ryder said, and slipped into his shirt.

"Yes, but I should like to follow the course I believe he would have wanted. He was an honorable man. . . ."

Ryder's fingers stopped moving on the buttons of the shirt. He thought of his own father, erect and motionless: *Listen, don't you hear it?*

Krylov said, "My mother and I were in Paris when the news came from Ekaterinburg. She wept for weeks. Do you know what seems strange to me? She was only fifty—the age I am now. She lived another dozen years, but I think her life really ended that day when we learned about the tsar's death. She's buried outside Paris, on a hill that faces to the east, toward Russia. . . ."

At noon Serova returned from the cooperative. She had queued in three lines, but there were no fresh vegetables or tinned meat and she had only a loaf of black bread, the flour laced with sawdust to make it stretch further.

"There are some cabbage leaves left," she said. "I'll make a soup."

The afternoon waned with excruciating slowness, as if it had been sedated on the sky. They had an early meal, and Ryder smoked a cigarette at the window while the evening aborted itself in a final tiny hemorrhage of twilight on the panes. The drift of darkness took the city off the horizon. Already the first stars burned on the clear night.

"Anton Stepanovich," Krylov asked in Russian, "what do you see in their arrangement?"

Ryder looked at him and replied, "It's not up to the stars to decide."

In the half darkness Serova smiled at his answer but said nothing.

Chapter
20

SHORTLY before ten on the morning of April thirteenth, Chernov arrived at Stalin's war room. Two guards checked him at the door. As always, he opened his briefcase, removed the papers, and lifted out the two sections of the pointer.

"My baton." He held up both pieces and smiled as one guard ran an enormous hand gingerly inside the empty briefcase. The guard handed it back and nodded for Chernov to proceed.

The high-ceilinged room, paneled in oak, contained a long conference table and chairs. Portraits of Marx, Engels, and Lenin had been joined by pictures of Kutuzov and Suvorov, heroes of the wars with France and Turkey. Chernov would have preferred Metternich and Massenet, but Stalin's sense of decor did not extend beyond revolutionary politics.

This morning Chernov would brief Georgy M. Malenkov, Stalin's deputy and adviser, and half a dozen lesser commissars. The briefing would cover the general order of battle from the Gulf of Finland and south to the Sea of Azov; it was the same presentation Chernov would give tomorrow evening to Stalin and the members of Stavka, the General Staff. Malenkov had requested a preliminary briefing. Not hard to guess why. He wanted prior knowledge of the material so that he could impress Stalin on some strategic point.

The others stood up when Malenkov came in. Two minutes and twenty seconds late, Chernov noted. Tomorrow night, with Stalin present, the pudgy deputy would be more prompt. He would sit with his fingers together, eyes downcast under their fatty folds, while the slack face assumed an expression of subservient devotion.

But not today. Now he flung himself into Stalin's chair with an air of surly power and gave an imperial nod—the signal to begin.

Chernov spoke faultlessly and with clipped precision. He required no supporting notes. His inexhaustible grasp of detail always astonished his audiences. Even Stalin.

Tapping the charts with his pointer, he tried to imagine that it was Stalin at the head of the conference table. A dress rehearsal for tomorrow evening's performance.

At the finish there were no questions. Chernov went over to his briefcase under Lenin's portrait, stooped down, and buckled the flap. Normally, after a Stavka briefing, he broke down the pointer. Today he would carry it out in his right hand. He went through the imaginary motions of twisting the rod twice, counterclockwise, but did not actually arm the device.

Absorbed in fresh discussion, the men at the table hardly noticed him. The exit he would take lay behind Stalin's chair to the far left. Chernov started for it. Going out, he passed directly behind Malenkov's seated figure. The deputy's fat neck bulged over his uniform collar. Chernov imagined that it was Stalin's neck. His concentration became so intense, he could nearly detect the slow throbbing of the carotid artery, and like a surgeon, he saw precisely where he would place the dart.

* * *

At five that afternoon Chernov crossed the square where Balov and Natasha, a few days earlier, had sat and talked. He walked up the side street, bathed in cold shade, to the secondhand shop. A bell went off as he stepped inside. He heard the click of beaded curtains in the rear, and Natasha appeared among the gloomy shadows.

Chernov said, "I've come to pick up Apollo's head."

"You aren't the same person who left it," Natasha said.

"No. Were you able to repair it?"

"Yes, but it's rather badly flawed. Perhaps we could find you a new one."

"I have use for a flawed Apollo," Chernov replied, using the coded response.

Natasha went back through the curtains. Chernov heard her on the stairs. She returned cradling a bust of Apollo—a hollow ceramic—and placed it on the counter.

"The vials are inside," she murmured.

"Where?"

"Taped to the bottom."

"What kind of venom?"

"It was taken from a Gaboon viper," Natasha said.

"How quickly will it act?"

"That depends. If you strike a vessel or artery anywhere near the head, it should be only minutes. A small amount is extremely toxic."

Chernov glanced at the ceramic face. Hairline cracks ran across the glazed surface where fragments had been glued together. He took the bust from the counter and went out.

In the street the cool breeze touched his face, and he remembered the way Malenkov's fat neck had looked above the tight collar. What an easy target Malenkov would have made. Stalin would be more difficult. Stalin was from Tiflis, in Georgia, and Georgians were typically wary and suspicious, like Beria.

Chernov paused in the square, smiling up into the clear April light. It rather pleased him that Stalin's death would come from a spoiled Apollo. It gave the event a classical touch. Now he would return to the barracks, relax with Caruso, read Marcus Aurelius, and not think anymore about the Georgian target.

Chapter
21

O N April thirteenth at two in the morning, NKVD officers had arrested Shevchenko. They took him directly to an isolation cell in the basement of Lubyanka prison.

Balov assigned two of his best interrogators, Larichev and Krenek, to work around the clock.

Larichev had a pear-shaped figure and soft white hands. Some imbalance of hormones had produced the apple-cheeked face where the beard grew hardly at all, and a cherub's smile concealed bad teeth. The colonies of bacteria eating into the enamel were the basis of a joke—that Larichev cringed from the pain of a dentist's drill.

Krenek's chunky strength and glowering underlip made a striking contrast, and they called him "The Mechanic." Clearly, he seemed the one whose sadistic enthusiasm had to be restrained.

In fact, it was the other way around. Krenek possessed the sharper intelligence and was entirely detached from the pain his muscular hands inflicted. It was the angelic-faced Larichev who drew some inner pleasure from his work.

Balov said, "You have only thirty-six hours to get the truth out of him."

"Don't worry," Krenek said. "I'll give him back to you before that."

Normally an interrogation spanned many weeks. Sleep deprivation, starvation, and indefinite confinement were as much an interrogator's tools as a hot wire drawn through the nose. Crimes had to be choreographed in the mind of an accused before a confession could be wrung from him. Such was the nature of political heresy.

But Shevchenko's case involved no games, no subtleties. The hard information was there. It had only to be extracted like a diseased molar, and this was exactly why Balov had selected Krenek for the task. Krenek was an expert with the truncheon and could find the sciatic nerve or break a bone with one blow. He had a surgeon's instinct for the amount of trauma the body could absorb and still remain in a conscious state.

But by the morning of the fourteenth, Balov had reason to worry. After thirty-six hours the interrogators had nothing from Shevchenko.

Balov brooded at his desk. Impossible to delay any longer. Stalin would have to be alerted. The investigation would then be taken out of Balov's hands. The opportunity of a lifetime—lost! He might even face a reprimand for failing to come forward sooner with the information. Panic would surely descend, and the investigation would achieve nothing in these final hours except to drive the conspirators to cover and preserve for them the chance to try it again.

Still, he could wait no longer. Stalin had to be notified. The quickest way would be through General Vlasik, who had direct access to Poskrebyshev, the head of Stalin's personal secretariat.

Balov telephoned twice. The general was out. On his

third attempt he reached one of Vlasik's deputies, Colonel A. V. Andreyev. The voice sounded brisk and efficient.

"General Vlasik is out of the city. I have responsibility in his absence."

"When will the comrade general be back?"

"I can't say," Andreyev replied. "A day, or maybe two. What is it you require?"

More complications! Where could he start?

"There is a certain military operation," Balov said. "The code name is Grey Wolf. Does it mean anything to you?"

Did he imagine the startled silence at the other end of the wire? Or was the fool only taking time to think?

"Grey Wolf?" Andreyev repeated. "I don't know about any Grey Wolf."

Perhaps, after all, Balov could turn Vlasik's absence to his own advantage. He could claim that he had informed the general's office of the threat, but those in charge had failed to take it seriously.

"We have reason to believe," Balov said, "that certain officers disloyal to the State may be involved in counter-revolutionary activity."

"Who are they? What are you talking about?"

Balov explained in a halting voice, giving the impression that he did not really believe the story himself. He concluded by saying, "There are indications it might take place some-time this evening—assuming it's true, of course."

"An attempt to kill Comrade Stalin?" Andreyev scoffed. "That's unlikely. He won't be leaving the Kremlin at all. I have his schedule."

"Still," Balov said, "you might want to post extra se-curity."

"He has a Stavka meeting at twenty hundred hours. I doubt you'll find an assassin at the table. Or under it, either."

"I'm glad to hear it," Balov said. "General Vlasik briefed

Comrade Poskrebyshev several weeks ago. You might want to pass on this latest bit."

"Have you any other factors that would be useful?"

"I'll call you," Balov said, "if we develop any."

The conversation with Andreyev satisfied Balov that he would have another six to eight hours to operate without interference. Andreyev would hardly go to Poskrebyshev before he checked with Vlasik.

Where could Vlasik be? Out of the city? He generally left Moscow only when Stalin did, and then he traveled in the convoy of sleek black Packards shielded by bullet-proof glass. The general's absence disturbed him. Some jealous corner of his mind began to wonder if it had anything to do with Natasha.

Later Balov rang up the motor pool for transportation and drove out to the field headquarters of General Sinilov, Military Commandant of Moscow. Sinilov, in the company of three commissars, was inspecting the fortifications that ringed the capital. This tour had been hastily arranged at the time of Shevchenko's arrest. It would occupy the commandant for the next twelve hours.

In the operations bunker Balov studied the defensive positions on terrain maps and spoke to a senior aide.

"Are any new units scheduled into the city over the next twenty-four hours?"

The aide had a long nose and two vertical creases in his cheeks, which made his expression more one of an aristocratic hauteur than outright cockiness.

"New units?" he said. "No, only the usual replacements coming in by rail."

"No heavy armor? No units being shifted from the Moscow front?"

"It hasn't been coordinated with us." The aide frowned. Clearly he didn't appreciate questions from NKVD officers.

Only a little daylight seeped through the observation ports

of the bunker and gleamed on the dark timbers that formed the walls and ceilings. Outside and on top, sandbags were piled to a thickness of three feet. The timbers had a smell of creosote.

Balov said, "Has anything that size passed through your checkpoints in the last few days?"

"Nothing."

"What about your own armored units?"

"They're in static positions."

Balov was a little tired of this passive cooperation. He stared hard at the aide, not in a threatening way, but only to insure that his meaning had been communicated. He said, "I'll leave a telephone number. I want to be informed of any large troop movements. I'm giving you the responsibility—you, personally. If anything slips through and I don't hear about it, I wouldn't want to be in your place. Understand?"

At four o'clock Balov was back in his office over Lubyanka prison. The arrest of Krylov and Ryder was to be handled by Major Siren, an experienced security officer, and a squad of NKVD. The operation had been planned over blueprints of the building and a scale diagram of the apartment itself.

Balov went over the details a final time with Siren, who sat erect, his stocky legs crossed, nodding through a heavy-lidded stare.

"Be sure you take them alive," Balov warned. "Their corpses won't be any good to us."

After Siren had departed, Balov took the stairs down to the basement. The stink of latrine buckets drifted from the cells into the dimly lit corridor. At a checkpoint Balov sent the turnkey for Krenek.

In a short while he heard a distant clang of iron and the echo of approaching boots, and the interrogator appeared. The sweat shone on his neck at the open collar.

"Nothing?" Balov could already read the verdict in the fatigue on Krenek's face.

"This Shevchenko—he's a brute." Krenek shook his head. "I've never met one like him yet."

"That's not the answer I'm looking for."

"He's reached the point where he loses consciousness," Krenek said. "Anyone else would have cracked. We've got to ease off for a bit or we'll kill him. The heart won't take the strain. I've seen it happen before. I'll need more time. . . ."

"We've run out of that."

Krenek only looked at him, angry defeat etched into his face. Balov smiled. How alike they were, he and Krenek. Their egos couldn't tolerate failure. But ego became a liability when it interfered with judgment.

"What about his wife and daughter?" Balov said.

"Our last option." Krenek shrugged. "I wanted to hold off on it. . . ."

"Get them down here now," Balov said. "We can't wait any longer."

Chapter
22

AT five o'clock on the fourteenth of April, Ryder and Krylov were alone in the Kishkin apartment. Half an hour earlier Serova had said good-bye and left for a safe house near Komsomolskaya Ploshchad. Both men watched from the window as the familiar figure walked away through the park, the trees wet and dripping from a spring shower. Finally she passed out of sight, and the park was bare.

"Will she be all right, do you think?" Krylov said.

"She knows how to take care of herself."

A convoy of military trucks rolled down the boulevard, splashing through puddles.

"I wonder if they're part of it?" Krylov said.

"We'll know soon enough."

In a little while the sky closed again. The rain knifed down, blurring objects in the downpour.

"Look." Krylov came in from the other room. "Serova forgot her pendant."

"Careless."

"She'll be disappointed."

"Keep it," Ryder said. "You'll see her again."

Krylov nodded.

"Yes, of course."

Ryder gazed down at the pendant in the outstretched palm. The gold leaf took him back suddenly to a jeweler's window on Regent Street. Among the reflections—another pendant—a soiled white cuff stretching toward a velvet case: *This one, sir?* The pendant was to have been a surprise for his wife.

"Perhaps I could find another one," Krylov said, his voice pulling Ryder away from the image.

"What did you say?"

"A Russian pendant—like this one."

"Why?"

"A present," Krylov said, "to take back to your wife. But I don't even know her name."

"Catherine."

"You never speak of her."

"She's dead," Ryder said.

"Forgive me, please." A look of genuine distress twisted across the bearded face. "I did not mean to intrude on something painful. I know so little about you. It occurred to me, in view of what we're facing together, that I ought to know more...."

"Maxim Nikolayevich," Ryder said, shaking his head. "It's better that you don't know anything about me."

The rain slackened again, leaving no break in the cloud cover. A few tiny figures moved among the watery reflections on the boulevard where the street lamps rose, each with its cluster of three bulbs, useless now under blackout rules. A number of shops had their windows boarded over, and some had sandbags stacked in front.

Ryder said, "Better have something to eat."

"I'm not hungry," Krylov said. "I suppose it has something to do with nerves."

"It may be a long time before we get another chance."

"That's true."

They ate the last of the sausage that Serova had brought that morning from the cooperative, and the leftover black bread. The bread had turned hard overnight, and they dipped the pieces in *braga*. Afterward Ryder smoked a cigarette at the table. Twice Krylov went to the window, looked out, and came back again.

"It's too early," Ryder said. "They won't be here for a while."

Later they both stood at the window and watched the afternoon burn itself out on the horizon.

Krylov smiled reflectively and said, "One day, after the war, I should like very much to go home."

"The villa? Outside Leningrad?"

"Maybe it's gone now. I'm not sure I could even find it."

"Someone would know. Anyway, there must be old records."

"The fall would be the best time. After the first snow, when it's dry as powder, and the skies turn cold and clear. That's the way I remember it."

"The last time you saw your father?" Ryder said.

The sad gaze seemed to reach beyond the pale glow in the west to some larger distance, lost to view. Finally he looked at Ryder and said, "Anton Stepanovich, perhaps you could visit someday. We could take a walk in the woods. I could show you the pond where we saw the wolf."

Storm clouds smothered the twilight. The boulevard paled, dark and empty under a sheen of water. Krylov sat down at the table in the dusk-filled room and arranged the chess pieces on the board.

"Any sign of the car?" he said.

"No."

"It's after seven. They should have been here."

Another twenty minutes slipped away. The blackout shades

were open, the room unlit. In the semidarkness at the table Krylov's face had a tense, distracted look.

"They're not coming," he murmured. "Something's gone wrong."

"Maybe not," Ryder said from the window.

Below, a man crossed the street into the park and sat on one of the curved benches. Ryder watched him. It was a wet night to be out. But he might be waiting for a tram. They ran irregularly after dark and sometimes not at all.

A sedan cruised past the apartment building. It looped back, the filtered parking lights swerving across the window of the shoe repair shop. The black shape wheeled into a side street.

The park bench was empty. The man had moved out of sight. Then Ryder saw the red tip of his cigarette suddenly glowing out of the dark under a tree.

In the hallway a shadow passed across the crack of light under the door. Two knocks filled the silence of the apartment.

"Uncle Vanya . . ." A muffled voice that did not belong to Shevchenko followed the second rap of knuckles.

Krylov stood up, his hand clumsily overturning the white king. Ryder motioned him back and went to the door and unbolted it.

A shoulder slammed into his midsection, driving the wind out of him. The force of the man's rush carried Ryder backward off his feet. He rolled but could not break free of the arms clamped about his waist. Figures poured into the room. Ryder heard the shouts and pounding feet as he went for the pistol. A crack on the skull sent a silver flash miles into his head.

A flashlight only a few centimeters from his face brought him back. He blinked at the glare. Both arms were pinned behind him, and hair hung down in front of his eyes. The flashlight dazzled him, like spinning solar rings. He could almost feel the incandescent heat at the core of the bulb. Behind the blinding lens, the man leaning down was only a dark outline, featureless, indistinct. Over and over he shouted, "What did he take? What did he take?"

Ryder turned his head and saw Krylov on the floor, his extremities jerking. At first he thought the circle of figures must have beaten and kicked him. Then he saw the face, livid, eyes widened, teeth clenched, a white froth at the mouth. The men crowding around him were trying to hold down the convulsing figure. Two of them ran into the hall. Another one wadded a coat and slipped it under the head. The excited voices, all going at once, made little sense. But the panic mounted as the spasms stopped and the face turned blue. A dark stain spread over Krylov's trousers as he lost control of his bladder.

"What did he take?" A fist struck Ryder in the face. Blood flowed inside his mouth.

Searching him, they unstrapped the holster from his calf. Taped in one of the cartridge loops was his own L-pill.

"One of these?" The man who had hit him held up the capsule. "Did he swallow one of these?"

Ryder said nothing. The NKVD officer swore at him and punched his face again. The light went away. The officer shouted an order. Two men dragged Ryder to his feet. They cuffed his wrists behind him and taped strips of adhesive across his mouth. Obviously State Security had wanted both prisoners alive. Now they would make sure he had no chance to ingest any lethal substance.

He had a final glimpse of Krylov's upturned face. The pupils were dilated and fixed, and would see no grey wolf, ever, in the snow outside Leningrad.

Chapter
23

AT twenty minutes to eight that evening Balov followed Krenek into Shevchenko's interrogation cell. The windowless room had a sour reek. On a long table two battery-powered car headlights shone across the Soviet colonel's nude figure. The body slumped, unconscious, in a thick oak chair bolted to the floor. Leather restraints gripped his ankles and wrists, and a strap passed around his chest under the armpits to the back of the chair. Blood and vomit smeared the muscular trunk, and fecal matter left a dark ooze on his legs, the result of his having lost control of his sphincter. Blistered cigarette burns covered the head of the penis, and the squashed testicles were swollen purple from internal bleeding. That would be the result of Larichev's tender mercies.

Above one ankle restraint a shinbone pierced the skin. Salt water had been forced into the abdomen from a high-pressure hose, and in the lower left quadrant a large herniated mass bulged where the intestinal wall had ruptured under Krenek's truncheon.

Krenek clamped a hand into the scalp and raised the head

into the light. One eye dangled by bloody threads from its socket, the jellied pulp clinging to the cheek. The breath barely wheezed through the smashed nose and parted lips, which had been splattered against snags of teeth and had swollen to twice their normal size.

"Get him out of those restraints," Balov said. "He looks half dead already. You'd better be able to bring him back. . . ."

Fumes from a capsule of amyl nitrate drifted up. Shevchenko groaned. The head on the enormous neck turned slowly from side to side. He choked. A fleck of gore spilled down his chin. The remaining eye focused on Balov in a bewildered stare.

"Mikhail Vasilyevich," Balov said, bending close to the puffed features. "There is something I want you to see before we go on with this."

Shevchenko could not walk. Krenek and the turnkey dragged him down the corridor, the foot trailing at a queer angle under the broken shinbone. On the way he fainted again, his head bobbing.

The subterranean tunnel branched away to a heavy door. Instead of the usual iron peephole, a double thickness of glass looked into a holding area.

Inside, on a bench, sat Shevchenko's wife and six-year-old daughter. The woman's head was bent. She would not be permitted to look up. Larichev stood nearby to make sure, his smiling mouth leaving exposed the soft black holes in his front teeth. Balov scowled. How could one describe those red lips? Like biting through a candied apple into rot. There was something repulsive about them, the plump hips, too, and the white hands that had emasculated Shevchenko. One of these days, Balov thought, he would make it a point to see that Larichev got a taste of interrogation from a less comfortable perspective.

The girl's frail arms were tight around her mother's neck. The shining black hair of the child made Balov think of

Natasha. The mother's hand was buried in it, clasping the small head to her breast, and the little girl gazed at Larichev with a terrified expression.

Ammonia fumes from a second capsule brought Shevchenko back. Krenek got a shoulder into him and hoisted him to his feet in front of the window.

"Mikhail Vasilyevich," Balov said gently. "Don't you recognize your family?"

Shevchenko stared at them dumbly.

"Listen to me," Balov said. "We've picked up Krylov and the Canadian at your sister's apartment. Whoever was in the car you sent for them has been arrested too. The Kremlin Guard has been put on full alert. Armored units are rolling into Moscow right now to put down any armed resistance. I'm telling you these things to make you understand. It's over for you. No attempt to bring down the government can succeed. You've lost the element of surprise. All it can do in the end is spill more Russian blood. Will that serve any purpose?"

The thick lower ridge of Shevchenko's sloping forehead rested against the glass. His free hand was clamped hard against the loops of herniated intestine bulging into his lower abdomen.

"You still have one option," Balov went on. "Give me the information I want, and I promise you a quick release from any more pain. As for your family, look at them. Don't you have any feeling for them? Can you imagine the price they'll pay for your silence? Your wife in a labor camp for the rest of her days. Your daughter—how old is she? Six? It's the last time she'll see her mother. We have a criminal element with a sick fondness for children. One man in particular you ought to know about—an untreated syphilitic. His crime involved the rape of a two-year-old. He couldn't get his penis into her, she was too small, so he cut her.

"Now, look at me, Mikhail Vasilyevich." Balov's tone had no malice, only regret. "I want you to see that I'm altogether serious. You have my word, that's only the beginning for your daughter."

The gouged socket oozed watery matter. Balov couldn't tell if the discharge came from tears or the suppuration of serous fluid. The lips parted, and the name of his daughter was hardly more than an escaping breath from them.

"Tanya..."

Balov shook his head and said, "But it doesn't have to be that way. Tell me what I have to know, before it's too late, and I can promise you the protection of the State for your family."

Balov waited. Everything hinged on Shevchenko's reply, though he seemed almost too pale and far gone to speak at all. Another gout of black blood erupted from the crushed mouth.

"It may already be too late," he mumbled, and Balov felt the tension slide out of his own nerves in a silent rush. It was two minutes before eight o'clock, and he had broken Shevchenko.

Poskrebyshev, Stalin's secretary with the humped back and withering gaze, would not come to the telephone at first. When he finally did come on the line, his manner was abrupt and irritable. More valuable minutes were wasted in explanations.

"A Gaboon... *what*?"

"A Gaboon viper. A deadly snake. Don't let the briefing officer near Comrade Stalin. The venom is inside his baton."

"He's briefing now!" Poskrebyshev exclaimed.

"Then stop him." The more excited Poskrebyshev grew, the more Balov was overtaken by a strange calm. "Don't hang up. This is important. You'll have to arrest Andreyev."

"Andreyev?" The mounting panic took the secretary's voice into a higher register. "Vlasik's deputy?"

"Don't let Andreyev give any orders. Shoot him if you have to. Whatever happens, don't let him near the communications room."

"Stay on the line!" Poskrebyshev cried. "Stay on the line!"

The receiver, banging down on the tabletop, hurt Balov's eardrum. Even as he waited he could hear the secretary shouting and the trample of feet past the phone. . . .

Chapter
24

IN the war room Chernov was finishing his briefing. He stood beside his charts on the tripod. The tip of the pointer traced German positions along the Kerch Peninsula in the Crimea. To the west lay Sevastopol, cut off by von Manstein's Eleventh Army. Artillery units were moving into place for the expected spring offensive, and Chernov indicated these as well as new troop concentrations.

The light gleamed on the wall panels of Karelian birch and on the faces of the men flanking Stalin at the conference table. They were all familiar to Chernov. On one side were the senior military commanders, Zhukov, Vasilevsky, Voroshilov, Timoshenko, and Marshal Boris M. Shaposhnikov, Chief of the General Staff and Chernov's own superior. Shaposhnikov sat on Stalin's right. To the chairman's immediate left was Georgy Malenkov. Next came Lavrenty Beria, the icy schoolmaster; no infraction would slip past his stare. Only the polite attention of Nikolai A. Voznesensky, Chief of War Production, could be safely ignored.

But Chernov was conscious only of Stalin. The other faces were blanks of flesh. Stalin sat stiffly erect, the beige tunic buttoned all the way to the heavy neck, which swelled above the collar. Both hands were on the tabletop with its cover of crimson baize, and a Hertzogovina Flower smoldered between two blunt fingers. The streamer of smoke prowled upward across the shrewd, bright stare and low forehead where the thick quills of hair plunged straight back.

Chernov lowered the pointer and asked if there were questions. No one raised a hand or spoke.

Stalin gave a curt nod. It meant the briefing officer was excused. Throughout the presentation Chernov had fought against his own impatience. Now his nerves were numbed by a cold purpose, his mind totally locked into the problem. All the targets for the spring offensive had been briefed, and there remained only one—the Georgian target.

Chernov moved to the wall behind Zhukov's chair and squatted over his open briefcase. Instead of breaking down the pointer and dropping it into the briefcase, he merely twisted the upper section of the rod two turns, counterclockwise, exposing the needle at the tip and arming the plunger.

Shaposhnikov was talking. Something to do with the Baku oil fields on the Caspian. Chernov straightened, grasping the briefcase. No one noticed that he still carried the pointer.

He started for the exit behind Stalin to the far left. Timoshenko's stone-bald head passed out of sight on the right.

Everything struck him now as dreamlike, decelerated to slow motion. This was due in part to his eagerness, a desire to get the thing done, and the fact that he had rehearsed the scene a dozen times in his imagination.

All the while he was aware of Stalin's face coming closer. The others at the table were like marionettes with the strings cut—exactly as he had choreographed them in this pas de deux between Stalin and himself. Now the dictator was close enough for Chernov to distinguish the tiny pock marks in his flawed skin like a dead asteroid coming up in a telescope.

Suddenly, from the far end of the war room, the door to Poskrebyshev's office burst open and a voice shouted, "Stop him!" For a split second it broke Chernov's concentration, and he had a lightning glimpse of Poskrebyshev and, two security guards bolting forward.

At the table faces jerked around at the same instant Chernov lunged. He went for the thick neck just below Stalin's left ear above the collar of the tunic. But Stalin's head, whirling in the direction of Poskrebyshev's warning, gave him the millisecond needed to react. His left hand darted up instinctively. The needle jammed into the fleshy zone between the thumb and forefinger, discharging its fluid into the fatty tissue.

Malenkov had ducked away from the scuffle, bringing up both hands to shield himself. It was Shaposhnikov who sprang from his chair with surprising quickness and slammed into Chernov.

Both security guards were on him. One clamped a choke hold around his throat from behind. Chernov's hands clawed at it as he was dragged away, but the arm had the power of steel. At the table all the Stavka chiefs except Beria were on their feet, their faces horrified. Stalin himself yanked out the dart.

A fist slammed into Chernov's belly, driving the breath out of him. His glasses flew off and shattered. The faces at the table were pulled into a myopic blur. A blow to the head from a solid object buckled Chernov's knees. Blood shone in his scalp. He did not lose consciousness but remained stunned and unaware of his surroundings as the guards dragged him, gasping for breath, down the hallway.

Three minutes after the attack Stalin was in the infirmary, one floor below the war room. Luckily for the Soviet leader, two physicians were present, A. A. Voikov, the clinic chief, and a staff doctor, B. Larin. A second bit of luck was that

Dr. Voikov's specialty lay in the field of toxicology. In fact, his recent assignment to the Kremlin post owed itself to Stalin's pathological fear of poisoning.

Dr. Voikov had a rather austere and distinguished air, notwithstanding his diminutive stature, and his features, under the thick silver pompadour, were unwrinkled and deceptively boyish.

Dr. Larin, in contrast, had a hulking figure, and his features were a study in acromegaly, the head, hands, and feet oversized in proportion to the rest of his body. A heavy lantern jaw and poor skin exaggerated the condition. He was held by his peers to be an excellent physician, though somewhat absentminded and rather careless about his appearance. His shoes were always scuffed and worn, and he could be counted upon to miss a loop in his belt, and sometimes he would appear in mismatched socks. His shaggy thatch of hair always looked as if it needed combing.

It was Poskrebyshev who now blurted out to the two physicians the facts of the attempt on Stalin's life, and who identified the toxic substance. Even before the secretary finished his account, Dr. Voikov was issuing clipped instructions to Dr. Larin and the nurse who had just come in. Then, with Poskrebyshev trailing behind and gesturing excitedly, the clinic chief hurried to the telephone in the outer office and put through a call to the Institute for Herpetologic Research.

The nurse looked quite young and wore her hair tucked up under a white surgical cap. She darted behind a screen to prepare a mild solution of permanganate crystals in water.

Stalin sat upright on an examination table under a light that had the shape of a kettledrum. He appeared deathly pale and winced as Dr. Larin pulled the sleeve of the unbuttoned tunic over the injured hand.

"Is there much pain?" Dr. Larin used a coil of IV tubing to tie a tourniquet above the elbow.

"There is burning pain," Stalin said. "Quite severe."

"How far does it extend?"

"Above the wrist."

A scalpel flashed in the light. Dr. Larin made a crosscut at the site of the puncture, already discolored and swollen from the rush of serum and lymph to the area. Blood spewed over Stalin's knuckles. The doctor cupped a suction device over the wound and drew fluid from the incision.

The Soviet leader started to slump forward. Dr. Larin steadied him and called for the nurse. The two eased him back onto the examination table. The nurse pulled off his boots, unfastened his belt and trousers at the waist, and covered the stocky figure with a blanket.

"Dizziness," Stalin murmured. "Great dizziness."

Dr. Voikov reappeared, followed by Poskrebyshev. The clinic chief had donned a white coat over his uniform. A stethoscope dangled from his neck, and rubber tubing bulged from a waist pocket. From the pillow Stalin looked up at him. His eyes were two oblong slits of bright Georgian wiliness.

"Tell me, how serious? Be truthful."

"I haven't seen the attack device," Dr. Voikov said. "There was a hollow needle apparently designed to act hypodermically by injecting a substance into your body. As yet, I can't determine the quantity that was absorbed into the tissues."

"But you have identified the poison?"

The doctor nodded and said, "I think we can be reasonably certain it is a serpent's venom. *Bitis gabonica.* An African viper. The poison is of extremely high toxicity. Had it penetrated at the neck, it would have produced death very swiftly. The hand is a different matter."

"Is there a serum?"

"Not for this particular species. At least, not in Moscow. I've been on the telephone to our Institute for Herpetologic

Research. I talked to the director, Metlin, an international authority. He's on the way here with several antivenins that can be used to good effect."

"Several?"

"Venom of a Gaboon viper contains both a hemolytic and neurotoxic poison. It destroys blood and tissue at the same time it attacks the nerve centers and respiration. Since we have no access to a specific antivenin for *Bitis Gabonica*, treatment will require a combination of sera to counteract neural and vascular damage."

Dr. Voikov lifted his patient's right wrist and checked the pulse. The rate had risen to 84 beats per minute. The respiration count was 25—too fast. He wrapped the blood pressure sleeve around Stalin's arm, inflated the cuff, and recorded a reading of 115/70—at least 20 points below the norm.

The clinic chief scrawled this information on a chart. He noted that the tourniquet had been in place for ten minutes and ordered the band loosened. The nurse sponged the wound from the solution of permanganate. Then Dr. Larin tightened the ligature and resumed cupping with the suction device.

A frost of sweat covered Stalin's face. His forearm looked thickly swollen, blue from extravasated blood flowing into the tissues.

"Shooting pains," Stalin murmured through clenched teeth.

"Where?"

"The left side of my chest."

"Anything else?"

"Some trouble breathing, and headache."

"Describe the headache, please."

"Pressure," Stalin said. "Great pressure at the top of my head."

Dr. Voikov once again checked pulse and respiration. The heart rate had now dropped to 68, and the respiration count had increased by five. These changes alarmed him, and he scribbled them on the chart. Completing the entry, he wrote: "Pain in left chest wall radiating toward heart."

Time to loosen the tourniquet again. He directed the nurse to take over that function and drew Dr. Larin to one side.

"Look at these changes," Dr. Voikov said, tapping the chart. "The neurotoxic reaction is more rapid than I expected. We need the sera now."

Dr. Larin frowned and said, "Pain in the chest wall and difficulty breathing. That would appear to indicate some infiltration into the vasomotor system."

"I would say marked infiltration. In the absence of antivenin we'll need something to stimulate musculature activity."

"Caffeine sodium benzoate?" Dr. Larin suggested.

"I should think about seven and a half grains," Dr. Voikov replied. "Let's try it with one-thirtieth of a grain of strychnine sulphate."

No sooner had they injected medication than the Soviet leader began to vomit. The nurse cradled his head above a shallow pan until the spasms passed. Immediately he complained of chills. Dr. Voikov spread another blanket over his patient. He observed that the discoloration and swelling had passed well above the tourniquet and into the upper arm.

He said to the nurse, "Give me a pulse and respiration count at ten-minute intervals, and better have a temperature reading as well."

"Do you want to continue the tourniquet action?" Dr. Larin asked, his unruly brows knitted above the slab of his jaw with its pocked surface.

"Yes, continue it until we have the sera."

Turning, Dr. Voikov bumped into Poskrebyshev. He had forgotten about the Secretariat chief with the bent back and crooked nose. It was crowded enough in the clinic without

curious onlookers, and the doctor suggested to Poskrebyshev that he wait outside.

From the examination table Stalin turned his head. The
bloodshot gaze communicated some furious suspicion.

"Let Poskrebyshev stay," he murmured.

Dr. Voikov's neck reddened above the stiff collar. The
last thing he needed to complicate treatment was an attack
of paranoia in his patient. The Soviet leader mistrusted his
doctors almost as much as his generals.

The doctor ran a hand across his silver pompadour—a
gesture of resignation rather than impatience. Where was
Metlin from the Institute? Where was the sera?

There were voices outside in the anteroom, and Professor
Metlin strode in with a satchel. He was short, plump, and
out of breath. Wire spectacles were hooked across the nose
in the bearded face.

"I've brought units of two different sera." He opened the
flap of the satchel, gulping breaths as he spoke. "The yellow
tabs identify the antibothripic, processed from the fer-de-
lance. It will retard destruction of the erythrocytes and capillaries."

"The green tabs?" Dr. Voikov pressed him.

"Cobra antivenin," he replied breathlessly, "for the neurotoxic reaction."

Dr. Voikov checked his watch. Thirty-two minutes had
elapsed since the attack. Working swiftly, the doctor mated
the antivenin to the syringe and injected his patient. He
injected 2 cc. of the hematic agent into the dorsal region of
the hand above the puncture site, 3 cc. into the arm, and
the rest into the left pectoral muscle. This he followed with
10 cc. of cobra antivenin injected into the abdomen.

Dr. Larin loosened the tourniquet. The nurse used a gauze
pack to sponge the perspiration from Stalin's face, which
had turned even more pallid. His lips had a bluish cast and
were slightly parted. His breathing seemed more labored.

The nurse completed another pulse and respiration count. Wordlessly she lifted the chart for Dr. Voikov to read. Respirations were holding steady, but the pulse had dropped to 60.

The clinic chief said to Dr. Larin, "I would like preparations under way to transfer our patient to hospital."

From the examination table Stalin regarded both men. He was now bathed in cold sweat, and his voice, hardly above a whisper, shook hoarsely.

"I will not leave the Kremlin. You doctors have your responsibilities. You will carry them out here. Poskrebyshev! Where is Poskrebyshev?"

The misshapen figure shuffled forward and bent his head close to the face on the pillow.

"Poskrebyshev," Stalin rasped. "My old friend, my true comrade. Do not let them take me from here. I won't leave these walls, and there is to be no mention of the attack. No mention at all. Are my orders clear?"

"Everything will be done as you say," the bent figure replied with a nod.

Damn his paranoia, Voikov thought. If the venom didn't finish him, suspicion and mistrust would do the job. And if he died as a result of this stupid obstinacy, where would it leave the attending physicians? Probably exiled to a labor camp, treating inmates for frostbite and scurvy. Stalin's behavior, in times of personal stress, seemed to cross back and forth over some thin edge of psychosis.

The tourniquet had not been reapplied after the second series of injections, but Dr. Larin continued intermittently, over the next fifteen minutes, to suction the puncture site.

Later, as the nurse applied a blood-pressure cuff, the Soviet leader complained of severe pains in the kidney region. Before Dr. Larin could insert a catheter into the genitourinary tract, the patient became incontinent. A dark stain spread over the trousers, soaking the crotch. He was now in too much agony to move, and the nurse used a surgical scissors to cut away the garment. The urine was thick with blood. Dr. Voikov noted the time. Fifty-eight minutes had now elapsed since the attack.

Stalin vomited again. This time the stomach disgorged only blood. The nurse sponged his face. The vomiting left him weakened.

The nurse lifted his wrist, staring at her watch to check the pulse rate.

She glanced at Dr. Voikov and said, "It's down to fifty, and thready."

The half-lidded eyes, staring at the ceiling light in confused vacancy, slowly closed. The mouth remained open, the respirations shallow. The chest seemed not to lift at all.

"I can't find a pulse," the nurse cried.

Dr. Voikov seized an ophthalmoscope, forced Stalin's lids apart, and shone the light into each pupil. Both were maximally dilated and would not react.

"He's dying." Dr. Larin's voice cracked. "We're losing him."

"Be quiet," Voikov snapped. "Get me another antibothropic syringe! Hurry!"

Before Larin was back, Dr. Voikov had already scrubbed the surface area with an alcohol patch. Now he injected the hematic agent directly into the right median basilic vein. He called for another 10 cc. of cobra antivenin and injected this into the right deltoid.

"Still no pulse," the nurse said.

"He's cyanotic," Dr. Larin murmured tensely.

"Another seven and a half grains of caffeine sodium benzoate." Dr. Voikov held out a hand, never taking his gaze from the Soviet leader's face.

"Strychnine sulphate too?"

"Yes."

"Same dosage?" Dr. Larin said.

"Increase it to one-fifteenth of a grain."

Seconds after the injection of strychnine sulphate, the chest lifted perceptibly.

"I still can't find a pulse," the nurse said, shaking her head.

"Keep checking for it. Let me know."

The respirations were less labored. The left arm had swollen nearly twice its normal size, from blood and lymph intruding into the tissues. The discoloration extended along the length of the arm. The interior portion from wrist to axilla was almost black.

"I have a pulse," the nurse said. "Rapid . . . very weak."

Dr. Larin glanced at the clinic chief and said, "Better try to relieve pressure on the arm, don't you think?"

"Agreed," Dr. Voikov murmured, even as he shone the ophthalmoscope light into the eyes once again. This time the pupils were only partially dilated, the right larger than the left. The left was mildly responsive to light. Both sockets exuded a slow hemorrhage, which forked down the cheeks in pink rivulets. A bubble of blood formed on the open mouth. The nurse turned his face sideways so he would not choke on the red froth.

After novocaine infiltration of the swollen arm, Dr. Voikov made two incisions with the scalpel, both about five centimeters in length. One extended over the dorsal side of the forearm, the other along the underside of the upper arm. Black blood poured out in the wake of the blade. Soon the tissues began to herniate through the incisions. Dark matter sloughed down into a shallow pan.

Forty-three minutes after the onset of unconsciousness, the patient stirred.

"*Vahdi*," he whispered. "Water."

Dr. Voikov checked the eyes. Both pupils had returned to normal and equal size and reacted to light. He noted on his chart that hemorrhagic activity had ceased in the eyes and mouth, though the urine draining from the catheter tube remained bright red. He also recorded severe anemia, coldness in the extremities, and weakness.

"Let's set up for a transfusion," the clinic chief said, "and, I think, hot saline packs for the arm."

For the first time in nearly an hour Dr. Voikov moved away from his patient. He scrubbed the perspiration from his own face with a towel and tossed the solid linen carelessly toward a receptacle. Poskrebyshev, lurking close by, stepped into the light. Exhausted from his own long ordeal, Dr. Voikov stared at the bent, sinister little figure with genuine hatred. The question dancing across Poskrebyshev's piercing gaze needed no articulation. It was just there—waiting for a response.

"Don't worry," Voikov said. "I think we've saved him. He's past the first crisis. We'll deal with the others as they occur."

Chapter
25

A S soon as Balov broke off the connection with Poskrebyshev, he telephoned Trubetskoi Barracks. The
NKVD troops in Trubetskoi belonged to the special
security force rushed into Moscow during the October panic
to check looting and restore order. Now these units would
proceed to strategic points in the city where Shevchenko's
tanks were deployed, awaiting an attack order that would
never come.

Outside Lubyanka, Balov commandeered a militia van.
He turned down Kuibyshev Street and sped several blocks
until the faded stones of the old stock exchange loomed out
of the falling drizzle. The tanks were parked in Rybny
Pereulok, one of the narrow lanes that cut through to Razin
Street and the south tip of Red Square. Balov switched on
the headlights. The beams swept up the shining wet cob-
blestones and flung them sideways as he swerved into the
lane, blocking it. The first tanks came up, grey and glistening on their wide steel tracks. A helmeted crew leaned
against the sloping armor plates beneath the 76.2mm cannon
of the lead tank. They straightened in the glare of the head-

lights. Two of the men raised their hands to shield their eyes.

Someone yelled, "Turn off those lights! Don't you know the blackout rules?"

Balov ignored the order. Probably their machine guns were trained on the van. One quick burst would shatter the lights or cut him down when he stepped out of the vehicle. Too late for those considerations. He was committed. Nothing could work for him now but a brazen initiative to seize control of the moment. The slightest hesitation or sign of weakening on his part would be the end of him. Adrenaline, pouring into his blood, hammered out of his fingers on the steering wheel.

"Stay in your vehicle!" the same voice called out.

Balov heard the steel snick of the machine gun going into battery even as he crossed boldly in front of the headlights to the crew. But the burst of fire never came. The dazzling radiance behind his advancing figure gave him a momentary advantage. The men stood, motionless, not sure how to react. They had no idea how many others might be in the van. Balov had a glimpse of more crews waiting beside their tanks down the lane. Cigarettes glowed out of the dark where the lane narrowed to an incision between the buildings.

"Who is your officer?" Balov demanded.

The faces stared back dumbly.

Balov singled out the largest man in the group and said, "Answer my question."

"Major Platonov," the man stammered.

"Where is he?"

"Checking the column."

"Go find him."

The man hesitated, looking at the others. He was only a boy, really, no older than nineteen.

"Do as I say," Balov said.

The young crewman glanced at his companions once more. Balov saw the last resistance break in him. The boy lowered his gaze and slipped into the lane.

Another figure appeared in the open hatch above the turret of the T-34. This man was a sergeant named Vavilov—the man who had held Balov in the iron sights of his machine gun for several seconds, so that he might have altered a small piece of history with only the slightest pressure of a fingertip. Now he dropped to the pavement.

"Who the hell are you?" The sergeant glowered at Balov, who wore no insignia of rank.

"Balov. Lieutenant Colonel. People's Commissariat of Internal Affairs. . . ."

A flash of fear loosened the sergeant's scowl. He stared past Balov at the headlights of the van, trying to pick out anyone in the darkness behind them.

Balov said, "Do you know why these tanks are here?"

"No, Comrade Colonel. We're waiting for orders. That's all I know."

"What kind of orders?"

"Something big, but who can say? I only take orders, I don't question them. I'm only a sergeant. Besides," he added, "there's a reason for everything, isn't there? That's what the officers told us."

"Did they tell you it was a mutiny? Against your own government? Against the Soviet people?"

Now the tough sneer cracked altogether.

"But that's impossible. How could it be?"

"If you don't want to be shot for counterrevolutionary activity and treason in wartime, you'd better listen. Get back in your tank. Don't move it until I tell you. Your officers don't command here anymore. I do."

The sergeant glanced away helplessly. He was looking for his officers. A shifty opportunist, Balov decided, who might go either way. He watched the noncom climbing up out of the light.

Several figures ran down the lane toward Balov. The pounding of their boots against the cobbles rose in the dark between the buildings. Balov watched the moving shapes and unsnapped the flap of his holster. The men slowed as they came into the light. The leader was nearly as tall as Balov, but rail-thin and breathing hard.

He said, "I'm Major Platonov. Who are you?"

Behind Platonov stood a captain and half a dozen crewmen. Except for the two officers all were helmeted, and one crewman had an automatic weapon slung, muzzle down, from his shoulder.

Balov identified himself and said to Platonov, "I'm placing you under arrest. The other officers too. In the name of the Party and the People."

"On what charge?"

Balov smiled derisively. He was remembering that, in tsarist times, fish peddlers had brought their sturgeon and carp into this lane, piling them into heaps and, in the winter, packing snow into the chinks. He said, "You didn't come here to peddle fish."

Platonov spat, then looked at him. "I don't take your orders," he said.

Balov drew his pistol and fired point-blank. One moment Platonov's face was there, implacable and determined under its grimy shine. Then one side seemed to explode, pieces torn away. The head jerked sideways from the impact at the same time his legs gave way. He lay on his back, his arms flung outward. Dark blood poured from the gaping hole onto the wet cobbles. The shell had taken one eye and some of the brain out through the skull. His mouth hung open, and the white of the other eye was rolled up under the half-closed lid.

"Who else has difficulty taking orders?" Balov said.

The thin-lipped captain, whose name was Ramzin, went down on one knee beside Major Platonov. He touched the dead officer's tunic in shocked disbelief and stared at the red and grey mash draining from the cavity in the skull.

A nerve fluttered at one corner of the captain's mouth. He rose, shaking his head at Balov, and finally managed to choke out a command: "Shoot him."

"No," a voice above them said. Braced against the open hatch of the turret was Sergeant Vavilov. The light glinted off the circular magazine seated in the breech of a 7.62mm PPSh submachine gun. Now the blunt muzzle shifted from Balov and came to a stop, pointing carelessly at Captain Ramzin's breastbone. Once again the events of the night turned on the sergeant's decision, and the outcome of this final crisis, and its mercurial history, too, shifted on the front sight of the weapon.

Balov stepped forward with his pistol and struck the captain hard on the side of the head. The officer slumped against the tank and slid to the pavement, moaning.

"Pick him up," Balov said.

Two crewmen lifted him. His legs were unsteady. The crewmen had to hold him under the arms. His head sagged forward. Blood shone wetly in his scalp and streaked down one side of his face.

"Are there more tanks?" Balov said.

"No," Ramzin murmured.

"It's not true," Sergeant Vavilov called down from the turret. "We have more units in Khrustalny Lane."

Balov said to Ramzin, "How many officers besides yourself?"

"Two."

"Five," Vavilov corrected.

"Do you have radio contact?"

This time the captain managed a nod.

"Tell your officers to assemble here—without their sidearms."

Balov called Sergeant Vavilov down from the tank.

"You're no longer a sergeant," he said. "You're promoted to lieutenant. Can you choose five tank crews that you trust and then follow the orders I give you?"

"Of course, Comrade Colonel."

"I want them deployed at each of the five Kremlin gates. You'll be in command. Take the Spassky Tower yourself. Tell the guards you're there to reinforce them in case of attack."

"Anything else, Comrade?"

Vavilov was comrade-ing him now with all the zeal of a peasant Bolshevik.

"Pick a reliable man to guard the officers."

"One who isn't afraid to shoot, you mean?"

"Yes." Balov looked at him. "That's what I mean."

"I never trusted those fucking officers," Vavilov said, showing his yellow stubs of teeth in a grin.

"Maybe being one tonight will soften your attitude," Balov started to say, but thought better of it. Instead he said, "The rest of the tanks are to proceed to General Sinilov's field headquarters and stand by for orders. Captain Ramzin will issue the necessary commands over the radio."

The radio message went out. In a short while Balov heard the low throb of diesel engines down the lane. Once more a light drizzle fell. The splinters of rain flew across the glare of the headlights where the officers sat in a circle on the pavement. Legs crossed, backs curled, they stared into the rain with that odd despair common to soldiers in defeat.

Chapter
26

A T the reception area in Lubyanka, the major in charge ordered Ryder to strip. The bare, window-less room contained only a long wooden table and chair, which the officer used for a desk. A paper-shaded lamp threw Ryder's shadow across the unfinished wall as he shed his clothing. Guards searched him. They handed back his shorts. He buttoned them and straightened, the light gleaming against his corded brown neck. One guard rolled the rest of his clothing into a bundle and put it to one side.

The major opened a logbook and asked his name. Ryder said nothing. The officer leaned back in his chair, tapping the log with his pencil. A patch of styptic plaster covered a new razor nick on his cheek. He growled a command. The guards led Ryder out to a bench in the corridor.

The swelling underneath his left eye puffed it to a slit, and his mouth, cut on the inside, felt sore. He was sure in his own mind that the whole thing had failed. There had been no hammering of machine guns, no firing from the big 76.2mm cannons mounted on T-34 tanks. The silence only confirmed failure, smothering his hope a little more with each passing moment.

His guards lounged against the wall. One lit a cigarette. Ryder listened to their low voices. The murmuring drifted in and out, losing itself in the fatigue backed up in his nerves. His eyes closed.

A boot cracked into his shinbone.

"Sit up! Leaning against the wall isn't permitted."

Twice during the night the guards escorted him into the office and the major asked his name. The daub of plaster over the razor cut had caked and fallen away. Ryder only stared back while the officer tapped the logbook.

On the bench he fought sleep. His eyelids turned to lead. A dark bruise swelled across his shin where the guard's boot had landed half a dozen times.

The third time they marched Ryder into the office, a lieutenant colonel had relieved the major. The lieutenant colonel did not even look up from his work.

"Your name is Antony Ryder," he murmured. The pen in his fingers scratched across the silence. "To be precise, it is Anton Stepanovich Rydorov."

Still the officer did not raise his head. The scowling concentration conveyed the impression that the prisoner's existence was a matter of total indifference. Never glancing up from the papers, he waved the men out of the room.

The cell had no bed, and the walls were of solid mortar. A ceiling light burned under a protective grate. A lidless pail served as a latrine bucket. Every two minutes the olive cover at the door slid back and a pupil appeared at the peephole.

Ryder lay on the stone floor. The cold sent a shiver through him. Later the guard unlocked the cubicle and threw him a soiled blanket. Ryder wrapped it around himself. He could smell the sour reek of dried vomit in the fabric. Despite the pain in his shinbone, the light, and the constant scrape of the peephole cover, he slept.

He woke, blinking, and pushed up on one elbow. The cuts inside his mouth had ulcerated with pus. A dozen inflamed patches covered his legs and arms. He picked a tiny flat bug from his calf. The insect's belly looked swollen with blood. The jointed legs wriggled until he cracked the head between his nails.

Ryder urinated in the bucket, one hand braced against the wall above his head. Lack of fluids had turned his urine to a dark amber. He had a sudden recollection of Rosewall in Hyde Park, and the wind gusting across his words. If Cleopatra's nose . . .

He thought, If Stalin's killer . . .

In both cases, the failure might enrich history with its irony, but it would not change it.

Chapter
27

IN another cell block of the prison Chernov was dreaming about his mother. The dream had no continuity but was like a film, carelessly cut, the different frames spliced together. One moment she was seated in her long white dress at the Bosendorfer grand playing a Brahms waltz, and the next they were both hurrying through the sunlit birch woods by the lake in search of wild berries. The light flashed in the leaves streaking past her face, and her breathless laughter rose and was lost among the gleaming motes.

In the dream Chernov couldn't see himself clearly, only the crimson berry stains on the pressed white linen of his sailor's blouse. Lizaveta Mihalovna called out to him. He turned from the berry thicket toward the sound of her voice and saw her standing off at a distance in the trees, the beautifully formed hand resting just below the brocaded lace of her high collar. Over and over she called his name, and he couldn't distinguish her expression, for the sparkle of the sun in the leaves around her face dazzled him.

Chernov woke in pain on the plank bed where he had been lying facedown with his head on his arms. He wished he could be back in the dream. Gruff voices came from the corridor as a key turned in the lock. The cell door swung open, and the guards hurled a figure to the floor. The door clanged shut again. Chernov blinked at the crumpled figure who swore at the turnkeys. Then the man raised his head, and the ceiling light fell across the features of Sergeant Vavilov.

Chernov sat upright on the plank bed, his back against the wall, and gazed at the other man. His dispassionate stare contained no emotion whatsoever. The NCO had no more importance in Chernov's scheme of things than one of the stone seams in the flaking mortar or the grate bolted across the ceiling bulb.

Vavilov picked himself up from the floor, brushing the sleeve of his tunic with a square hand on which the knuckles stood out prominently. He sat down on the other plank bed opposite Chernov.

"I'm Vavilov," he said. "Sergeant. Tank battalion. What's the matter? Can't you speak?"

Chernov's face was puffed and raw. Behind a badly swollen lip several teeth had been knocked loose. It hurt to talk, but he gave his name and said, "What are you doing here?"

"The same thing you're doing here, Comrade."

"There are no comrades in these cells," Chernov said. "Prisoners forfeit their right to that exalted form of address. Didn't they explain that to you?"

"They were too busy asking questions."

Give them time, Chernov thought, and they'll get around to the fine points of etiquette. He said, "How were you arrested?"

"I was with a tank column near the Spassky Tower. We were supposed to go in as soon as word came that Stalin was finished. Something went wrong—I don't know what. The NKVD stopped us cold. They arrested the officers and senior sergeants. I was interrogated for twenty-four hours without a break. There's only one way to beat it. You have to play dumb, see? You pretend you didn't know what was going on and were just taking orders."

The sergeant's face bore the usual relics of barracks life: a joy of brawling, a nose that had been broken more than once by fists and healed crookedly. The flashing seeds of his eyes above the misshapen cartilage reminded Chernov of Sergeant Gritsky from the Leningrad Military School. There was a wiliness in the pupils to match the smile that lay twisted on the thin mouth, and even the cockiness in his patterns of speech sounded like Gritsky. His feeling of contempt for Vavilov, Chernov decided, had to do with that association. Why shouldn't the NCO have been thrown into the same cell with him? The NKVD would make mass arrests, building cases against the innocent as well as the guilty, if only to impress Stalin with their thoroughness.

Chernov said, "Why did you get involved in it?"

"Have you ever seen a disciplinary battalion?" Vavilov said. "I did three years in one. Eating dust all day in the summer, freezing my ass in the winter, and nothing but gruel seven days a week. I'll tell you how it was. One day a tank rolled into camp. Everyone was handed an entrenching tool and told to dig, see? Four minutes, they said, and the tank was going to roll over us with its track. You learn to dig fast under those conditions. The guy who didn't shovel deep enough got his spine crushed. That's how they create vacancies in a disciplinary battalion. But I did my time, and they sent me back to my unit to start over again."

"Unfortunately your rehabilitation didn't last," Chernov said, no more able to control the sarcastic disbelief in his tone than the pain in his body.

"I was never rehabilitated," Vavilov said. "I just got smarter. The disciplinary battalion gave me that. In the end it didn't matter who sent you there. You wound up hating that bastard, Stalin, above everything else. He was responsible for the whole stinking system." Vavilov glared at him, and Chernov had the impression that there might be the tiniest bit of truth in his animosity for the Soviet leader. The sergeant shook his head and said, "You were supposed to kill him, and you bungled the job. . . ."

Chernov said, "How do you know it was me?"

"They brought up your name a dozen times during my interrogation. I know all about you."

Chernov only shrugged.

Vavilov reached into his tunic for a cigarette, but his hand groped through an empty pocket.

"They took my cigarettes and matches," he complained.

"Don't worry." Chernov's mouth hurt when he smiled. "They'll give you a couple of drags on one while they adjust the blindfold."

"And you?"

"There'll be no bullet for me," Chernov said. "It's too quick."

Chapter
28

O N the third day guards led Ryder to a shower and handed him a piece of lye soap. He stood under the stream of tepid water in the open stall, soaped himself, and rinsed. The clothing that had been taken from him lay folded on a bench. Missing were his belt and the laces from his boots.

The lift rose to the fourth floor. They stopped at the desk of the section supervisor. The supervisor wrote in his log: "Rydorov, A. S."

The turnkeys escorted him into the cell block, unlocked a door, and motioned him inside.

The door slammed behind him. From the plank beds three other prisoners stared at him. They were Chernov, Sergeant Vavilov, and Natasha Ivanovna.

Chernov's face was still badly swollen, the purple bruises turning dark under the skin. He noticed Ryder staring at the damage and said, "Resisting arrest. And you?"

"The same."

Chernov nodded and said, "It is what they mean by universal justice."

Vavilov said, "What have they got you for?"

Ryder glanced at the tough, inquisitive face and immediately mistrusted it. He said, "Anti-Soviet thought," and saw irritation gather behind the other man's grin.

The sergeant pointed to Chernov and said, "Well, this is the fellow who tried to kill that bastard Stalin. Think of it. He may be famous someday. Here we are, together in the same cell."

"It didn't succeed," Chernov said.

"Poison?" Ryder said.

"I was as close to him as I am to you," the officer replied. "The poison was in a special syringe at the tip of a lecturer's baton. It struck the hand instead of the neck."

"What type of poison?" Ryder said.

Vavilov broke in, gesturing toward Natasha. "She milked venom from a snake."

"The doctors saved him," Chernov said. "He's recovering."

"How do you know?"

"My interrogators."

"Maybe they're lying," Ryder said.

"No, he survived the attack," Chernov said. "Otherwise we wouldn't be here."

"Me," Vavilov said, jabbing his chest with a thumb, "I was with the tank column in Rybny Pereulok. We were ready to roll into the citadel. There was supposed to be a code signal that Stalin was dead, but it never came over the radio. Then we heard that NKVD units were moving everywhere in the city and arresting the leaders. They got all the officers at the top. Nobody was left to take command. That was the end of it. . . ."

Ryder stared at the faces. Already he was sure one must be *nasedka*—an informer placed in a cell to scavenge information. But which of the three? The sergeant struck him as too obvious. Chernov? Maybe. Or the girl?

"Where were you," Ryder said to her, "while all of it was happening?"

She raised her head. The black hair streamed diagonally across her cheeks away from the fullness of her mouth.

"Kuntsevo," she said.

Ryder frowned. Hadn't Shevchenko mentioned Kuntsevo? Something to do with the commander of the Kremlin Guard, Vlasik, sleeping with a girl . . .

Vavilov said, "We heard they arrested the son of Nicholas Romanov."

"Where did you hear it?" Ryder said.

"From our officers."

Now Ryder faced a choice—how much to tell them. If one of the three happened to be an informer, that person would be testing his responses. Better to be truthful about facts already known to the NKVD.

"He's dead," Ryder said. "Suicide."

"You're sure?" Chernov looked surprised.

"I was with him."

Vavilov shook his head and said, "Bad for British Intelligence."

"British Intelligence was never involved," Ryder said. "We acted on our own, for personal reasons. But what's the difference? This is the last stop for everyone, isn't it?"

He glanced from Vavilov to the girl and saw her eyes fill.

"It's my father," she murmured. "He's ill. Who's going to look after him now? He can hardly get around anymore."

Ryder found himself gazing at the white hands crossed in her lap. She looked to be about the age of his wife. A familiar resentment twisted through him, and the cold anger of it had nothing to do with her at all, for it was an independent emotion, like some chronic affliction that caused pain before it went into remission.

Within the hour the guards came again. A key turned and the door swung open.

"Kozlova," they called out her name.

She stood up slowly, more resigned than frightened. Ryder watched her go out. Before the door closed, she glanced at him, and he could feel the telepathic attraction of some embittered feeling in the dark of her eyes. It made him wonder once more if she might be *nasedka*.

Chapter
29

NATASHA did not return. Ryder thought she might have been taken to the female wing on the second floor.

"Or shot," Chernov speculated.

"Too bad," Vavilov said. "I wouldn't have minded a woman for company. Did you get a look at her ass on the way out? Built for fucking, I tell you."

That evening the guards returned for Ryder. The section supervisor logged him out, and once more he inhaled the dank mustiness of the corridors as the guards escorted him to an interrogation room.

The officers assigned to his case were Larichev and Krenek, the same team that had broken Shevchenko in thirty-six hours. But their instructions for the Canadian would require altogether different methods.

"No permanent injuries," Balov had warned them. "Your job is to wear down his resistance. Nothing more, is that understood?"

In the airless room Ryder sat on a stool. Above him, in front, and on either side, lamps were fastened to stanchions.

They beamed down like klieg lights on a film set. He was aware of a plump shape at the table on the other side of the blinding glare.

A second man sat behind Ryder, only his crossed legs visible. A rubber truncheon lay in his lap.

The questions centered on his activities in Stalingrad as a foreign engineer before the war. Clearly State Security had monitored all his movements. From time to time a pair of soft white hands, which belonged to Larichev, would reach into the light to draw a surveillance report from a dossier.

Three hours into the interrogation the line of questioning shifted.

"We know that British Secret Intelligence Service is behind Operation Grey Wolf. How did British Intelligence get involved?"

"They had nothing to do with it."

"You deny your own connection with the British Secret Service?"

"No."

"When were you recruited?"

"Hired," he corrected. "Not recruited."

"When?"

"In 1939," Ryder lied.

There was a silence. Behind the desk lamp, the hands shuffled through papers.

"Aren't you forgetting Spain?"

"I went to Spain on my own account," Ryder said. "I fought on the Republican side. It had nothing to do with intelligence operations."

"In what capacity were you recruited?" Larichev said.

"As a translator," Ryder lied again. "I translated documents from Russian into English."

"Does British Intelligence send all translators to the special operations school on the Montagu estate in Hampshire?"

Ryder stared at the white hands folded on the sheaf of papers. It unnerved him a bit to realize that they had this much data on him. He shrugged and replied, "Maybe they do. They didn't confide their training policy to me."

"But they did send you through their agents' school."

"Yes, before I went to work as a translator."

"We know about your work in MI-6."

"Then you must know when I left the service. What good are your files if they don't tell you that?"

The plump silhouette stiffened. Ryder could feel the stare burning across the heat of the metal-sheathed lights.

"I hold Canadian citizenship," he went on. "I was planning to return home."

"Why?"

"I'd lost my wife in the blitz. There wasn't anything to keep me in London."

"But you didn't go to Canada. The Soviet Union is not a province of Canada. You have an awkward sense of direction."

Behind him, Krenek said, "How did you meet the reactionary traitor Krylov?"

"Socially."

"Where?"

"At a private residence in Mayfair."

"Do you mean he just happened to be there?"

"At bridge," Ryder said.

Larichev said, "This is how you met?"

"I speak Russian. We had that in common. Other things too."

"What other things?"

Ryder wondered how far he could push. To what limits would their patience extend?

He replied, "Contempt for Bolshevik murderers who shoot women and children in basements."

He heard the scrape of a chair behind him. Krenek's

truncheon smashed into his elbow. The pain shot all the way into his fingers and left his hand paralyzed.

"Please be more careful," Larichev said, "how you speak about the Soviet State."

"I was only trying to answer your question with the truth," Ryder said, and half expected another blow. But it didn't descend.

"And you wish us to believe that you and this scum, Krylov, acted independently, without the help of British Intelligence?"

"Believe what you like. It's the truth."

Krenek said, "Then how were you approached?"

"A Latvian exile who had monarchist connections in the Red Army."

"His name?" Krenek said.

"The only man who could tell you is dead."

"Who?" Larichev said.

"Krylov," Ryder said.

"You yourself were never in contact with this Latvian?" Krenek said.

"It's true," Ryder said. "Give me a paper. I'll write it down and sign it. You'll have a statement."

Larichev said, "You were taken by a Royal Navy escort vessel into Murmansk, isn't that so?"

"No," Ryder lied. "By a merchant freighter that was under Royal Navy escort. The freighter had a Panamanian registry."

"How did you get aboard?"

"A bribe." He added, grinning, "In pounds sterling, not kopecks and rubles. It shows you the power of a sound currency."

The truncheon cracked across his elbow in the same spot. Again the pain numbed the nerves in his fingers.

"Don't turn around," Larichev said. "We were discussing the ship's passage, not economic theories. The discomfort in your elbow is only meant to encourage a more serious response."

"I'll try to be suitably grave," Ryder said, and was conscious of a third presence entering the room—a smell of burning tobacco. Now a few sinews of smoke drifted into the beam of light. But the person with the cigarette remained out of sight, a bit to the rear, beyond the blinding incandescence of the lamps. Someone in authority. Ryder could pick up a certain deference in the manner of his two interrogators. There were no more stunning blows to the elbow.

"If you had severed your connections with British Intelligence," Larichev began, "how do you explain your presence in London's Hyde Park with a senior officer of SIS two weeks before you sailed to Murmansk?"

"I don't remember being in Hyde Park. I may have been." Already his mind was recovering the image of a man feeding pigeons near the statue of Peter Pan. He said, "What senior officer? Don't you have a name?"

"Rozwell," Larichev said, mispronouncing it.

"I don't know any Rozwell."

"You were seen talking to him."

"It has to be a mistake."

"There is no mistake. Rozwell's face was disfigured by fire. A burned face is easy to identify—like a fingerprint."

"Wait," Ryder said. "You must be talking about Graham Rosewall. We were friends. He knew my wife. Now that I think about it, we had a farewell drink in a pub, and we did take a walk in Hyde Park."

"The man you call Rosewall," Krenek said, "is a senior aide to Sir Stewart Menzies, known as C—the Commander of the British Secret Service. . . ."

"Who answers directly to Churchill," Larichev added.

"At the risk of a broken elbow," Ryder said, "I don't know the identity of C. You've overrated my importance. I've never heard of Sir Stewart whatever-his-name-is, and

I haven't the faintest idea what position Rosewall held in the service. The few times I saw him were usually over a gin and tonic, and we talked about cricket and football."

"And Operation Grey Wolf," Krenek said, "planned by Churchill and Menzies."

"The British Prime Minister may have his share of human failings," Ryder said, "but stupidity isn't one of them."

The cloud of cigarette smoke hung motionless in the light. Somewhere behind Ryder a door closed softly.

His throat burned. He needed to relieve his kidneys and asked to be taken out to urinate.

"Time for that later," Larichev said. "Let's begin over again—with Stalingrad."

Chapter
30

A T six each morning the *vertukhai*—the turnkeys—woke the cell block inmates by banging mess tins against the doors. The prisoners filed down the corridor to the latrine. An inmate from each cell carried the pail of watery excrement to be emptied.

Later the *vertukhai* brought the morning meal—gruel and a ten-ounce ration of spongy bread baked with potato flour.

Twenty minutes each day, prisoners went to the roof of the fifth floor for exercise. Concrete walls formed an enclosure six meters high. The guard looked down from his watchtower, a submachine gun slung over his shoulder. The patch of sky had the sparkle of spring in its blue light, and sometimes a cloud, immaculate and white, drifted into view above the wall.

Vavilov said to Ryder, "Enjoy it while you can. It's going to be a hot, stinking summer in this hole."

Always the sessions with Larichev and Krenek took place after bed check. The key would twist in the lock, and a guard, standing outside the cell, would call out his name. Sometimes they called for Chernov or Vavilov. Once, when they took the sergeant out and the door slammed shut, Chernov told Ryder, "Don't trust him."

"Why not?"

"Because I know his kind—from a long time ago."

Both men were stretched out on the plank beds.

"An informer?" Ryder said. "The same thing could be true of you—or me."

"Yes," Chernov said. "It's possible. But, you see, there is one important difference. I expect to betray you before it's over. It doesn't matter whether you worked for British Intelligence or not. I'll write it in my confession before they shoot me."

"Then why tell me?"

"Listen. Try to think it through. It's pure logic, and they are logical people. What is the signature of a dead man worth? Or twenty dead men who confess that British Intelligence was involved? It's *you* they need the admission from, and it has to be freely given. They can't afford to shoot you. An interesting stalemate, eh? This time," Chernov said with a smile, "you are the star pupil in the class. As for me, I don't expect to graduate."

Chernov lay on his side, his head on his left arm, which stuck out from the bed. He was staring across the cell at the other man.

Ryder lay on his back and spoke to the ceiling.

"Remember the girl they took out of here?"

"Kozlova?" Chernov said.

"They've questioned me about her."

"Of course," Chernov said. "Trying to link her to British Intelligence too."

Ryder said nothing, but it was true. The nature of their questions confirmed it.

"She'll confess to it," Chernov said, "even though she had no knowledge. The amusing thing is, I don't even know myself if it's true. Only a few people at the top would have known. I knew the person above me and my own part of the operation—that's all. It was a question of security."

"Then how did it fail?" Ryder said.

"There's only one explanation. They got their hands on somebody at the top who knew the details and made him talk. They didn't crack it until the very end, either, or I never would have gotten into the war room with Stalin."

Ryder laced his hands behind his head on the boards and stared up at the dim light on the cracked walls. He was thinking about Natasha Ivanovna.

After a while Chernov spoke again. This time his tone had a far-off, reflective quality.

"Sometimes, now, I dream about a summer house in a birch wood on a lake. We went there by droshky every year when I was a boy. I can see my mother in the dream, and she calls to me. I find myself wanting to go back. Maybe death is just another dream, eh?"

It was as if Chernov had predicted accurately his own future. The frequency and length of his sessions with Krenek and Larichev suddenly increased, as did the physical punishment inflicted on him. Once, Krenek's truncheon splintered a tooth. Within twenty-four hours Chernov had developed a severe toothache. An infected pocket in the gum below the crown left his jaw swollen.

"Nothing to lance it with," Ryder said.

"It doesn't matter. They're already writing out my confession. One day soon it'll be ready for signature. Then I'll get a bullet behind the ear—the most reliable painkiller of all."

Two days later the Soviet officer, who had come within a hair's breadth of altering history, was led away. He was now thin and hollow-cheeked and limped stiffly from pain and inflammation caused by constant beatings. Going out, he turned in the doorway, grasping the waistband of his trousers, which would no longer stay up.

"I signed my obituary last night, and you were mentioned in it," he said to Ryder. The smile clinging to one edge of his mouth had the same derisive scorn in it as when he had put the revolver to his temple unnecessarily and squeezed the trigger that day, so long ago, in the brothel. He added, "The funeral service will be private."

In the exercise yard Ryder inquired about him. No one had information. Chernov might have been locked in a punishment cell or transported east to a labor camp. Or he might have been executed. In the end it would make little difference. He might never have existed except, perhaps, as a boy in his own dream.

It left only Sergeant Vavilov for company. Ryder no longer doubted that Vavilov was *nasedka*. Though the sergeant often went out for interrogation during the night, he exhibited few signs of sleep deprivation. Nor did the meager prison ration cause him to shed weight. He complained of beatings and came back once with a black eye, but when they stripped once a week to shower, Ryder saw no marks on him.

"Now I see that the whole thing was stupid," Vavilov complained one evening over the greasy mess tin of cabbage soup. "It had no chance from the beginning. And look at you. Didn't you even have an escape plan if something went wrong?"

Ryder shrugged and said, "We weren't able to follow it."

The scrape of the peephole cover at the door interrupted them. Vavilov brooded impatiently. Finally the eye pulled away from the slot, and the cover dropped into place.

"Well, it sounds like more nonsense." The sergeant dipped a dirty spoon into the soup and stirred the weak broth absently. "How did you expect to make it back to a northern port without getting caught?"

Ryder looked at the cocky noncom, who waited with suppressed expectancy.

"By going south," he said.

"South? Are you crazy?"

"Into Iran. It's not hard to get across the border passes in summer after the snows melt. We planned to pick up the rail line at Tabriz."

"But how would you have reached the border?"

"Safe houses were set up for us, all the way to Stalingrad. I had old contacts near the city. They would have gotten us down river to Astrakham, then south to Baku by oil barge. From there it would have been an easy hike in the mountains."

Vavilov nodded appreciatively.

"Quite a plan," he said.

"Too bad we'll never be able to try it," Ryder said. He was sure the sergeant would pass the information. It would worry somebody—perhaps even the man who had smoked a cigarette behind the klieg lights in the interrogation room.

But his interrogators did not bring up the subject of safe houses and escape plans. They seemed deliberately intent on avoiding this line of questioning, as if their silence would cast doubt on his own judgment of Sergeant Vavilov.

Still, the night sessions continued, calculated always to deprive him of sleep. The key would grind in the lock, and the guards would call out his name. At night their footsteps rang down the corridors. The half-lit emptiness would not digest the sound. Then he would be on the stool in front of the lights, rubbing the fatigue from his eyes.

Early on Larichev held up a gold pendant. It swung back and forth on its chain, and Ryder recognized it as Serova's.

"We have Shevchenko's statement," Larichev said. "The woman, Serova, left the Moscow apartment a few hours before your arrest. Where did she go?"

"I don't know."

"You must have been curious. Didn't you ask?"

"Maybe she told Krylov."

Always the questioning came back to British Intelligence.

"Your orders came from Whitehall."

"No."

"From Churchill."

"That's even more absurd."

"What do you know about Churchill?"

"Probably less than you. He smokes cigars and has a liver."

"And is the great enemy of socialism."

"But an ally against fascism."

"Allies don't plot against each other. . . ."

He grew more curious about the third man who was sometimes present but always out of sight. His closest glimpse came one night when he turned his head sharply and tried to see past the lights. He could distinguish, just for an instant, a pair of shoes and a tall shape leaning against the wall. Immediately the figure dissolved in the blinding lamps, which left their afterimage bursting on Ryder's pupils.

The restraint of his interrogators seemed only to confirm Chernov's remark. They can't afford to shoot you. Even when his replies antagonized them, they reacted more often with punitive threats than with physical abuse.

But during one session the pear-shaped Larichev came around into the light, shaking a document he claimed was Chernov's confession. His cheeks had a darker hue than usual, like the skin of a Winesap, and the enraged mouth hovered only inches away.

"You are implicated," he shouted over and over.

"Get stuffed," Ryder said in English.

"Speak Russian," Larichev exploded. "What did you say?"

"Comrade Larichev, the phrase does not translate well into Russian. But the general meaning is that you are urgently requested to file that paper in the lower bowel of your fat ass."

Krenek's foot knocked the stool out from under him. Ryder was on the floor, squirming away from kicks and blows. He crossed his forearms in front of his face. More boots pounded into the room. A lamp stanchion crashed. He heard the crunch of glass underfoot as the guards dragged him out into the hall.

"Punishment cell," Krenek ordered.

The lift descended, cables creaking. The cell might have been the same cubicle in which he had been confined on his arrival, windowless, lice-infested.

He thought a rib must be cracked. Each breath hurt as the lungs pushed against the rib cage, and a sore ache developed in his kidney region. Later he stumbled over to the latrine bucket and urinated blood.

Pain mounted by the hour. He huddled in one corner, holding his ribs and breathing shallowly. The peep-hole grate opened and closed once every minute, but no one came in.

After several days of isolation they led him out to the exercise pen—a low courtyard between the walls, too deep for the sun to reach. He no longer urinated blood. Apart from a searing discomfort in his lower ribs, most of the pain had passed into stiffness.

Among the prisoners circling the courtyard were half a dozen females. He recognized Natasha Ivanovna. She raised her head and caught sight of him. She gave a tiny nod. He worked through the crowd until he was beside her. Talking in ranks was forbidden, but it was possible to communicate in a low voice with the head down.

"So you're alive," he murmured.

"For now," she said. "I don't know how they'll handle my case."

Circling past the guard, they fell silent.

"And you?" She picked up the conversation again. "What have they done to you?"

"I've been moved into a private suite."

"Did you hear that Shevchenko is dead?"

"Are you sure?" Ryder said.

"I talked to someone who was in the infirmary when they brought him in."

"What happened?"

"They beat him too hard. His intestines ruptured. Peritonitis..."

"How much did he tell them?"

"Who knows the answer to that? It was enough to save Stalin, anyway."

"What have you heard about Chernov?" Ryder asked.

"Chernov?" she said. "Nothing."

"They took him away. I thought it might have been to a punishment cell."

"I would have seen him in the exercise yard."

"Maybe they shot him, after all," Ryder said.

"Every day you hear rumors of mass arrests and executions. They say Stalin was out of sight for three weeks. Probably at his villa, but now he's recovered."

The guards stared at them. Ryder noticed his frown and dropped back a pace. Natasha walked in front of him. He watched the curve of her shoulders and her hair, bound by a bit of dirty twine into a black sheaf. The guard's face drifted past on the edge of the crowd. Ryder drew beside her again.

"Any news of your father?"

"They promised me he'd be sent to a clinic and given medication for pain."

"Promised you?"

She hesitated and replied, "In exchange for information."

"Did you give it?"

"I confessed my own part in it. Why shouldn't I? They knew all about it, anyway, and the names I gave belonged to people who were either dead or arrested—Shevchenko and Chernov. Why should I add my father to the list?"

Ryder shrugged and said, "You're right."

"The guard's watching us," she warned.

They walked in silence. Once, her fingers brushed his, and he felt her recoil from the physical contact.

"Maybe I'll see you in the yard again," he murmured. "If not—good luck, Natasha Ivanovna."

But the next day he was sick and did not go to the exercise yard. That night he forced himself to eat, then vomited in the latrine bucket. Nothing would stay in his stomach, and pain stabbed into his ribs every time he retched.

By the second day diarrhea and fever left him weak. He barely had the strength to crawl across the floor to the slop pail.

During the night his fever mounted. The heat burned out of his cheeks where a week's black stubble had gone to seed. A rash of bites covered much of his body, lice had invaded his scalp, but he was beyond caring. He slipped in and out of feverish dreams. In one of them Larichev stole into the cell and offered medical attention in exchange for his confession. Awake, Ryder couldn't be sure it hadn't happened.

A chill shook his body. He shut his eyes and pulled the blanket around him.

Later voices woke him. He thought they came from a great distance. Then he realized they were outside in the corridor. The door swung open. In his delirium Ryder wasn't certain of his perceptions. He blinked at the light. Balov's powerful figure filled the doorway. He gazed down at Ryder. Then he turned back, speaking to someone in the hall.

"Why wasn't I called?"

"I don't know." The high voice sounded like Larichev's. "I don't understand. Someone didn't follow orders."

"If anything happens to him, you'll answer for it."

Balov ducked into the cell and squatted beside him. The ceiling light seemed to float miles above the face that stared down at him with genuine concern.

"Well, Anton Stepanovich," he said warmly. "What a sight you are! Don't worry. I'll see you have a doctor. Some decent food, too, when you can keep it down. Then we can talk about old times."

Chapter
31

HE stayed four days under guard at the hospital on Serehryansky Pereulok. By the second day aspirin had broken the fever. An orderly treated his scalp with a carbolic solution, and a doctor taped his ribs.

On the morning of the fifth day, bathed and wearing clean clothes, he rode in a sedan between two guards back to Lubyanka.

The lift carried them to the fifth floor and a new cell. It had a high ceiling and one elevated window covered by a wire grate. The bed sported clean sheets and a pillow. A wooden table contained a chess set and books. There was no latrine bucket—no ammonia fumes from standing urine. The sun beamed through the open slats of the blackout shutter and lit the room.

Later Balov appeared. A turnkey brought tea and slices of fresh lemon.

"Before the revolution," Balov said, "these buildings belonged to the Rossiya Insurance Company. The big executives drank tea in this room."

"It's nice to receive some benefit from the redistribution of wealth."

"Sit down, Anton Stepanovich. Let me look at you. I think you haven't changed so much. You are thinner, perhaps. These Lubyanka kitchens aren't widely acclaimed for their fattening cuisine, eh? But no, it's something else. You've grown more serious these six years."

"The prospect of a bullet behind the ear doesn't sharpen a sense of humor."

"You expect to be executed?"

"They're not going to decorate me with the Order of Lenin."

"You won't be shot," Balov said, "if I can help it."

"No?"

"Your case is too important. Only the unimportant fools get shot. Have some tea."

The tea tasted bitter. Ryder sucked on a slice of lemon.

"Was Chernov one of the unimportant fools?"

"Not unimportant." Balov shook his head. "Dangerous, but still a fool in the end."

"The distinction might have amused him."

"It didn't amuse the State. Quite apart from everything else, Chernov was a traitor in uniform."

"The only thing that separates a traitor from a patriot is whether he chooses the winning or losing side."

"Whoever loses," Balov said, "has to pay the check."

"I expect to."

"In your case we haven't presented the bill for collection."

Ryder sipped more tea.

Balov said, "Why did you get involved in this stupid business, Anton Stepanovich?"

"Are you taking over my interrogation?"

"I ask the question as your friend, not your interrogator."

"Friendship and politics don't always mix," Ryder said. "Conviction gets in the way."

"Shall I give you the formula for conviction?" Balov said. "It breaks down into equal parts of delusion and stubbornness."

"What would you replace it with?"

"Reality and reason."

"Reason can be twisted to fit any reality."

"But at the core of every reality there is always one simple truth. In your case it is that you are Russian."

"That isn't what it says on my passport."

"Does a passport change anything inside? Listen, Anton Stepanovich, why did you come back before? Shall I tell you? Because your past is here. Your past is Russia."

Ryder said nothing. Balov's manner grew light again.

"Remember the old days," he said, "in Stalingrad?"

Ryder shrugged and said, "A long time ago."

"Remember the park? The dark-haired girl who used to come out and sit at the fountain in the evening?"

"You wanted to sleep with her."

"So did you," Balov said, laughing.

An image flashed in Ryder's memory of a yellow shine of sunflowers reflected on a girl's skin.

"Did you succeed?" Balov winked.

"Did you?"

"It is one of the wasted opportunities of my life," Balov said. "Remember young Sasha with his accordion box? What music, eh? And the smell of summer in the trees—it was never quite so intoxicating again, was it?"

"No," Ryder said, shaking his head slowly.

"And those stone lions under the stars," Balov said. "We never could decide what they meant."

Ryder looked across the table at the other man.

"Maybe it's better to wonder about the meaning of things," he said, "than to know the truth."

Balov came several times to the cell. They talked of politics and the war, and even argued the dialectics of socialism. Once, they played chess to a draw. The game only reflected the psychological stalemate of their larger conflict.

Going out, Balov asked, "Is there anything you need?"

Ryder ran a hand across the blue-black stubble on his face.

"A razor."

"I can't let you have one."

"Why?"

"If your hand were to slip and the blade accidentally cut your throat, I could not bear the sorrow of my own grieving conscience."

The next morning a barber came to shave him. He was an old man, stooped from mustard gas in the 1914 war. He honed an antique straightedge on a strop hooked to his belt and wiped each scraping of lather on the back of his own hand while a guard hovered next to him. After that the barber came every other day but never spoke.

One afternoon Balov called for a limousine, and they drove out to a park on a hill above the Moskva River. Crossing the bridge, Ryder caught sight of a sedan trailing in the rear glass. At the park it pulled off the road not far behind them and four men climbed out. They were taking no chances with him. The hillside sloped gently through a birch wood, the white trunks shooting up into the speckled glaze of leaves. The men fanned out into the woods but remained in easy shouting distance.

Ryder and Balov walked out under the trees and looked down at the river streaming in the leaves. No more than a hundred meters away, Ryder decided. Already the impulse to bolt for it was backing up in his nerves. The possibility of freedom was mixing with the adrenaline blocked up behind his heart, and some of that excitement escaped into the blood.

"Another summer," Balov said. "Smell the air."

"Better than Lubyanka."

"I thought you would appreciate the improvement."

Ryder smiled and said, "Valery Vasilyevich, nothing comes free. We're here for a reason. What is it?"

"Shall we be frank? I hope so. Anton Stepanovich, you are an officer in British Intelligence. Whether you deny or admit this, we know it's true. We also know about Operation Grey Wolf. If Churchill didn't order it, he at least sanctioned it, which amounts to the same thing."

"If you believe it, why question me?"

"For your confirmation."

"I acted independently," Ryder said. "Krylov too."

"The men who interrogated you could have beaten a confession out of you. Why do you suppose they didn't? Because you would only have repudiated it later. I want a statement made freely, as an act of conscience."

The leaf shadows pulled at their faces as they walked. Ryder glanced downhill toward the river. Two of the NKVD men trailed along near the bank. Higher up, close to the road, a third figure moved in the trees. Probably the fourth man lagged just behind them. Ryder could feel the valve opening still more, pouring the useless adrenaline into his system.

"Our Foreign Office," Balov went on, "has been pressing Whitehall for a meeting between Comrade Stalin and Churchill."

"Where?" Ryder said.

"Moscow."

"For what purpose?"

"To persuade the British to open a second front."

Ryder shook his head and said, "It would be impossible. Churchill can't do it."

"We know about Churchill. Churchill talks openly of the great Anglo-Soviet alliance, but nothing would please him more than to see Germany crush the Soviet Union. Let the two armies destroy each other. Then he will open his second front."

"You don't give him much credit for honor."

"It's not a question of honor. Powerful men have always shared a compulsion to gamble recklessly with history. Powerful men are above honor."

"Stalin too?"

A grin pushed down one corner of Ryder's mouth. How right Chernov had been! So Balov needed him, after all. Alive, he remained the key exhibit of British treachery. A nice bit of blackmail. Stalin would use him to try to extort a second front out of Churchill.

"A second front is vital," Balov said. "Without it millions of Russian lives will be lost."

"What about British lives if Churchill mounts a second front before he's ready?"

"You are Russian," Balov said, "not British."

Ryder did not reply.

"Listen," Balov said, "haven't we paid our share of blood? Why shouldn't someone else bear part of the cost? Anyway, here's the point. Unless a second front is opened soon, the war in Russia could be lost by winter."

They stopped in a sunlit patch, and there was a fine view of the river bending into the horizon. Escape was suddenly as impossible to grasp as the sky reflections drowning in the distant sparkle of the water.

"Anton Stepanovich," Balov said. "In the beginning they wanted to shoot you. I persuaded them not to. Now you have a chance. There's still time. But time runs out, and once it does, I won't be able to help you."

Ryder smiled and said, "Then maybe we'll know what the lions meant."

Chapter
32

WHILE Balov and Ryder were in the sedan cruising back to Lubyanka, Natasha was standing, naked, in a line of female prisoners waiting to shower. Only two fixed spouts stuck out from the wall above a drain hole, and the stones were slick from soap scum and chinked with mold.

The time allotted each inmate to bathe was rigidly curtailed. When it came Natasha's turn, she moved quickly under the stream of water and lathered her skin with the chip of communal soap. Her hands worked downward over her breasts, smooth and rounded in their bareness, and descended to the dark, triangular pelt where her fingers became suddenly hesitant and awkward. The specks of black fungi shining in the grout reminded her of the pustules on Vlasik's chest and back where the enlarged skin pores had been plugged with cheesy matter. She rinsed away the soap film and stepped from the cubicle, her body gleaming and dripping. She dried herself and dressed at the bench where her clothing lay folded. All the while she kept her head lowered and talked to no one.

Alone in a cell, she sat on the plank bed, one cheek pressed disconsolately against the wall, and wept silently. She felt unclean inside, perhaps even diseased, though there were no positive signs, as yet, to indicate a venereal infection.

Vlasik had hurt her, and the first glimpse of his peasant's foreskin, swollen purplish, had sickened her. She had closed her eyes as he clumsily drove the stunted thickness of it into her, and she was aware only of the crushing weight of his body and the pain of her own vaginal membrane, which seemed to stretch but never to tear.

"You must learn how to arouse a man," he insisted later, taking her hand, and the contact of her fingers with the hooded flap in its flaccid state triggered another sick rush of feeling.

In the long hours alone with him at Kuntsevo he had forced her to do things to him, and then to submit her own body to acts she considered unnatural. If she protested, he only laughed or grew crudely sarcastic until she consented unwillingly, and in the dark the smell of carnal sweat and the sounds coming from him made her think of a rutting animal.

She was convinced that she had contracted an infection, and now imagined a burning sensation each time she passed urine. Very soon, she thought, the fear would be confirmed by a purulent discharge as the contamination spread into her life-bearing female organs. Psychologically her feelings were already quarantined and shut off. She could never again bring herself to be sexually intimate. The shame of her experience overwhelmed and shattered all desire.

For a long time the tear-streaked face remained pressed to the wall of the cell. The sense of revulsion dominated her mental state, and only a few thoughts flickered on the other side of it. These were mostly about her father, memories that retreated far back into childhood.

There was a snow sled, the varnished slats of the frame fitted with long steel runners and a steering mechanism, and she could remember going into the park in winter, and the snow packed in the trees and blanketing the hilly rise, and sitting on her father's lap on the vehicle while he grasped the steering ropes. "Hold tight," he cried as they flew downhill, the blades slicing the frozen crust. She wore a fur cap on her head, and mittens, and her hair streamed below the brim where the cold wind cut her face. The trees fled by, and she squealed delightedly as the sled plunged downward. Sometimes it overturned, pitching them into the snow with a powdery explosion. Then her father would lift her above his head, his hands strong and sure, and there would be laughter on his face.

"Shall we go again?" he would cry. "Shall we go again?"

"You will have to keep Vlasik occupied for at least twelve hours," Shevchenko had told her. "That part is critical."

"Shall we go again? Shall we go again?"

The key turned in the lock, and the cell door swung open.

"Kozlova," a voice called.

Back in his office, Balov had sent for Natasha. Documents cluttered the desktop. He found her case file and lit a cigarette.

A guard brought her in. She stood before the desk, and finally Balov raised his head. His gaze held steady through the plume of the cigarette in his mouth.

Eight weeks of prison had drained the color from her face. The eyes seemed larger in it, the cheekbones more prominent.

"Was he a good lover?" Balov said.

"I don't know what you mean."

"Vlasik."

On the surface her expression remained impassive, cold

above the recent pain. She made no reply, and Balov misconstrued her silence.

"Very sentimental." He smiled around the cigarette. "I applaud your patriotic sacrifice."

"I prefer not to talk about it."

"Naturally," Balov said. "But you should understand, Natasha Ivanovna, that the topic of discussion is not yours to choose. That burden was lifted from you permanently after your arrest. Whether you'll be shot or sent to rot in a labor camp will be someone else's decision."

He motioned her to sit, and she obeyed, staring past him at the cracked plaster, her hands folded in her lap. What a waste, Balov thought. On the other side of his regret lay a resentful anger. He should have taken her that night, after the ballet, in his apartment. Would it have changed anything?

"Look at me," he said.

The dark eyes engaged his, then slid away. Balov circled the desk and sat on the edge of it in front of her. He cupped a hand under her chin and lifted her face until she was forced to look at him. Immediately he felt a sense of retreat and flight in her.

"You're a fool," he said.

There was no resistance in her stare, only that blank emptiness. Balov moved to the window and looked out. Below, in the square, the traffic crawled.

Behind him, Natasha said, "Certain guarantees were given when I signed my confession."

"Guarantees?"

"That my father would receive treatment for his cancer, and medication to stop the pain."

"The bargain was kept."

"How do I know it isn't a lie? He was supposed to be brought for a visit."

Balov came back to the desk. He took a long time stabbing out the cigarette.

"Would you like to see your father?"

The spires of the Kremlin sank on the sky behind the limousine. There was heavy military traffic, most of it moving south to reinforce Timoshenko's army. At Stavka Headquarters talk persisted that Hitler would mount his summer offensive any day with a strike on Moscow. If it happened, Balov planned to move Ryder to the prison at Vladimir, one hundred and fifty kilometers to the east. And Natasha? He still hadn't decided.

"This isn't the way to the clinic," Natasha said.

"No," Balov said.

They reached a suburb. The driver turned down an unpaved lane. A stone wall, low and crumbling, ran alongside a hill, wooded, overgrown with gorse and wild blackberries, and steeped in shade. The golden cupolas of an abandoned church and monastery lifted above the trees.

The driver stopped on the road below the church. Balov leaned across to open the door and motioned Natasha out. Higher up, in the trees, grave markers took shape in the dappled gloom.

Balov took her arm. They followed a footpath into the green stillness past an occasional bright blossom ciphered into the capillaries of twisting vine. Finally they halted before a new stone tablet above a grave.

"Your father," Balov said.

Her body stiffened as the nerves absorbed the shock. A delayed shock, Balov decided, for surely she had already guessed. It needed only the visual reality of the marker to release her mind from the irrationality of hope.

Natasha knelt, touching the stone with one hand. Balov couldn't see her face, only the curve of her back. The thicket formed an arbor overhead in the branches, and the motes of afternoon sun, spilling through it, were streaked with copper light where dead leaves from other seasons were impaled and moldering on thorny barbs. Natasha made the sign of the cross. Then she turned her head sharply.

"So this is how you keep your promises."

"What were you promised? That he wouldn't suffer for lack of medicine, that's all."

"I wonder," Natasha murmured, "if it's possible to hate all of you any more than I do now?"

"Ivan Nikolayevich took his own life," Balov said, "twenty-four hours after your arrest."

"Couldn't you have told me?"

"The State needed your cooperation. Besides, you couldn't have done anything."

"Tell me how he died."

"He opened his wrists."

Natasha turned from him once more. This time she wept.

"I arranged for him to be buried here," Balov said, "on church ground."

He waited for her to regain her composure. Finally she nodded, her face still averted.

"We can stay a while longer if you like," Balov said.

A breath of air stirred the leaves, the glint of copper light went to pieces in their movement, leaving her face solemn and sad. She only shook her head, indicating she did not wish to stay.

Darkness had fallen over Moscow when Balov called for a guard to take Natasha back to the cell block. Intensive questioning had uncovered nothing new, yet some instinct convinced him she was withholding information. Alone, he stretched both hands against the window frame and stared at the rooftops, dark against the blue evening.

Later he took a tram to the apartment off Karl Marx Prospekt where Serova was staying. The apartment was assigned to an actress who belonged to a theater brigade touring the Moscow front. Her absences now served a convenient arrangement, and Balov had his own key.

He let himself in. Only the clock's ticking from the mantelpiece drifted out of the shadows. A night breeze unfurled itself on the lace at the open window. He wondered if Serova had stepped out. Then he caught sight of her in the stuffed chair. He couldn't see her upper body, only the gleam of her crossed legs in the moonlight, and the smoke from her cigarette rising in the pale radiance.

"What delayed you?" Her voice came out of the dark.

"I had business to finish."

"You could have called." Her tone reflected cool disinterest. Only her fingers, demolishing the cigarette, gave a clue to her irritation.

"There was no telephone," he lied.

"You take too much for granted, Balov."

"Do I?" He watched the long legs uncross as she got up from the chair. He said, "Then perhaps you should know I was with another woman."

Balov caught her wrist before her fingers could rake his face. He twisted it and pinned both hands behind her. Serova's head was thrown back. She could not tear herself free. He smiled in a coldly insolent way and, almost as an afterthought, kissed her antagonistically on the mouth.

"Damn you," she murmured through the kiss, but he could already feel the resistance break in her as something altogether different replaced the angry violence.

"You're wasting time, Katya." He smiled at her again. "We both know what you need."

Later her curled fingers trembled and slowly relaxed their grip on his shoulders as he started to withdraw from her. She moaned, "No, don't," and the sudden constriction of vaginal muscles sent another spasm of pleasurable feeling through him.

Finally her hands slid down his arms to the pillow where her hair, unpinned, spilled over the fabric. Balov grazed her throat with a kiss.

"Now we have other business to discuss," he said.

"What business?"

"That damn information of Gritsky's—the safe houses, the escape plan."

"You don't believe it, surely?"

"No, which is the thing that bothers me. It's just improbable enough to be true. Exactly the kind of gamble British Intelligence would take because it's too stupid to be believed."

"What got you started on this?"

"Questioning Kozlova."

"So that's what occupied your day."

"Most of it."

"I've heard she's pretty."

"Pretty enough."

Her hand moved under the bed sheet. She grasped his sex, stroking it with warm fingers.

"But I've got the part of you she doesn't have."

Aroused, he began to harden again. Immediately she dug her nails into the swelling erection, laughed, and reached toward the night table for a cigarette. Her bare shoulders flickered. She turned back, propped on an elbow, leaving a distance between them. Even her breasts, pinned by the perpendicular line of her arm, were chastely out of reach behind the cigarette smoldering in her curled fingers.

"Since you have such a burning desire for conversation, suppose we talk for a while. Did this girl you had to unmercifully interrogate all day say anything about General Vlasov?"

"No," Balov said. "Not that it makes much difference at this point."

"Why?"

"What's left of Vlasov's army is encircled south of Leningrad. They're finished."

"And Vlasov?"

"Moscow sent a plane to bring him out, but he refused to leave his men."

"Doesn't that indicate something?"

"Everything points to him as one of the leaders. But the evidence is circumstantial. If we could get our hands on him..."

"Why can't you?"

"Because the decision's already been made to let him die with his men. Stalin wants it that way. After all, Vlasov was the savior and hero of Moscow last winter. It wouldn't do much for morale if word got out that he was an anti-Soviet traitor."

"Maybe he was the only general officer involved."

Balov scoffed and said, "Not likely."

"*Valya*," she said, smiling, "you're starting to see counterrevolutionaries behind every tree."

"Then we'll chop down the forest."

"But maybe they're only hiding in your imagination."

"The safe houses too? Well, there's still one way to find out."

"How?" Serova asked.

"An escape," Balov said. "Kozlova and the Canadian. It shouldn't be hard to arrange."

"Let them go? Are you crazy?"

"Not a bit. You'll be with them."

"Me!"

"Don't worry, I'll have someone else along to back you up. Not that you need it."

"I don't like it, Balov," she said, frowning. "If anything should go wrong..."

"We'll have to make sure nothing does." He smiled and

leaned back, his heavy fingers laced behind his head. "Besides, I can almost see it happening. A transfer from Lubyanka to Vladimir—just the two of them in a closed van, on their way out of the city. . . ."

Chapter
33

THE van pulled away from Lubyanka after midnight. Ryder and Natasha sat opposite each other on boards mounted against the side panels. A wire grate screened a window in the front partition, and a shade, drawn on the other side of the glass, concealed the driver and guard riding in the cab.

"Chernov's dead," Ryder said.

Natasha was silent, not bothering even to glance up.

"A lot of men are dead," she replied finally, as if death were commonplace, no worse than a bad cold.

Above the rear doors a missing stove bolt left a hole. Ryder got up and pressed an eye to it but could distinguish little more than the unlit boulevard racing back into darkness, and the buildings spinning across the aperture each time the van swung through a turn. He went back to the bench and sat down. Natasha's face made a pale oval in the dark.

"Maybe they're going to shoot us," she said in a disinterested way.

Ryder shrugged and replied, "When they're ready."

"Why would they move us to Vladimir?" she went on in the same monotone.

"They're worried about a new German offensive against Moscow."

A faint smile, more embittered than amused, broke from the corner of her mouth. It might have been trying to escape from the sadness of her face.

"Do you believe it?" she said.

"No," Ryder said.

The vehicle turned frequently, slowing, then picking up speed. For a while they cruised along a thoroughfare. Later the van slowed again, turning off the paved road. The wheels bounced over a pitted surface, gravel stinging the fenders. They had gone about two kilometers when the driver slammed down hard on the brakes. Ryder's head banged against the side panel, and Natasha was nearly thrown to the floor.

They were stopped, the motor idling. The driver had his head out the window, shouting at someone. Ryder peered through the rear slot. A stretch of unimproved road took shape in the settling dust. On either side the ruined shells of buildings rose darkly.

"What is it?" Natasha said.

"Trouble. Maybe a roadblock."

They heard the driver cursing. Abruptly the string of obscenities broke off. There was a cry of surprise—aborted by a pistol shot.

The horn was blaring. It seemed to blare forever, filling the night with decibels of outrage. Finally it went dead. The engine still idled. Someone switched off the ignition.

The running board creaked under the weight of the guard climbing out of the cab. They heard muffled voices outside, and the crunch of gravel. The panel doors swung open, but instead of the guard, Serova confronted them.

"Hurry," she cried, beckoning, "out of the van!"

"Serova." Ryder frowned. "But how . . . ?"

"Don't ask questions," she pleaded.

Ducking out, Ryder looked for the guard and saw him standing, unarmed, beside the cab. The guard had both hands clasped behind his neck, and alarm showed in the whites of his eyes.

Two meters away, a red-haired giant pointed a pistol. His soldier's tunic would not accommodate his massive shoulders and arms. Even the pistol had the look of a toy in the huge hand.

"The driver's dead," Serova said. "Help me get him out from behind the wheel. We have to move the van."

The driver was slumped, his forehead on the steering wheel. His eyes and mouth were open. The blue hole in his cheek was puffed around the edges. It hadn't bled much, only one thin ribbon like a party streamer.

They pulled him out by his clothing. His head rolled back and his cloth cap fell to the ground. Serova stooped to pick up the cap.

"Get him into the back," she said.

Ryder dragged the dead man by the feet. The slack mouth and half-lidded stare were beyond caring. Natasha turned away, shutting her eyes.

The man holding the pistol waved it at the guard.

"You too," he ordered. "Get into the back, facedown on the floor. Be quick!"

As soon as the panel doors were secured, the man in the soldier's tunic stuck the pistol into his belt and climbed into the driver's seat. The steering wheel looked as if it would fly loose with one wrench of the powerful hands. His neck, Ryder decided, would surely measure twenty-one inches. The cords standing out in it had the thickness of steel cable.

"This way." Serova motioned to Ryder and Natasha. "We have a truck. Hurry."

Ryder took Natasha's arm, only to feel her draw it away. He saw they were not among ruins, after all, but on an abandoned construction site. It appeared to be another sprawling complex of apartments. Probably work had been halted early in the war when the big factories were dismantled and moved east to the Urals.

Behind, in the dark, the van's engine finally kicked over. The vehicle backed down the road, stopped, and turned off. They heard it moving, in low gear, loose debris crunching under the tires.

"Who is he?" Ryder said.

"Ilya Pavlovich," Serova said. "He's a deserter from the Army. You can trust him."

Ahead, the truck drifted out of the shadows. It was a military stake bed, and it blocked the road.

"How did you get it?"

"Stolen," Serova replied. She looked around in the dark with an anxious frown. "Both of you had better ride in the back. There's no one around at this hour, but sound travels at night. Someone might have reported the shot. We don't want to take any chances."

She held up the tarpaulin while they crawled under with the cargo. It was a cargo of horse blankets and bridles. The leather was newly tanned and glistened under a coating of oil. In a few moments they heard the scuff of boots as Ilya Pavlovich hurried back on foot. He swung heavily into the cab and started the truck.

Ryder lay with his shoulder squeezed against Natasha's. He said, "It's all right. I know her. She's the courier who brought us out of Murmansk."

"Where are they taking us?"

He raised the edge of the tarpaulin and saw the dust, white in the moonlight, trailing off in a knight's plume. He let go of the canvas and turned to Natasha. In the dark her face was close enough for him to distinguish the anxiety and confusion in it.

"I don't know," he said, "but it's bound to be an improvement over Vladimir, isn't it?"

Chapter
34

THE truck stopped on a road beside a stone wall. Serova unhooked the grommets holding down the tarpaulin and motioned to Ryder and Natasha.

"Where are we?" Ryder said.

"A monastery," Serova replied, "or what's left of it. Don't worry, there's only a caretaker."

"What about the driver?"

"He'll leave the truck somewhere and come back on foot."

The truck rumbled off. The grounds inside the wall were wooded and overgrown. The moon shone in the tops of the trees, but underneath it was gloomy. Ahead, the church took shape in the slumping leaves, the gilded domes ablaze in the summer night. They crossed a courtyard to the monastery and went in under the arches.

The caretaker, limping stiffly, met them with a candle. Grey stubble bristled over his face, and his clothes were rumpled where he had slept in them.

"Where is Ilya Pavlovich?" He peered at Ryder and Natasha.

"Coming later," Serova said. "I'll wait for him, Aleksei Sergeyevich. Give me the candle and go back to sleep."

The old man nodded, his brows drawn together in confused vacancy, and limped off. In the cavernous shadows a door closed.

"He's a little soft in the head," Serova said. "He thinks he has holy visions, but he's harmless enough."

They followed Serova down a hallway. The monastery was one of the state museums, closed since October. Frescoes from the seventeenth century flickered by on the walls— saints and angels in the struggle against evil. The figures were faded. Perhaps evil would outlive them, after all.

In a narrow wing were cells where the religious had once lived. The women would share one, the men another. Serova lit a lump of tallow. Straw mats rested on two plank beds. Higher up, a slot in the bricks served as a window. Wooden shutters opened on iron hinges.

"There's a toilet across the hall," Serova said. "Only a chamber pot, I'm afraid."

Natasha said, "Is there water to drink?"

"We have to draw it from a well in the courtyard. I'll bring the carafe when I come back."

They left Natasha sitting on the bed. In the room Ryder would occupy with Ilya, Serova lit another candle. The light bloomed on the bare walls. There were faded places on the stone where icons had been taken down.

Serova turned from the flame, a smile curved into her broad mouth. She stepped across to him, touched his cheek with her fingers, and said, "You have a beard. As I recall, it scratches."

Ryder drew her wrist down but did not release it.

"You've gone to considerable trouble," he said, "for a beard that scratches."

"Would you prefer I hadn't?"

"I'm only curious why you took the risk."

"You have a skeptical nature," she said, and her manner struck him as evasive. "Mine is purely physical."

Ryder let go of her wrist and sat on the bed. The candle flexed across the barb-shaped scar indented into his cheekbone.

He said, "How did you know about the van?"

"I've known where you were for weeks. The night they came to arrest you and Maxim Nikolayevich, I saw the whole thing."

He gave her a questioning stare.

"I'd forgotten my mother's pendant," she went on. "I was sick about it, so I went back. I saw the NKVD dragging you out. That's when I decided it wouldn't be safe at the address Shevchenko had given."

"Where did you go?"

"To a family we'd known before in Moscow when I was growing up. Ilya's a nephew. At first they were afraid. I found out why, soon enough. They'd been hiding him for weeks. He'd deserted from the army."

"Why?"

"At Smolensk his commander ordered a retreat. The unit was only carrying out orders. The NKVD arrested them. The officers were shot, and the men were tried and sentenced to labor camps. Ilya Pavlovich escaped during an attack. He hates Stalin and the NKVD."

"Enough to risk his neck for two strangers?"

"His family has connections in Lubyanka. We knew about the transfer to Vladimir three days ago. Risks become more acceptable when you know in advance what your enemy is going to do."

On the other side of his doubt lay a deadly fatigue. His mind was too tired to distinguish between truth and a rehearsed response.

"Krylov found your pendant," he said. "He was going to keep it for you."

"Poor Krylov," she said, shaking her head, and he could almost believe her quiet grief.

Ryder said, "He told me once that he always wanted to be part of some noble undertaking—to find out about himself. I wonder if he would have changed his mind in the end?"

"At least he didn't live to see it fail," Serova said.

"Yes." Ryder nodded. "I guess that's something."

"You'd better sleep now," Serova said. "We have more important things to worry about."

Ryder woke at daybreak. Ilya lay curled on the second bed, his boots off. Above the flannel strips wrapped around his feet and ankles, the calf muscles bulged. His tunic was rolled into a pillow, and the pistol made a lump under the straw mat next to his head.

Ryder heard the snap of a dead limb outside. He rose, pushed open the shutter, and looked out. The caretaker, Aleksei Sergeyevich, limped from the orchard cradling fruit and fresh eggs in his cap.

Later the old man gave him soap, razor, and a hand mirror, and Ryder went out into the courtyard. He drew water from the well, stripped off his shirt, and washed his face and arms.

The morning sun bathed the stone arches in lemon light. He fitted the mirror into a crevice and shaved off his beard with the razor. In back of him were trees, the church, and the cemetery. The headstones and marble monuments, obscured in shade, lingered in the mirror.

He ducked down to rinse, straightened, and this time, among the reflected graves, he saw Natasha. She was suddenly just there, as unmoving and still as one of the marble figures in the speckling of leaves.

He dried his face and buttoned on his shirt and walked down to her.

"What is it, Natasha Ivanovna?"

She stood gazing down at an unmarked headstone and did not look up. Her tone was flat, covering the emotions underneath.

"It reminded me of something—my father's grave."

"You've seen it?" Ryder said, surprised.

"They took me once," she said, "from Lubyanka. It was a cemetery like this one. There was a monastery too."

Natasha turned from the stone tablet. She leaned against a tree with both hands, her forehead pressed to the papery bark. Then he saw that her shoulders were shaking.

A breath of air stirred the leaves, and on the ground the shadows of leaves flickered.

"He took his own life," she said, "after my arrest."

Another sob lifted her shoulders. Grief and anger were squeezed together inside her, and a third emotion, too, but it was unidentifiable, like a fingerprint lacking enough points for classification.

"He didn't know what I did at Kuntsevo unless they told him," she murmured. "If they did, then I'm as responsible for his death as the cancer."

Once more the despondent sorrow wrenched at her body. The sight of it touched a place inside him that had been tightly shut since he had sat beside his dying wife and gazed helplessly at her motionless figure with the gauze pads and dressings. The tremor of feeling passed through him like the first sensation returning to a nerve that had been blocked off. But compassion was too easy to confuse with despair. It had been so at Coventry. Why should it be different at Kuntsevo? Whatever had occurred there with Vlasik, she could do nothing to change it, any more than his wife could change the fact of her charred flesh.

"You did what you had to do at Kunsevo," he said gently.

She nodded faintly and turned back to the grave, wiping her tears with the backs of her fingers.

"He always wanted to go back," she said reflectively, "to the way things were. Before the revolution he owned a fine droshky with leather seats and bells from Gstaad. In the fall he used to take my mother riding in the country."

Another draft of air shook the leaves. Already the memory seemed lost in the dissolving shadows flung to the ground.

"Toward the end he couldn't sleep. He sat up in a chair next to my mother's picture. Maybe he was dreaming about those fall days and the droshky." Natasha shook her head sadly. "Now he'll sleep forever."

Someone called out. They glanced up and saw Serova under the stone arch.

"We'd better go up," Ryder said.

In the dim, high-ceilinged kitchen they sat on benches around a table of heavy plank boards.

"By now they've found the truck," Ilya said.

"The van too?" Serova said.

"I would think so, yes."

The angles in the soldier's face did not match, as if the wrong parts had been forced together. One eye looked larger than the other. Even the heavy dimple notched into his chin appeared slightly off center.

Serova said to Ryder, "Last night you were curious why we took the risk to help you escape. The British Secret Service got you into the Soviet Union. Surely it can get you out—the rest of us too."

"The way out was supposed to be a potassium cyanide pill."

"But what about the safe houses?"

Ryder looked at the woman across the table and wondered who she was. So Vavilov had passed the information, after all.

Now, finally, the circle came closed. Where was the real Serova? Dead, probably.

He said, "Who told you about the safe houses? Krylov?"

Her stare didn't flinch under his, and he felt only a cold admiration for her nerve.

"He mentioned them once," Serova said, "but he was vague, and I didn't really want to know about them."

Ryder shrugged and said, "For all I know the safe houses have been compromised like everything else."

"Still," Ilya said, frowning, "if there's a chance for us . . ."

"To get yourself shot," Ryder said, and wondered which section Balov had tapped to find the giant. It would not have been a random selection. Too much was at stake.

"We've already taken one risk and succeeded," Serova said. "Why not another? Besides, what other option is there?"

Ryder asked for a cigarette. Ilya slid the packet and matches across the table.

"I don't like the odds," Ryder said as new smoke streamed away. He tossed the cigarettes and matchbox back in quick succession. Ilya caught the cigarettes but not the matches. His reflexes were a bit slow, Ryder decided. But size and strength would compensate for them. No, the NKVD wouldn't send a man who couldn't handle himself. And there was the pistol in his belt. The pistol would have to be taken away from him.

Chapter
35

THEY were still in the kitchen at the table of thick larch boards when Ryder said to Serova, "You'll make contact from the same telephone kiosk you used before."

"But why must it be the same kiosk?" Serova protested. "It's hours away."

"My guess would be that they have someone in the area to spot the caller."

"What do I say to them?"

"You'll pass a coded message, then hang up and wait. Someone will ring back with instructions."

"Well, then, give me the code and the number to call."

Ryder glanced at the other two people, then back to Serova.

"I'll give it to you when you're ready to leave," he told her. "But only to you, understand? If we should get separated or caught on the way, the fewer who know, the better."

"He's right," Ilya said. "It's just good security."

"Then I'd better get started," Serova said. "I'll have to take a tram into the city."

"No," Ryder said. "The call can't be made until after dark."

The look she gave him was suddenly questioning and suspicious.

"Why not?" she said.

He smiled at her across the table. "I don't make the rules," he said, rising to leave.

Outside in the hall, Ryder paused before the fresco of St. Michael driving Lucifer from Heaven. Pillars rose up into the dark. A voice startled him.

"They say he fell to earth as lightning."

It was Aleksei Sergeyevich. Ryder hadn't heard the caretaker come up.

"I've seen him." The old man spoke haltingly. "The angel in the painting."

"Where?"

"In the trees, near the graves."

"Maybe it was only a marble angel," Ryder said.

"No," the other insisted. "He had a sword in his mouth. It's the Angel of Death." The seams in the leathery skin deepened behind a grin. "He's among us now. You'll see, you'll see."

Aleksei Sergeyevich limped away. Later, from a window, Ryder watched him talking to Ilya in the orchard. Gone from his manner was the stumbling vacancy. The old man spoke animatedly, his expression tough and shrewd, while Ilya nodded like a subordinate taking instructions.

At the same time Ryder caught sight of Natasha alone at the well in the courtyard. He slipped outside to her. Beyond the stone archway the leaves of the orchard were green and sun-burnished. The two men did not see him and remained in conversation under the trees.

Ryder dipped a cup into the water and murmured to Natasha, "The safe houses don't exist. It's a trick, do you understand? As soon as it's dark I'm getting away from here. We can try it together, or not, whichever you prefer."

She frowned and replied, "What are you saying?"

"The transfer to Vladimir and our escape—the NKVD arranged it. They were gambling that I could put them on to something—an escape network. Only it doesn't exist."

"But they killed the driver of their own van," she protested. "He was dead, you saw it."

"Probably another *zek*, like us. They set him up to make it look convincing. He didn't know it until the gun went off in his face."

She gave him an anguished look, but Ryder was staring past her at the two men under the trees.

"This could be the only chance we'll have to talk alone," Ryder said. "You've got to make up your mind. The whole thing is a game. We'll go on playing it until Serova makes her call this evening. Then it's over for all of us. If you don't believe me, stay behind."

Natasha shook her head quickly.

"What do you want me to do?"

The two men were coming back from the orchard. The giant had to stoop away from branches.

Ryder said, "We'll wait until Serova leaves. Then you'll have to distract the old man while I do something about Ilya. Maybe you could get him to show you the church. Tell him you want to light a candle—for your father."

They had an early meal of beet soup, wild mushrooms, and greens from the garden. Serova was impatient to be off. Ryder walked out with her past the archway. Her departure needed only this last improvisation of actors' dialogue to complete the performance. The cast was largely posthumous. Only real blood had been let, and Krylov and other key players would not get up when the curtain rang down.

How did the NKVD deal with failures? Unpleasantly, he hoped.

"Good luck, Katerina Alekseyevna."

"I don't believe in luck," she said, "only in doing what has to be done without any mistakes."

"You've risked enough already. The pity of it is that I won't ever be able to pay you back what I owe you."

"Don't talk such nonsense, and stop looking so worried. I'll be all right. Would you like to kiss me before I go?"

The cool mouth stirred under his with just the right mixture of lust in conflict with higher duty. The grey stare held some erotic promise above the smile, and even the pressure of her fingers on his back had a sexual inference. Then she was gone, past the church and out of sight where the fading light hung in the trees.

Ryder walked back into the monastery. In the reception area, a big room with fretted panels and French windows, he found Natasha sitting with a book open on her lap, her head bent. Not far away stood Ilya, his shoulder tipped against the wall, watching her through the wreathing of a cigarette.

In the garden beyond the open French doors Aleksei Sergeyevich stooped beside a trellis of roses. The snip of his pruning shears clipped at the gloomy silence.

"A game of chess, Ilya Pavlovich?" Ryder said, pointing to the board.

Natasha closed her book, got up, and stepped out into the garden.

"Yes, why not?" The giant dragged the cigarette from his mouth, glancing from Natasha to Ryder.

They wandered over to the table where ivory chessmen gleamed among their own long shadows. Ryder held out both fists. Ilya tapped the left one. A white pawn spilled out.

"White moves first," the giant said.

As the two men sat down, Ryder could overhear fragments of the conversation outside in the garden. Natasha was asking Aleksei Sergeyevich to unlock the church. She wanted to offer a prayer for her father. The caretaker replied that it was already too dark inside.

"But we could light some candles," she insisted.

He limped after her across the courtyard, shaking his head in displeasure, yet clearly unwilling to let her out of his sight. Probably Balov had given orders to that effect.

Ryder said, "How was it at Smolensk?"

"A slaughterhouse," Ilya said. "The German panzers went into a circular defense. They were supplied from the air. We were ordered to go against them in waves. If anyone tried to retreat, NKVD troops were there to shoot them."

Ryder looked at the other man. Maybe Ilya *had* served at Smolensk, but it would have been as one of the executioners. His speech patterns, when he could be made to talk, were more like those of an officer than a soldier-conscript. Usually he remained sullen and uncommunicative. He struck Ryder now as alert and dangerous but still not suspicious.

"You were lucky, Ilya Pavlovich."

"The NKVD took the boots from the bodies before they froze," Ilya said, "and then stacked the corpses like cordwood. I thought I was a dead man."

On the board, the opening advance of pawns was under way. Across from Ryder, the giant's heavy fingers tapped the table. His other hand rested high on his leg near the pistol in his belt. It was a short-recoil Tokarev automatic with the five-pointed Soviet star in relief on the grip, and the magazine carried eight cartridges. Ryder saw that the hammer was half cocked. That would mean a round was already seated in the chamber.

Ryder shifted his queen's knight to a square in the queen's file and said, "The light's going. We'll need a lamp."

He got up and in a moment was back, gripping a rush

lamp. A metal band secured the thick glass to the solid brass base. He made a point of studying the chess board and said, "Let me have one of your matches, Ilya Pavlovich."

The fingers ceased drumming against the table and went for the pocket of the tunic. Ryder had hoped he would use the other hand, next to the pistol. He swung the lamp.

Perhaps the giant had been wary all along. The pistol was halfway out of his belt. His face jerked away from the blow. The lamp caught him above the ear as he was coming out of the chair, and the glass shattered against his skull. The room shook as he crashed to the floor, and the pistol slid across the hardwood boards. He pushed up slowly with both hands. The severed flap of an ear hung loose. Stunned and confused, he blinked at Ryder, unable to concentrate vision through the bloody film. Ryder had already snatched a chair and now brought it down hard across Ilya's head and shoulders. The force of it snapped a wooden leg, and once more the floorboards shook as the giant collapsed.

Ryder threw the chair aside and turned to look for the pistol. He heard a grunt and whirled. The staggering rush of the other man caught him off-balance, driving him backward into the table, which overturned.

Ilya was on top of him. The fingers at Ryder's throat might have been steel, choking off oxygen. He punched at the face, jabbed his thumbs into the hollows below both ears, but the other man was insensitive to pain. The eyes staring down were dispassionately absorbed in their purpose. Ryder struggled to wrench the arm away and could feel his windpipe cracking.

Broken glass glittered on the floor beside his head. He groped for a daggerlike shard and drove it into the heavy neck where the carotid swelled.

Ilya made no sound, but the shock registered on the whites of his eyes. For a moment nothing seemed to change. Then some of the strength melted from the fingers clamped on

Ryder's throat. Ryder slammed a fist into the chest wall under the heart and felt the fingers loosen more. Finally he shoved hard with both hands, and the giant went over, like a toppled slab of granite, onto his back.

Ryder rolled shakily to one knee. His breath came in hoarse gasps. He retrieved the pistol, drew the hammer to full cock, and squatted beside the prone figure, running a hand gingerly over his pockets.

Among Ilya's effects he found an NKVD identity card, money clipped together in large bills, and a letter on official stationary. The letter read: "Captain I. P. Kruglov is granted special authorization to travel freely within the USSR in the course of a secret assignment of highest priority. All units are enjoined to provide him full support upon request." The document was signed by Major General V. Ivanov and bore the stamp of the People's Commissariat of Internal Affairs.

Ryder kept the money and papers. He uncocked the pistol, thrust it into his belt beneath his coat, and dragged Ilya by the legs across the hallway to the kitchen. The giant was still alive but his pupils were fixed, staring straight up, and the breath made a bubbling sound in his throat. His mouth was open, his jaw slack, and the piece of bloody glass protruded from the side of his throat.

Ryder left him in the larder and shut the door, dropping the pin into the hasp. He darted down the hall to the office and tore the telephone cord from the wall. Suddenly there were voices. Natasha and Aleksei Sergeyevich were coming from the church. Ryder slipped back to the reception room and watched them enter from the garden.

Natasha had a tense expression. The old man glanced around sharply. The eyes in the hooded pouches narrowed as they took in the overturned table, broken glass, and bloodied floor.

"Where's Ilya Pavlovich?"

"He knocked over a lamp and cut himself," Ryder said. "He's lying down."

Aleksei Sergeyevich glared at him, then limped quickly into the hall. Ryder considered going after him, but decided it was safer simply to try to get away.

"He was getting suspicious," Natasha whispered. "I couldn't keep him away any longer. I think he knows."

"Let's go," Ryder said, taking her arm.

"What about Ilya? What about the pistol?"

"I have it."

They darted across the courtyard, steeped in the shades of evening. Behind them, Aleksei Sergeyevich called out.

"Kozlova! Rydorov! I order you to stop!"

They ducked into an alcove. Ryder thrust Natasha into the recessed wall and flattened against her. A torch flashed across the courtyard. Natasha stiffened against him, hardly breathing. Ryder had a glimpse of Aleksei Sergeyevich, surprisingly nimble on his stiff leg, the torch in one hand, an automatic in the other. The old man hurried past the archway into the orchard.

"We'll go out through the cemetery," Ryder murmured.

Crouching, they bolted for the trees beyond the church wall. Ryder half expected the crack of a pistol shot across the stillness. The woods came up fast in the dusk. They followed a hedgerow overgrown with strangling vines. He heard a soft cry, looked over his shoulder, and saw Natasha down on her hands. He darted back.

"I've twisted an ankle."

"Can you make it to the wall?"

"I'll try."

Ryder had an arm around her waist. The headstones and marble figures fled by in the leafy darkness.

The torch bobbed in the woods above them, the tree trunks swinging back and forth in the beam.

"He's coming down," Natasha cried.

Ryder pulled her into the clumped scrub spilling down behind a marble angel. They lay flat in a spiraling tunnel of bramble and vine. The pistol was a reassuring weight in his hand. Still, he had no desire to kill the old man if it could be avoided.

They heard the crack of dead limbs and brush as the other man drew close. Beyond the slumping leaves, the angel gleamed in the torch. The beam jerked again. The pale glow touched the thicket where they lay, then swept away. They heard Aleksei Sergeyevich cursing as he climbed toward the church.

"He's going back up," Natasha whispered. "He'll telephone for help."

"I cut the wire. It gives us some time, but we'll have to move fast."

He helped Natasha to her feet. Above, in the dark, the angel stared straight ahead out of blind sockets. But there was no sword in its mouth, Ryder thought, and it was not the Angel of Death, after all.

Chapter
36

IN the bombed-out ruin the windows gaped blindly, panes smashed. Incendiaries had taken out part of the roof, and stars glimmered in the opening above the girders.

The concrete floor was strewn with rubble. The turbines and machinery that could be salvaged had been shipped east. A few twisted ends of steel rods protruded from the cement.

They rested in the shadows beneath a collapsed scaffold and looked up through the iron at the night sky.

Natasha said, "Do you think they'll search this far from the monastery?"

"Tomorrow. After it's light."

"A pistol won't be of much use if they find us."

"It will to me," Ryder said. "I'm not going back to Lubyanka."

He grew conscious of her stare, though her features were touched out in the shadow under the dark iron.

"Are you so anxious to die?" she said after a moment. There was no derisive irony in her tone, only curiosity.

He shrugged and replied, "We all have the same appointment to keep, don't we? No matter who pulls the trigger, it was a fixed reservation from the beginning."

A cut had opened on his hand. He saw now that several raw gashes ran across his fingers at the lower joints on the palm side. They must have come from the hunk of glass in that second when he had tried to work the jagged point deep into a vital artery.

"What's the matter with your hand?" Natasha said.

"Nothing."

"But you've cut it."

Ryder flexed the fingers.

"It's not deep."

"Still, you ought to have a dressing for it."

He smiled and said, "My dirty handkerchiefs never came back from the laundry, but then, everything in Lubyanka was unreliable."

"Here." She reached up with both hands, her breasts lifting in the dress, to unfasten the dark kerchief tied behind her head. "It's something to keep the dirt out, anyway."

She wrapped the kerchief around his palm and joined the tips in a soft knot behind his knuckles.

"Is it too tight?"

"No. Fine. But you shouldn't trouble."

An odd feeling of gratitude, disproportionate to the act, swept over him. Having kept his emotions shut away for so long, he couldn't even handle a normal one. Like an infidelity, it left a sense of guilt. He drew his hand away awkwardly and said, "It won't be easy to get clear of Moscow."

"I wish we could go now. I'm afraid."

He shook his head and replied, "It wouldn't do to be caught out after curfew. We'll have a better chance of slipping through in daylight."

"Yes, I suppose so."

They were silent. Natasha leaned back, staring up at the twisted gap in the ceiling.

"Stars," she murmured. "What a long time since I've looked at them."

Her face and arms were pale in the dark. Ryder took off his coat and rolled it into a pillow for her. As he slipped the garment under her head their fingers brushed and the anxiety, tensed into hers, made him wonder again what could have happened to her at Kuntsevo.

"Better sleep, Natasha Ivanovna. Tomorrow could be a long day."

In the morning Ryder woke and looked at her. The over-ripe mouth matched exactly an unfurled rose. He got up silently and mounted a pile of loose rubble to the top of the wall where the windows had been blown out.

The remaining shards of glass reflected the first streaks of dawn. The heat of the day was still pent-up in the east. Here, where the factory ruins stretched off in the first light, it was windless and cool. A railway spur was stitched along the boundary. The tracks and ties had been torn up. Only their indentation remained like a missing trilobite.

At the railhead, beyond a row of warehouses, the roofs of a suburb ran out to the horizon. People crowded around the loading dock of the nearest warehouse. Some carried tools. Their voices drifted across the morning silence, fading in and out.

Ryder slid down the bank of loose rubble and woke Natasha. Both climbed back to the windows.

"It's a timber brigade," she said. "Or they may be going outside the city to dig tank traps."

"Are you sure?"

"Yes. See the trucks? They'll be loading soon."

"Volunteers?"

"Most of them."

"Are their papers checked?"

"Mine weren't."

"Then it could be a bit of luck for us."

The truck ground along the road, and the canvas top flapped in the wind. Most of the talk was about Voronezh on the Don. Pravda reported heavy fighting. Usually that meant that defeat was imminent. Perhaps Voronezh had fallen already. No one in the truck expressed the thought openly, but it was understood.

"And Moscow?" someone said.

"Moscow! That's different!"

"Zhukov will chew them up and spit them out!"

The truck slowed for several military checkpoints. Each time the guards waved them through without stopping. They crossed a bridge into timber. The road followed the river and they could smell the woods. Ryder looked at Natasha. She was looking at the country where the canvas flaps were tied open above the tailgate. Perhaps it was the same country where her father had taken her mother in the droshky. Ryder could see it, too—the whole memory—circumscribed into Natasha's dark stare.

The road dropped down close to the river, and they stopped at a landing. The driver came back to lift the pins from the tailgate, and the passengers jumped down. An empty lumber barge was tied into the bank. By evening the flat deck would be stacked high with timber.

More trucks rolled into the clearing. The brigade assembled, and a party official assigned individuals to work crews. Ryder watched helplessly as Natasha was directed to a different group from his.

"That's my wife, Comrade," he told the supervisor. "We wanted to work together."

"Don't worry." The man treated it as a joke. "You'll be reunited before the end of the day." He added with a smirk,

"When you've been married as long as me, you'll welcome a chance to get away from the old lady for a few hours."

"But—"

"No more talk," the official said. "Did you come to work or to picnic in the woods?"

Natasha marched off with her crew. She shook her head, a quick movement, warning him not to protest.

Ryder was paired with a man who looked to be about fifty. He had a petulant doll's mouth wedged between slackly hanging jowls. The eyes under the cap bill bulged from a thyroid condition. It exaggerated the curiosity in them.

"Why isn't a young fellow like you at the front?"

"I'm on leave. Convalescing."

"Wounded?"

"I took some German steel at Kholm."

"You're supposed to be in uniform."

"It's being patched and washed."

By mid-morning Ryder was sweating, and blisters had formed on his hands, though Natasha's scarf gave some protection. The cut on his palm had opened again and bled into the fabric. When the men exchanged the ripsaw with its double hand grips for two axes, Ryder tried to work away from his companion, but the man stayed with him.

Later the crews broke for a rest. They wandered in to get a drink from the water bag, its canvas skin sweating, slung from a tripod. Natasha opened the spigot and drew a cup of water. She drank it, refilled the cup, and handed it to Ryder. All the while Ryder's partner watched them, his cap pulled forward so that they could not see his eyes but only the band of sun across his irate doll's mouth.

Ryder said to her, "Which section of timber are you working?"

"Over there." She glanced in the direction.

"Alone?"

"Yes."

"Go out past the others as far as you can. I'll try to meet you."

"What's the matter?" Natasha said.

"The man wearing the cap and standing by the truck—I think he's suspicious."

"NKVD?"

"I don't know. An informer, maybe."

"He's watching us now," Natasha said.

"Better go back to your work crew."

A whistle shrilled, ending the rest period. Ryder and the other man walked back to the spot where they had left their axes. The pistol was strapped to Ryder's leg inside his boot. Using it would be out of the question. No, he had to bluff his way out. He picked up his coat and said, "Wait for a bit. I'll be back."

"But where are you off to?" The other man frowned under the cap bill.

"One of nature's emergencies."

"It's the exercise," the other said, nodding. "Always gets the bowels working."

He tramped off in a wide arc through the sun's hot dappling. Overhead, birch leaves shimmered. There was no sign of Natasha. He circled a meadow where a creek cut through the bending grass. The ground lifted through a stand of pines. Several figures came into view. Their voices drifted from a distance. Then he caught sight of Natasha, farther out from the others. She was bending over to collect dead brush. Straightening, she scanned the woods. He stepped into the open and raised an arm. She glanced back over her shoulder, then hurried to him. Ryder took her hand, and they ducked low through the woods. The sound of axes and saws faded behind them. Both were breathing hard when they finally stopped in the shade of a rocky outcropping.

Natasha said, "Do you think anyone saw us?"

"No, but we'd better keep moving."

"Where will we go?"

"We'll have to cross the river. The bridges are guarded. We may have to swim."

"Then what?"

"We'll swing north and try to strike the main railroad line."

"To where?"

"Archangel," Ryder said. "On the White Sea. There's a chance that the senior British naval officer can get us out."

"Archangel." She shook her head despairingly. "But we're days from it—even by train."

"Think about Lubyanka," he said, "and it won't seem as far to you."

Chapter
37

IT was purely a matter of time, Balov knew, before he himself would be arrested. The meeting with his superior, Colonel A. N. Postychev, only reinforced the conviction.

A diminutive figure with steel-grey hair, Postychev was a nervous perfectionist and Party doctrinaire. He spent hours brooding over unimportant details, avoiding decisions, afraid of making a mistake.

Not long ago Balov had imagined he would take Postychev's job and the other man would be demoted back to the field. Now the prospect seemed remote. The same neurotic caution that had kept Postychev from controversy in the past would shield him from this latest crisis.

Adorning the walls of the office were the standard photographs of communist leaders, living and dead. Postychev exhibited them like a sign of faith. Balov smiled wryly at a painting of Lenin, arms outstretched like a messianic savior, stepping from a train on his return to Russia. Behind, in the coach door, stood a beaming Stalin. Surely Stalin had not been there, but history would give way to artistic license.

Art would indulge and glorify those who succeeded in their coup. Only the failures, like Vlasov and Shevchenko, would be ignored.

To start the meeting Postychev called in his stenographer—a young woman named Anna with whom Balov had been intimate several times. The light flashed on her glasses as she crossed her plump legs and rested the notepad on them. Were all myopic women so passionate? Thanks to Anna, Balov knew the purpose of the meeting beforehand. It was Postychev's attempt to disengage himself, in front of a witness, from the actions of his subordinate, which had led to the escape of the Canadian.

"Valery Vasilyevich," he began gravely, "you acted in this foolishness without my knowledge or approval. Why did you do this?"

"You were busy with other matters," Balov said.

"Other matters? Be specific, please."

"Reports," Balov said. "Conferences."

"Couldn't you have interrupted them?" Postychev chided him. "Didn't you stop to think about the potential consequences of this decision you were taking on your own?"

What was there to say? Postychev was making a record of his own noninvolvement. Pilate washing his hands before the Jews—or, in this case, the Party.

Balov glanced at Anna's heavy legs. When she uncrossed them, they would leave a pink mark above the knee. He could visualize the perspiration and heat between them, and in the crease where her breasts pressed together under the blouse. Anna perspired heavily. It intensified the effect of the cheap perfume Balov had bought for her on the black market. He became aware of the scent now. Anna sat, altogether aloof, but Balov knew he would have a copy of the transcript later, just as he would feel the indolent weight of the legs astride him. It was this reversal of sexual positions that gave her the most pleasure, and he could measure the intensity of it in the way she threw back her head, moaning with her eyes tightly shut, while he handled her breasts and stiffened within her.

"Don't you see, Balov?" Postychev picked up a letter opener to occupy his hands. "This could have been avoided if you had come to me first. The whole scheme was foolhardy and reckless. A terrible gamble, letting them escape, a terrible gamble. I would never have sanctioned such a plan."

"Sometimes gambles are necessary," Balov said, "especially with counterrevolutionary elements still at large. As long as they exist, what's to prevent another attack on Comrade Stalin? That's what I was trying to stop. Isn't Comrade Stalin worth the risk?"

Postychev tapped the letter opener against his palm. The conference had taken an uncomfortable turn. He cleared his throat and said, "In any case, you've prevented nothing, arrested no one. But you've lost an important prisoner, our one link to British Intelligence—gone!"

"Temporarily," Balov replied, nodding, "but I'll get him back, and the woman too. They can't get out of the Soviet Union without help." He paused, waiting until the stenographer's pencil stopped moving on the notepad, and added, "Of course, Comrade Colonel, I understand your concern. Any mistake or failure on my part reflects on this section and on your leadership."

Postychev dismissed the stenographer. Evidently he had changed his mind about a written transcript. As Anna uncrossed her legs, Balov noticed the pink mark above her knee, exactly where his imagination had choreographed it.

He turned back in time to catch some flicker of cruel pleasure in Postychev's stare. Apart from the danger it posed to his own position, Postychev was enjoying Balov's fall from favor. It occurred to Balov that he had underestimated the personal ambition behind the pathological fear of failure.

Postychev said, "I tell you this, Valery Vasilyevich: *You'd better find them*. This escape—it hasn't reached Stalin yet, but when it does, the responsible people will have to pay."

"*Neizvestino kogda vernesh'sia domoi*." Balov made the familiar joke, which was a play on the NKVD acronym. It meant, "You never know when you will get home."

The letter opener stopped moving. Balov half expected it to fly out of Postychev's angry fingers, cross the desk by some telekinetic force, and lodge in his heart. Instead of a smile the remark brought only a surge of resentful alarm to the pallid features.

After the meeting Balov went down into the street for a breath of air. He strolled into the Old Quarter where buildings rose narrowly on the sky, drenching the lanes in shade. A walk through this district usually cleared his thoughts, but today that alchemy was missing.

Anton Stepanovich, what a clever bastard you are, after all. Now where would you go?

The answer wouldn't come. He had alerted State Security in Astrakhan and Baku on the Caspian. At Stalingrad, all known contacts from the early days were under surveillance.

But fresh factors complicated the operation. The anticipated German strike against Moscow had not materialized. Instead the Second and Fourth Armies of Field Marshal von Bock had roared east out of Kursk to take Voronezh on the Don. In the south, Paulus's Sixth Army had joined the push. Clearly the German High Command had targeted Stalingrad and the Caucasus for its summer offensive, not Moscow.

Inconceivable, he thought, that the Canadian would head south into the fighting. On the other hand, who could have foreseen the unexpected tactical shift? The news in *Pravda*, censored for morale, always lagged behind events. A British spy on the run might even take advantage of the movement and confusion around Stalingrad.

The safe houses—the damn safe houses—did they exist? The information passed to Sergeant Vavilov in the prison cell struck everyone as too deliberately obvious. No one believed it. Only Balov could appreciate the subtlety. What better way to conceal the truth than by so obviously making it seem a lie?

When he returned to his office, he found Serova waiting. He could gauge her impatience by the number of broken cigarette cylinders in the ashtray.

"Balov!" She jumped up. "Where have you been? They're out looking for you!"

Fast work, he thought with a smile. *You're about to be arrested and shot. Well, it's a fine day for it.*

Serova said, "The Canadian and Kozlova. They've been seen and reported."

"Where?" Balov exclaimed, truly surprised by this turn of events.

"North," she replied, "on the main rail line above Vologda. They were on a supply train. One of the crew discovered them, but they got away."

"Then it wasn't a positive identification?"

"No, but who else could it be? A man and a woman together. The descriptions fit both of them."

Balov went to the wall map. His fingers traced the route and came to rest on the green of printed forests stretching across the continent.

"Vologda," he murmured. "That's about four hundred kilometers."

"A long way from Moscow," Serova said.

"And Stalingrad," Balov said. "He's going out the same way he came in."

"Murmansk?"

"No," he said, frowning, "more likely Archangel. It's

closer, and the heaviest concentration of British PQ convoys will be there until winter."

"What's the next step?" Serova looked at him.

Balov smiled. "I'm going after him...."

Chapter
38

THE supply train passed through the switching yards at Vologda around five in the afternoon. The gondola Ryder and Natasha were in carried two big 76.2mm divisional guns. Only the long barrels protruded from the tarpaulins draped over the batteries. Camouflage nets were stretched to break the outlines from the air.

It was hot under the waterproof canvas, which was rotted and speckled with mold spores. A streak of light passed through a rip higher up. The glow fell across Natasha, who sat with her legs drawn up in front of her and her face buried on her crossed arms. She did not stir as Ryder climbed past her onto the undercarriage of the artillery piece and worked his way up to the rent in the canvas. Holding on to the armor-plated shield of the battery, he peered out. Standing freight cars slid past. A locomotive blowing steam and smoke chugged toward them-around a curve where a dozen tracks fanned out from a signal gantry. The engine took on the shimmer of a mirage in the thermal waves of afternoon heat. A few moments later it shook past with a tramping roar.

The supply train slowed until it was barely moving. Finally it ground to a stop, and Ryder eased himself down to the floor of the gondola.

"Where are we?" Natasha murmured, her face upraised.

"A railroad yard. It looks like a main junction. Probably Vologda."

Suddenly they froze. Outside, voices were calling to one another. Ryder put a finger to his lips, stretched out a hand to Natasha, and drew her back to the darkest pocket of the canvas behind the breech of the field gun. They crouched together in the cramped space, and the barrel of the automatic pistol made a dull shine resting against the slant of a guy wire.

Boots crunched in the loose cinders beside the track bed outside the car. They could hear two men talking. A third voice joined in and there was joking and laughter. Both of Natasha's hands gripped his arm, and Ryder could feel her trembling against him. Once, he turned his head to look at her, only to find her staring at him, her expression tense. Their faces, close in the mottled gloom under the canvas, were wet with perspiration. Natasha's lips parted, as if she wanted to speak but dared not utter a sound. Instead her fingers only tightened on his arm.

There were more shouts outside. The train gave a shuddering creak as coupling joints took up their slack against the steel pins, and the car was rolling again. Ryder could feel some of the tension go out of the hands clutching his arm.

Later they huddled on the floor beside the chocks and listened to the wheels of the gondola flinging the empty distances behind them. In a little while the dull gleam of the riveted armor plates of the field gun above their heads faded as the light went from the canvas. The sun was down, but the stifling heat remained, leaving Ryder drowsy.

Natasha shook his leg. The alarm in her fingers jolted him awake. Instinctively he groped for the pistol.

"We're slowing," she warned.

Half asleep, he hadn't noticed. The clicking of the wheels over the rails was long and drawn out.

Suddenly the flap of the tarpaulin jerked up. A parcel of pale light fell across Natasha's face.

"Come out," a voice ordered.

Ryder saw a hairy fist clamped on the canvas and a face bending down. It was a railroad crewman, not one of the armed guards, or it might have been over for them. The crewman was checking the cables that lashed down the field guns. Still, Ryder thought, the guard could not be far away. Otherwise the man would not be so overconfident.

"Go ahead," Ryder said to Natasha. "Do as he says."

She crawled out on her hands and knees. Ryder followed, straightening. The crewman saw the pistol too late. The cockiness fell from his expression, and he opened his mouth to shout. Ryder swung the pistol and could feel the skull crack under the steel. The man dropped in a heap, and the train whistle shrilled.

Ryder motioned to Natasha to get down. Camouflage netting was stretched above them on poles, leaving the sky gridded. Crouching, he looked both ways and saw no one. There were two gondolas in front, and one behind, then the high shapes of boxcars.

Suddenly the guard bobbed into view. He was in the second gondola, nearest the engine, and Ryder saw only his head, cloth forage cap, and the tip of the rifle slung above his shoulder.

Ryder ducked low and crawled with Natasha to the other side of the artillery piece. Overhead, a girder slid past on the sky, then another.

The train had slowed to cross a railway bridge damaged by bombs. The underside around the weakened piles had been shored with timbers. The trestle sagged under the weight of the train, the jointed iron creaking as the overloaded cars swayed and tipped. Ryder could see the river below the gaps in the ties. Beyond the bridge, etched on the red evening were an antiaircraft battery and several tiny figures.

"This is where we get off." He pushed Natasha toward the handrails.

"On the bridge?"

"There won't be another chance once we pick up speed."

They scrambled over the side, hugging the iron ladder, and dropped to the foot ramp beside the track. Ryder looked up at the train. The guard had spotted them. He was shouting but couldn't be heard above the grinding wheels. The rifle came off his shoulder.

Ryder lifted Natasha, flung her over the side, then vaulted the railing himself. The guard's shot from the moving car clipped splinters from a beam above Ryder's head but did not come close.

He saw the white explosion, thirty feet below, as Natasha disappeared into the water. Then the spreading concentric rings were shooting toward him. His boots and clothing took him deep, and he struggled up through a chain of bubbles and found Natasha treading water. The current carried them in under the piles, and they clung to the planking in the heavy shadows. The trestle still trembled under the weight of the passing train. Finally the caboose lumbered by, leaving the last evening light in the ties.

The train did not stop. Ryder didn't think it would. A train carrying armaments had a schedule to keep. It would take the guard awhile to find the unconscious crewman. By that time it would be too late to react. They could only report the incident.

"Listen!" Natasha murmured.

They heard the hollow pounding of boots on the ramp. Ryder pulled her in close. Natasha's arms were around his neck, their bodies tight together in the watery shadows.

Shouts came closer. Ryder looked up through the ties and saw soldiers running.

"The guard who shot at us..." he said, frowning.

"Would he have left the train?"

"He must have dropped off at the artillery position long enough to tell them about us. He could have swung back aboard before the train passed."

Two more figures ran past. Altogether he counted five. Only three came back, moving slowly along the track and staring down through the ties. Probably they had posted two men at the end of the bridge to spot anyone coming into shore.

Downstream, the river swung into a wide bend. Low hills lifted away. Woods were dark along the shore. The reflections emblazoned on the water were fading in the long twilight.

Brush and deadwood, swept downriver during the spring thaw, clogged the junctures of the shoring timbers of the bridge. An uprooted tree was jammed sideways into the piling. The current sucked at the root system and spilled over the partially submerged trunk in a watery sheen.

"If I could float it loose," Ryder said, "we might use it for cover."

"Suppose they see us from the bridge?"

"It's nearly dark. Their rifle sights won't be of much use. Besides, they've probably called for help, maybe even a boat."

He dived several times to rock the tip of the tree back and forth. At last the tangle broke loose with a heavy thump. They floated out with the debris. The trestle receded slowly. In the current the island of brush began to break up. They clung to the limbs of the tree. There were no shots from the bridge. It drifted away silently, the black iron hanging in the twilight.

Chapter
39

THE river bend took the trestle out of sight. They rode the current downstream, the shore sweeping past. A second curve carried them close in to the bank. Ryder called out to Natasha to let go of the log. They swam in, wading out of the sandy shallows.

The night air blew against their wet faces. They climbed, dripping, into the trees along the shore. Natasha's dress clung to her body.

"Better wring out our clothes," Ryder said, "or we'll be wet all night."

He went off a short way, emptied the water from his boots, took off his socks, wrung each one, then his coat, trousers, and shirt. The pistol was gone, lost the first time he went under. He still had Ilya's papers and money, and these he smoothed out carefully to dry.

Later he dressed in the damp clothing and went back to Natasha. He found her sitting on the bank, her face lowered into her arms, which encircled her legs in the same posture he remembered from the train.

They'll have a patrol out at daybreak," Ryder said. "We can't stay on the river."

She raised her head slowly, and he saw the tracks of tears on her face—a shadow of Kuntsevo, he suspected. A foolish urge swept over him, a homicidal wish that had to do with Vlasik, but the desire was only a compromise with reality. He dropped to one knee, put his hands on her shoulders, and said, "Natasha Ivanovna, it's just fatigue, that's all. Don't confuse it with anything else."

She stared at him and nodded gravely. Ryder smiled at her, using his fingers to wipe the moisture from her cheeks, and then he drew her gently to her feet.

"We're two or three kilometers east of the railroad," he said. "If we follow the line, we're bound to find settlements and farms."

They tramped north over the low range of hills under the stars. At the top of the ridge line they rested in the timber and looked back at the country they had come over. White thunderclouds, adrift on the horizon, seemed nearly level with them, and there was a fine view of the river, blazing and brilliant under a rising moon. The water streaming over rocky shoals had the look of smoke.

On the far side of the ridge the hills broke and stampeded away under the starry darkness. Scattered lights glimmered in distant valleys.

"Probably farms," Ryder said.

"Maybe we'll find something to eat by morning."

Going down, they picked up a dim echo of thunder from another valley. Before an hour had passed, a cloud dimmed the moon. The drifting shape was ragged and grey, torn from the edge of a storm.

Sometime before midnight the rain started. The first swollen drops spattered in the forest. Then the whole sky caved in, tearing pinecones and dead twigs from the trees.

They had come close to a farm. A lighted window shone

through the rain lashing down. Nearby the dark, high shape of a barn squatted in the downpour.

They ran for the barn. Inside it was dark and dry. The fragrance of newly cut hay came from the loft. A horse pranced nervously in a stall.

"I'll go have a look at the house," Ryder said, "just to be safe."

Between the barn and the house stood an open shed where firewood was stacked. He bolted toward it, ducking in under the roof, but the house was still too far away in the rain. Crouching, he sprinted for it and flattened against the wall outside the window.

A rush lamp lit the bare room. A woman under thirty and a wiry old man sat on either side of a small coffin. The woman wore peasant workclothes, her ankles were brown and dusty in the open sandals, and her hair, parted down the middle, was swept back tightly.

Inside the coffin lay a dead girl, no more than two, her eyes closed. A garland of pink blossoms had been arranged in her blond hair.

Candles burned around the coffin. The man and woman sat, unmoving in the slow flicker, holding a vigil over the dead child.

Ryder ran back through the rain to the barn.

"We'll be safe enough here until morning."

"You're soaked," Natasha said.

"You too."

They climbed the ladder to the loft. Hay from the summer harvest was stacked to the crossbeams. They crept back among the shocks. Natasha shivered.

"Better get out of your wet things," Ryder said. "I'll sleep over on the other side."

He crawled away to the joint of a crossbeam and stripped off his own wet clothing. Later he had a glimpse of Natasha, beyond the sheaves of hay, pulling her wet slip over her head. Her bare shoulders were pale in the darkness. He turned away.

The thunder had moved to the west, the torrent slackening. Ryder lay back and listened to the rain drumming against the roof close above his head in the dark. It brought back the memory of another night, the creak of a barn door on the windy darkness, the hooves of a horse flinging their sound into a boy's dream like a farewell. Hadn't he dreamed of a parade? The banners and flags still streamed in his mind, the marching feet still marched, but the tune . . . he couldn't remember the tune. . . .

During the night he woke. The rain had stopped. The wind blew hard under the eaves. The big timbers of the barn creaked. It seemed to him that his life had always been full of silence. He curled deeper into the hay and went back to sleep.

Asleep, he dreamed of his wife—the familiar nightmare in which he pursued her through the fire storm. Always some new obstacle prevented him from reaching her—an exploding bomb, the collapse of a flaming wall, a warden's hands restraining him . . . Once, in the dream, she turned back and it was Natasha, not his wife, trapped in the street between the billowing sheets of fire, and she had pink flowers in her hair like the dead child in the coffin.

Then he saw another coffin deep in the ground and Natasha's hair, damp and shining, with the garland in it. But the face on the satin pillow was badly burned, the gauze strips around the burned hands were brown like mummy wrappings, and he knew it was his wife. . . .

He woke with the outcry still corded in his throat. Natasha had her fingers over his mouth. The first morning greyness spilled through the cracks in the barn. She crouched beside him, one hand clasping the slip to her nakedness.

The troubled anxiety on her face gave way to a different

emotion. Tenderness? Concern? He couldn't identify it. In the dream the two women had been interchangeable. Already the effect was receding, leaving him empty.

Her cool fingers touching his mouth trembled slightly, no longer imposing silence, but lingering like a caress. The dark eyes were full of confused discovery. She understood it all, Ryder thought, a split second before he did.

His fingers slid back in her hair, drew her down. Her lips under his gave up something impossibly soft. Finally they opened, and the heat came quickly into the kiss. The garment had fallen away. Her bare breasts were heavy and hard against his chest. He put his hand between her thighs. Immediately her legs stirred, the thick rise of pubic hair already dampening under his stroking fingers.

In the soft crush of hay he heard the tiniest gasp at his entry. Then another long gasp was torn from her throat—and another—as his own sliding hardness within her unlocked a wet, straining response.

Chapter
40

STREAKS of daylight stole through the side boards of the loft. Natasha's head rested on Ryder's shoulder. Her hand lay lightly on his chest. One white breast was steeped against him, the tip swollen and pink.

They stared at each other in the calm silence. The expression in her eyes seemed to ask, "Is it real? Is it possible?" Why shouldn't she doubt it? He could hardly believe it himself.

A barn swallow flew up under the eaves and darted out again.

Below, the heavy doors swung open on their rusty hinges. Natasha stiffened against him. Ryder reached for the pistol and remembered it was gone. He leaned up on one elbow and peered over the edge of the loft.

It was the old man from the main house. His head and shoulders came into view as he stretched for a bridle slung from a peg. Then he stepped out of sight again. The latch on the stall gate clicked open. Ryder heard the horse stamping around on the hard-packed dirt. The old man led the animal to the hay cart and hooked the harness to the traces.

Later, from the vented opening high up under the eaves, they watched the man and woman carry the child's coffin from the house. The lid had been nailed into place. The woman rode in the cart next to the small pine box. The man walked beside the horse, holding the bridle near the bit.

"A dead child," Ryder said. "A little girl. I saw her last night."

Natasha made the sign of the cross. "We've intruded on the dead."

Before they left the farm, Ryder found fishing line and hooks, a small hunting knife and whetstone, soap, black bread, and a moldering block of cheese. These he packed into a blanket roll tied at both ends and carried under his arm.

They tramped through woods most of the day. There were breaks in the timber, the country rolling and sprawled out. Sometimes the roofs of farmhouses showed in the blue distance, along with the glint of hay stacked in fields, and a few cattle grazed in sunny pastures.

Once, less than a kilometer away, they saw a line of carts drawn by draft animals. The carts were loaded with burlap sacks of grain and tobacco, baskets of fruit and vegetables, and cloth bags of wheat flour—produce from the collective farms being hauled to a government collection point. Women and children walked barefooted beside the carts along the dusty road.

Later, from high ground, they watched a detatchment of cavalry canter down a long valley toward the railroad line. The rifles of the cavalrymen were slung across their backs, their capes lifting behind them. The thudding of hooves sounded very faint. The patrol, Ryder thought, could easily be searching for them.

At mid-afternoon, hot and dusty, they came to a stream and trudged along the bank until they found a pool deep enough for bathing. Beyond a sandbar the water swirled, cool and green, and the hardwood leaves of a shady glade dappled the surface.

"There's nobody around," he said. "Let's have our swim here. Then we can have something to eat."

"All right."

Her gaze touched his for only half a second and color came into her cheeks, but she smiled. They undressed with their backs to each other. Ryder heard water splashing, turned and had a glimpse of Natasha slipping, naked, into the stream. A breeze shook the leaves overhead, and the drowning gleams of afternoon light fell to the surface. He waded out into the channel. Sand, lifting off the bottom, drifted away in cloudy spurts.

He overtook Natasha in the cool shallows near the sandbar and snatched an ankle. She twisted back toward him, the water running down between her breasts. Her arms went around his neck, and her wet, laughing mouth on his opened a feeling that was like a secret to be shared, intimate and blindingly tender, until finally the centigrade of something altogether different came into the kiss, sweet and burning, like a delicious, impatient memory.

Natasha's eyes closed at the moment of his entry. Her legs locked slowly around him. It was strange to make love with their shoulders out of the water while the kinetic force of the current held them in its weightless medium. The contractions within her seemed to break for a long time against the flowing warmth of sperm, and he felt like the past had been washed away in the stream, as if in release from pain.

They lay with their bodies half out of the water where the grass vaulted up from the bank in the leafy dappling of shade and sunlight, and they talked in whispers. Both had slipped into the Russian familiar form of address as if they had always spoken to each other in that way.

"*Tosha*," she said, the fingers of one hand entwined tightly in his, "I've never loved anyone before. Now I'm frightened something could happen to us. Before, I didn't care."

He smiled and answered, "Don't you think I feel the same way?"

The tip of her breast pressed against his arm.

"What's to become of us, anyway? This stupid war! If we're caught by either side, we'll never see each other again. I couldn't stand it, could you?"

"We're not caught yet," he said.

Later they dressed, and Natasha trimmed mold from the cheese and cut slices to eat with the bread. After the meal they rested under the trees and considered which direction they should go from here. Natasha mentioned an uncle who was living near Kotlas.

"Kotlas?" Ryder said. "On the Dvina?"

"He's a yard supervisor at the sawmill."

Ryder leaned up on one elbow and said, "The Dvina flows into the White Sea—below Archangel."

"What's the difference?" Natasha shook her head. "Kotlas is almost as far east from here as Archangel is to the north. We'd be crazy, *Tosha*—crazy to go so far out of the way."

"*Nadia*, listen. Remember that cavalry patrol this morning? They're looking for us to go north from here. If we cut across country toward Velsk, we could pick up the main rail line east. The river might be our best chance, after all. It's full of barge traffic this time of year, isn't it?"

"That's true enough."

Ryder frowned.

"This uncle of yours in Kotlas—can you trust him?"

Chapter
41

THEY spent two nights in the woods near the river above Kotlas. Natasha left early the first day and went into the city to contact her uncle. By late afternoon she hadn't come back, and Ryder began to worry. Suppose State Security had assigned *topolshchiki*—surveillance men—to watch her relatives? Wouldn't Balov have thought of it?

But she turned up at dusk. The last fading light hung in the trees, and she called out to him from the river. He sprang up and ran to her.

In the blue darkness their bodies were tightly clasped. Natasha's head was thrown back, her lips opened under his, and for a while the river was a moving gleam beyond their faces.

He said, "I was worried you were arrested."

"No, everything's fine. Wait until you hear."

"You talked to him?"

"He'll have a small boat here in the morning before it's light. There's a barge downriver about six kilometers. It's taking a cargo of trucks and grain all the way into Archangel. The captain owes him a favor. We're in luck, I tell you!"

Ryder frowned.

"It almost sounds too easy."

"Look, *Tosha*, I've brought food." She held up a packet tied in newspaper. "Salted fish and bread and a fresh cucumber. Aren't you hungry?"

It was dark when they finished eating. They lay back on the carpet of pine needles and looked at the sky in the trees. Ryder laced his fingers together behind his head.

"Is there any chance of the barge captain going to the authorities?"

"I don't think my uncle would have approached him if there was. He's taking a big enough risk himself by helping us."

"Your uncle's not political?"

"If he was, he'd be a production commissar instead of a yard supervisor."

"How much did you tell him?"

"Only that there was an attempt by military officers to take power, and we were both implicated."

"Did he know about the attempt on Stalin's life?"

"There's been no word put out." Natasha shook her head. "It's as if it never happened. Sometimes I wonder myself. It seems so far in the past."

"There won't be any past for the Shevchenkos and Chernovs. They won't have existed."

"Or your friend Krylov."

"It was a dirty business from the beginning," Ryder said. "I think Maxim Nikolayevich was the only one who brought some dignity to it."

"Look." Natasha pointed up through the pine needles. "A shooting star."

Ryder saw it skating down the horizon. Hadn't the gods of mythology taken their favorite mortals and placed them among the constellations? Perhaps it was Maxim Nikolay-evich's star—totally alone, a streak of light going out.

Before daybreak they followed a footpath upstream to a wooded point. A log dock ran out over the water. An empty rowboat made a floating shadow at the end of the ramp. A thickset figure strode down from the trees lining the high bank.

"This is my uncle," Natasha said, "Pavel Nikolayevich."

In the dark Ryder could only distinguish a round face and heavy mustache.

"Hurry." The older man looked around nervously. "Into the boat."

A mooring line stretched from a steel eye-hook in the gunwale to a pier post. Pavel Nikolayevich loosened the half hitch and steadied the craft. Water sloshed against the hull as Natasha and Ryder climbed into the stern. The dock slid away.

The current grew strong where the channel deepened. Pavel Nikolayevich shipped oars, the blades dripping, and let the river carry them downstream. Scattered lights along the shore drifted past. It was cool on the water in the wind-less hush before daybreak, and the banks were high and dark on either side.

Ryder said, "How will you get the boat back to Kotlas?"

"I'll have it towed."

"And you? Won't they miss you at work?"

"I'll get a ride back and take the ferry across."

He sounded tense, uncommunicative. Probably he was anxious about the risk to himself and his family. Ryder made no further attempt at conversation.

In a little while the other man dipped the oars once more and began to row. The river dragged them another several hundred meters before the boat broke from the grip of the current. Ahead, more lights burned on the black water. They gave shape to tin-roofed buildings clustered along a wharf, and the dark iron of a loading crane. Paraffin lamps glowed aboard the barge tied up at the wharf.

"Is that the barge?" Ryder said.

The other nodded and replied, "Waiting for a load of grain from a government collection point. The rest of the cargo is already aboard."

"What did you tell the captain?"

"Nothing. It's better if he doesn't know anything. I don't even want to know myself."

"Then how can you trust him?"

"How? Because he spent five years in a labor camp for political crimes. I helped his family then. Now it's his chance to return the favor."

Ryder watched the bank gliding toward them. It came at an angle, rising on the sky, and he felt the soft bump as the prow went aground. The landing still lay downstream.

"I'll go in on foot and have a look," Pavel Nikolayevich said. "Wait here for me."

The first crimson was bleeding out of the sky in the east when he came back, breathing hard.

"The captain's waiting for you on board. You'll have to hurry. It'll be light soon and someone might see you."

Natasha embraced her uncle. She stepped back, tears shining in her eyes.

Ryder said, "We're grateful to you, Pavel Nikolayevich."

A frost of perspiration glistened on the round face above the mustache, and the older man's palm was slick with nervous perspiration. Clearly the instincts of family loyalty were in conflict with a healthy desire to distance himself from the problem.

"I wish you luck," he said, "and God's grace. But please go, now, and quickly."

Chapter
42

THE barge slid downstream. In a cargo compartment below deck, Ryder and Natasha rested against the bulkhead and listened to the dull throb of the engines. The hold was dank, stifling. Ryder climbed a pallet of grain bags and opened the porthole in the hull above the waterline. Warm air streamed in, and he looked out at the river bending into its own watery sparkle on the horizon. A string of barges, in tow, slipped across the distance. Powering upstream was a riverboat, its stack smoking. Soldiers crowded the upper deck, leaning on the rail.

Later the hatch cover swung open and the captain climbed down. His name was Radek, and he had silver hair, which was matted into points and curled over the grubby handkerchief knotted about his neck. Too much drink had spoiled his nose. It swelled at the base where big purple veins stood out. His eyes, close together and bloodshot, peered out from under the cap bill.

He grinned and said, "What an oven to sweat in, eh?"

"How long will we be on the river?" Natasha said.

"Four days," he said with a shrug. "Maybe five."

Ryder said, "Can you navigate at night?"

"There's not much darkness up here this time of year, maybe an hour or two, but we'll tie up somewhere. I'm running with a short crew. Six hands, and four of them women. They need rest."

"Does anyone know we're aboard?" Ryder said.

"No," Radek replied, shaking his head. "But we've carried passengers before. It's the captain's business who we take aboard, and nobody else's. Anyway, when it comes down to it, there's only one of the crew I wouldn't trust, and that's Strepnikova. . . ."

"What's the matter with her?"

"You know these Komsomol types, always talking politics to the others. She may have been put aboard to keep an eye on things."

"An informant?" Natasha said.

"Just stay out of her way if you can. You'll know her. She has short hair, like a boy, and a broad face. Not bad to look at, either, if you like them surly."

There was a latrine in the deckhouse passageway above the companionway ladder. The captain told them he would keep watch topside if they wanted to use it.

"The crew sleeps on deck," he said. "I'll bring something to eat once things are quiet."

At about ten that evening the engines stopped. Small waves splashed against the hull. They heard voices and the thump of feet as the crew scrambled to secure the lines. Soon the sounds of activity fell off. Probably the crew was eating the evening ration.

In a little while the sound of an accordion drifted down. The music lasted only a short time. Silence overtook the barge. Ryder climbed to the porthole. The sun was down, but the light remained on the horizon. Night, settling over the country, could not crack the pale dusk.

Another hour lapsed before the hatch opened and the

captain descended. The stubbled face, sweating through its grimy film, hovered in front of them in the shadowy gloom.

"I've brought smoked fish," he said in a rasping whisper. "Some vodka too."

"When will we get under way again?" Ryder said.

"A few hours." A band of shadow canceled out his stare, leaving only the lump of his nose and the rivulets of collapsed veins. "So you're on the run, eh?"

"It's that or a labor camp for us," Ryder said. "Maybe worse."

"I know about it. They sent me up for five years. Criticizing the government was my crime. I hadn't criticized anything, but someone trying to save his own skin denounced me, so I was arrested. They'd still be interrogating me in prison if I hadn't confessed. 'Save your health,' the other *zeks* told me. 'Sign a confession. It's the only way out.' That's how I got my fiver, and what did it accomplish? Here's sweet irony for you. I came out of it a real political criminal. I had plenty of time to cultivate anti-Soviet thought, let me tell you."

"Did you serve out your sentence?" Natasha asked.

"Four years, nine months, and two days. Then I was pardoned! Can you believe it? Because of the war, they needed pilots for these barges, men who knew the river. It's full of islands and sandbars. Not everyone can read the river. So I was declared rehabilitated and sent back."

"Lucky for us," Ryder said.

"For you?" Radek gave a hoarse chuckle. "It's the least I can do for the State, Comrade—to show my gratitude for its benevolent mercy."

After the Captain left, they ate. The fish tasted salty and dry, and they washed it down with vodka, which left their eyes watering.

"I could do without another fish," Ryder said, "for the rest of our lives."

"Vodka too," Natasha whispered, "that tastes like gasoline."

"We'd better try to sleep, *Nadia*, while there's no sun to heat things up."

"I've forgotten what a bed feels like, haven't you?"

"If our luck holds, maybe you'll be able to recapture the sensation."

They climbed onto the flat pile of grain sacks. As soon as Natasha was settled, Ryder stretched out beside her. The river splashed tiny swells against the hull, and each sound carried hollowly through the drum-tight silence of the hold. The moment Ryder put his arm around her, she turned to him, her face close. The porthole admitted enough of the night's pale radiance to pick out the restless anticipation in her parted lips, and she murmured, "I don't want to go any night without you in me. What if it's our last night?"

Ryder put his hand on her cheek. Immediately she drew toward him, pressing her lips to his mouth.

On the second day the barge put in to Verkhnyava Toyma to offload steel pipe and take on a cargo of tires. They could hear Radek bellowing orders through a megaphone. The captain did not appear in the hold until after dark. This time he brought tea and a jar of honey.

They were on the river most of the third day. Forests of larch and spruce were green along the banks, and many islands lifted out of the wide channels. The captain remained in the wheelhouse, navigating each new stretch of shallows.

On the morning of the fourth day the hatch cover swung back. They looked up, but it was not Radek. A woman stared down. Her hair was cropped short, and the bright, carnivorous eyes exaggerated the animal strength planed into the broad features. They showed neither fear nor surprise. There was no sound except for the throb of engines from the power plant. Then the face withdrew from the slot.

"She saw us," Natasha breathed, squeezing his arm.

"Yes."

"What should we do?"

"I'll have to go up."

Ryder mounted the ladder and opened the hatch. While he was still in the passageway to the deckhouse he heard the woman and Radek arguing. They stopped as soon as he appeared in the doorway.

"Your captain knows why we're aboard," Ryder said. "If he thought you needed to be told, he would have done that already. What's your name?"

"Strepnikova," the captain answered for her. "Anna Petrovna."

"He's following my orders," Ryder said.

Strepnikova was short, squarely built. The thick ankles and strong hands seemed deliberately constructed for hard use. Her skin was smooth and brown. Vitality glowed from it. She could have marched directly off one of those patriotic posters of the new Soviet woman.

"Your orders?" she said to Ryder. "Who are you to give orders?"

Ryder reached for the papers he had taken from Ilya Pavlovich. He held up the identity card from State Security. Then he handed her the letter authorizing unrestricted travel in the course of a special assignment.

"I don't mind your questions," he said to Strepnikova. "Everyone should be conscious of security these days. But we're on a special job. Our movement was supposed to be secret. Now it isn't, thanks to your prying. What made you look in the cargo hold, anyway?"

For the first time he could see doubt forming in the violent eyes.

"I saw him taking food down." She glared at Radek. "I thought we might be carrying unauthorized passengers."

"But you had no business in the hold. What's the matter

with you? Didn't they teach you about discipline in the Komsomol?"

The uncertainty dislodged a little more of the arrogant strength in the brown face.

"Now I have to decide what to do about you, Comrade Strepnikova. I could put you ashore and have them lock you up. But the captain's already shorthanded. There's no one to pull your share of the work, and we haven't time for unscheduled detours." Ryder paused, letting the silence have its effect. Finally he said, "You're to say nothing of this to the crew—or to anyone else. If our mission should be compromised, you'll regret it. I promise you. Understand?"

Strepnikova nodded, her face darkly flushed.

"Now get back to your job on deck and remember what I've told you."

She fled past them without a glance.

"The Komsomol bitch had me sweating, I tell you," Radek said. The creased pouches in his face were ingrained with dirt that flaked away when he dragged a sleeve across it.

"If anything comes of it," Ryder said, "be sure you stick to the same story. I showed you travel documents on official stationary. That's why you put us aboard with no questions asked."

"Yes, I've got it."

"Any more stops?"

"Kholmogory, below Archangel. We'll put in to offload two of the trucks."

"How soon?"

"Another hour."

"Can you keep Strepnikova aboard?"

"That shouldn't be hard. You've put a scare into her."

"I'm not sure she scares that easily."

Ryder descended to the cargo hold. Natasha had a worried look. He told her what had happened.

"Do you think she'll make trouble for us?"

"We'll have to wait and see."

Chapter
43

BALOV gazed down at Strepnikova's upturned face. Women, for him, fell into carnal categories. Sex for this one would be a proletarian duty. She would know all the textbook positions and still require a lubricant.

"But I've told my story twice to these others," she protested.

"Good," Balov said. "Now you can tell it to me."

No emotion, he decided, could survive for long on the blazing Fahrenheit of those eyes. Even her impatience was combustible.

In addition to Balov, two others were present—Serova, and B. Grigorenko, the NKVD officer in charge of operations for the Archangel district. Grigorenko was stout, with flesh-colored warts on his face.

Midway through Strepnikova's account Balov interrupted her.

"Never mind the descriptions. Where did they go when they left the barge?"

"We tied up at the north dock. There are some bombed

ruins of a sawmill about two hundred meters beyond the last warehouse. That's where they're hiding."

"How do you know?" Balov said.

"The captain sent me below to inventory the stores. I wasn't fooled. I watched them from a porthole. They went up to the sawmill offices, what's left of them."

"I know the place," Grigorenko said to Balov. "The Germans bomb it every time they come over. We think the pilots must have a bet among themselves. They've destroyed everything but the incinerator. From the sky it looks vulgar, just a big steel cone. The milling operation was shut down weeks ago."

"Then it's deserted?" Balov said.

"There's some unexploded ordnance that hasn't been defused yet. It would be a good place to hide, all right."

Balov said to Stepnikova, "Did the captain remain aboard the barge?"

"No, he left, and that's when I came here. I knew something was wrong. I've never trusted him."

Grigorenko said, "Do you want to search the place? I'll pull some men off the docks."

"They'll try to board a British vessel," Balov said. "Don't take anyone from the docks. I want a guard at every gangplank. You'll have to restrict allied crews to their ships except for emergencies and government business."

"What reason do I give?"

"That's up to you."

Serova said, "What about the sawmill?"

"We'll have a look at it ourselves," Balov said.

"Alone?" she said, frowning.

Balov turned to Grigorenko.

"Give me one armed man for a backup. But no shooting, understand? We want the Canadian alive."

From the high ground behind the sawmill Balov and Serova stared down at the yard. Nothing remained of the big open storage sheds but their stone foundations. Logs still floated in the bay behind a barrier. Jammed together, they looked the size of matchsticks.

Off to the left the long wharf shrank out to the horizon. Warehouses lined the quay. A railhead ran in close to the sawmill. More track glinted behind the warehouses.

Near the railhead rose the phallic shape of the incinerator. It was here that the armed man, assigned by Grigorenko, had taken up his position. He could intercept anyone trying to flee toward the docks.

Bomb craters pitted the yard between the incinerator and the mill office. The two-story structure was still standing, though it had received a direct hit. An outer wall was missing, the windows were blown out, and the tin roof twisted back on itself.

Balov nodded to Serova and said, "Let's go."

Signs posted around the building read: DANGER—UNEXPLODED BOMB. Inside, charred debris and broken glass were scattered everywhere. Balov drew his pistol.

"Better wait here," he whispered, "while I have a look upstairs."

The bomb blast had weakened the staircase. It sagged under his weight. The upper floors creaked with every step. He saw open sky in the mangled tin where the bomb had come through the roof. He had to skirt a gaping hole in the floorboards underneath it.

In the next room a shadow darted across the wall. Balov raised the pistol just as Natasha appeared in the doorway. Immediately some bright expectancy went out of her face and terror came into it. The expression told him the Canadian wasn't there but that she must be expecting him back.

"Where is he, Natasha Ivanovna?"

Chapter
44

THE wooded knoll overlooked a park. Beyond the promenade children swung on a primitive Ferris wheel made from skinned logs. Four swaying seats were attached.

Below, empty benches surrounded a flower bed and a bust of Lenin. A British naval officer paced back and forth. He paused to light a cigarette, then resumed pacing. From time to time he glanced at his watch.

From the knoll Ryder studied the officer. At last, satisfied that they were alone, he slipped downhill through the trees. The officer, tall and pink-cheeked, wore the stripes of a full lieutenant on his sleeve.

"I asked for the senior British naval officer," Ryder said.

"I'm Evans, sir," the Lieutenant said. "Assistant to the SBNO. He's tied up with the port authorities. Would have looked a bit odd if he'd broken away."

"Did he see my note?"

"Your Russian barge captain slipped it through to us at Norway House. Christ . . ."

"How much were you told about Operation Grey Wolf?"

"Nothing, except we're to give it highest priority." The lieutenant frowned. "But that signal came in four months ago. We'd nearly forgotten about it."

"You'll have to get us aboard a British ship. Can you manage it?"

"Us?" The frown deepened. "There's more than one of you?"

Ryder nodded and replied, "A Russian female."

"A Soviet citizen? Bloody hell, sir. The Admiralty didn't mention that bit. What I mean to say is, our instructions didn't cover—"

"You'll have to do it without instructions."

"Take some arranging, that." Evans shook his head. "Another fortnight and you'd have been out of luck, I'm afraid."

"Why?"

"The PQ convoys have been canceled."

"By whose order?" Ryder said.

"The prime minister himself. The last one, PQ.17, was a bloody disaster. Thirty-seven ships hit by a wolf pack and ordered to scatter. The Jerries picked off all but eleven. God knows how much tonnage went to the bottom. We're still calculating. . . ."

"I saw a British destroyer in port," Ryder said.

"The Admiralty's sent in four of them with ammunition and rations. We can't get anything from the Russians. It's *nyet* this, *nyet* that. Something's turned them sour."

A weary smile dragged at the corner of Ryder's mouth. A bungled coup, he thought. A failed assassination. A suspicion that British Intelligence was mixed up in it somehow. What right did they have to be sour? He said to Evans, "How much of a problem will it be getting aboard one of those destroyers?"

"The Russians have a guard at every berth. They check everyone leaving and boarding ship." He raised his head to stare at Ryder. "I think I'm beginning to understand why."

"How long will it take you to work something out?"

The young officer gazed off toward the distant docks. The shouts of children playing at the log wheel drifted back through the wood. Finally Evans shook his head.

"Give me three hours," he said. "At least that. I'll meet you back here, same spot."

Ryder waited in the woods above the knoll. He wondered periodically if Natasha was all right. The children were gone from the playground. Shade drenched the park, which was now bare and silent under Lenin's stare.

A little over three hours passed before Evans reappeared. Long, springing strides carried him out into the open. Once more Ryder left the knoll and went down to him.

"I have an address for you," Evans said. "A coffin maker."

Ryder smiled and said, "That's convenient if something goes wrong."

"We've had four survivors from PQ.17 die in hospital. The Russians have given permission for the remains to be put aboard one of our destroyers. We'll put yours aboard instead."

"In coffins?"

"Nailed shut."

"Can you trust the coffin maker?"

"He's a blasted capitalist," Evans replied. "Therefore corruptible."

"God save free enterprise."

Evans asked if the girl was nearby, and Ryder described the location of the sawmill.

"There's a spot of luck," the officer replied. "The coffin maker—you're practically on his doorstep. I've sketched out a map. He's in a lane behind the church. You can't miss it."

Ryder said, "When should we go?"

The naval officer struck him now as more high-strung than in their earlier meeting. The pressure of too little time, along with the possibility of something going wrong, would be working to the surface in his nerves.

"We'll have a bit of darkness tonight around midnight," Evans said, "perhaps an hour of it. That's the time to go."

"Let's hope it doesn't turn into a real funeral," Ryder said.

"Not to worry," Evans said. His tone had a note of forced optimism. "I used to do magic shows at school. Rabbits out of hats, disappearing scarves, the whole bloody circus. . . ."

"Were you any good at it?"

Evans frowned, his expression half amused and half serious. "Come to think of it," he said, "not very."

Chapter
45

THE sun was down on the horizon when Ryder came back to the sawmill. The debris in the yard rose, undisturbed, from the pale shades of the approaching evening. He called out from the stairwell.

"*Nadia.*"

She didn't reply, and his nerves bristled at the warning in the silence.

A shadow fell across the stairs from above. Ryder's glance jerked upward, and he saw Balov, his pistol drawn, step into view.

"Welcome to Archangel," he said.

The railing stopped moving under Ryder's hand. The front sight of Balov's pistol held steady on his chest. He could appreciate the simple physics of chamber pressure and muzzle velocity that would blow his sternum to bits.

He said, "You're a long way from Moscow, Valery Vasilyevich. Did you get lost?"

"Temporarily," Balov said. "But don't worry, we'll both be back before the snow flies."

"Will we?" Ryder was already thinking about the knife

inside his boot. The leather sheath, taped to his calf, formed a perfect image of itself at the core of his concentration. If he could get close enough to the man with the pistol... But Balov would be too experienced to let that happen.

"Come up, Anton Stepanovich, and take care what you do with your hands."

In the room where Ryder had left her, Natasha sat on the floor, her mouth taped and a scarf tied around her eyes in a blindfold. Serova stood behind, pointing a small-caliber pistol at the back of her head.

Balov said to Ryder, "Before I search you, there is something you should know. If you make even one dangerous move, Serova will shoot. You can see where the pistol is aimed."

Ryder glanced at Serova. The cold composure on her face only confirmed the homicidal promise. He faced the wall, his muscles tensed, but the pistol, a few centimeters from Natasha's head, left him powerless. He could feel the opportunity slipping away even as Balov's hand moved gingerly and expertly over sleeve and collar, around the waistband, down one leg, down the other. The fingers hesitated above his boot, then lifted the knife from its sheath.

Balov stepped back and said, "Turn around."

In the long shadows of the room the men faced each other.

"You could practice a little true socialism," Ryder said, "by giving me a cigarette."

Balov tossed him a packet. Hertzogovina Flowers—Stalin's brand.

"And a Marxist match," Ryder added.

"Take care the smoke doesn't turn you into a communist."

Ryder lit the cigarette and smiled. "I'll pretend it's a Woodbine."

Balov smiled too. His own reflexes were comfortably

taut. It seemed to him that the melancholy Canadian was most dangerous when relaxed and smiling.

"What a lot of trouble you've put us to, Anton Stepanovich," he said.

"I thought it was every citizen's job to guard against idleness in the workers' paradise. I've only done my bit."

"You'll be compensated for it."

Ryder grinned around the cigarette and said, "Buried in the Kremlin wall?"

"Somewhere east of it," Balov said. "Several thousand kilometers, I should think."

"See they don't put any cheap proletarian verse on the headstone, will you?" Ryder said, and his glance took in the stairs and the room's solitary window.

Balov smiled again. He knew exactly what the Canadian was thinking.

"You are wondering," he said, "if it's possible to make a run for it. Will I kill you? The answer is no. But I'll stop you with a bullet. In both kneecaps, if necessary."

"You have a way," Ryder said, "of taking the joy out of travel."

"Please don't force a practical demonstration."

"Don't worry," Ryder said with a low chuckle. "I've never fancied the sight of blood. Especially when it's squirting out of me."

"Good," Balov said. "We understand each other."

"We've always done that, Valery Vasilyevich."

"In the end," Balov said, "perhaps too well."

Ryder drew on the cigarette. He glanced at Natasha, who remained motionless, her back straight, the blindfold tight across her eyes.

"In Lubyanka," he said to Balov, "you made me an offer."

"You should have taken it."

"Maybe I'll reconsider."

"Too late," Balov said. "Time ran out. I warned you it

would." He shook his head in a sad, reflective way. "Remember the stone lions? Anton Stepanovich, you were right. Between men and lions there can be no covenants, and it's the same now with you and me."

"It was always that way," Ryder said.

Balov nodded and said with a smile, "If you'd gotten clear of the port, I'd be on my way back to Stalingrad. It's not so pleasant there now."

"No more parks and pretty girls?"

"Only advancing Germans."

"Too bad," Ryder said. "The parks in London don't suffer from that shortcoming. Just pretty girls. You'd like English-women. Even Marx had an eye for them."

Balov laughed and said, "Are you testing my incorruptible nature?"

"That would depend."

"On what?"

"The value you put on it."

"The value in loyalty?"

"The value in pounds sterling," Ryder said. "You can't deposit virtue in a Swiss bank. Only hard currency."

"Wouldn't I be a victim of capitalist exploitation?"

"That sounds like a Party slogan. Think of it. You wouldn't have to endure any more of that simpleminded rhetoric."

"But look!" Balov protested. "Here's poor Katya. Assuming you could negotiate away all my principles, what would we do with her?"

Ryder gazed at Serova. Above the loose smile on his mouth his eyes were flat, without pity.

"Shoot her," he said.

Balov tipped back his head and laughed.

Serova frowned and said, "Why must you laugh?"

"He's only joking," Balov said.

She looked at the Canadian. "Is he?" she said.

Ryder said to her, "Think of Valery Vasilyevich. You'll

be cooperating in the noble cause of a comfortable old age for him. Why don't you make the sacrifice?"

The smile twisted a little deeper into Ryder's mouth. Among the four of them Serova was the real killer. She would squeeze the trigger of the handgun touching the back of Natasha's head and would feel neither pleasure nor regret. He could remember the same absence of expression on her features the night they had pulled the driver from behind the wheel of the van. The blue hole in his cheek would have come from a small-caliber pistol—like the one in her hand now.

"You see?" Balov shrugged. "What's the use of talking? She can't be persuaded. Self-sacrifice isn't in her nature. Anton Stepanovich, please finish your cigarette."

"Listen," Serova said, turning her head sharply.

They heard the drone of planes, a formation of Junkers-88 twin-engine bombers coming in low out of the west over the White Sea.

Sirens wailed over the port, joined by the *choom-choom-choom* of antiaircraft batteries, but the roar of the planes only grew louder. In seconds bombs were falling on the nearest docks and warehouses. They whistled out of the sky, and the concussion from each explosion shook the room.

"Down . . . under the staircase." Balov waved the pistol. He said to Serova, "Get the blindfold off her."

He had to shout to be heard above the hammering drone. The walls shuddered and plaster sifted down as more of the big SC-250 bombs struck the railhead. Both men stopped on the stairs, their heads craned upward. The earsplitting whistle of another descending salvo seemed to hang over them forever.

The explosions came fast, one after the other, across the yard. The joints of the building gave a sickening wrench. A blinding orange flash sucked the air out of Ryder's lungs while the blast tore away the fragment of a woman's scream.

The blast...

Ryder stirred on the ground. He couldn't hear the planes for the ringing in his head. Dust and smoke billowed around him, lifting a stench of burned cordite into the air.

A dozen meters from Ryder, Balov staggered away. Incredibly he still gripped the pistol. He wiped a sleeve across his eyes. The drifting smoke took his figure.

Did Serova still have the pistol too? Ryder didn't know. He couldn't risk Natasha's life. Crouched low, he bolted toward the railhead.

Near the incinerator lay the body of Grigorenko's man. One arm was blown off, but the pistol was still in the shoulder holster strapped below the stump.

Skirting the craters of scorched terrain, Ryder passed within a few meters of the corpse and gun and saw neither.

"Anton Stepanovich!" Balov shouted.

A second wave of planes in tight formation drowned out the warning. Ryder looked back and saw Balov down on one knee, the pistol extended in both hands. He didn't hear the shot in the thundering roar of aircraft, but he saw the recoil as the gun jumped. Dust spurted near his feet. He cut behind the gutted ruin of a kiln where lumber had once been seasoned.

From the kiln it was a short sprint to the standing boxcars in the rail yard. The ground raced underfoot and the cars came up fast. He ducked under a gondola, slid down the ballasted embankment, and kept running.

A train rolled toward him as he ran. The engine chugged slowly around a curve past the signal tower. Beyond it, near the warehouses, a boxcar loaded with munitions took a hit. A fiery bubble swelled outward. Ryder flung up both arms as the explosion rocked the yard. The debris surged up, hung on the sky, and came down.

He saw Balov, behind, on the cinder embankment. From the west three aircraft roared low over the rail yards on a strafing run. Balov dove beneath the wheel carriage of the gondola. Ryder dropped flat. In the sky the planes had appeared slow. At low level they screamed past, their machine guns tearing long suture marks from the ground.

Ryder looked down the track. The engine was much larger now, coming straight on. He pushed up on his hands and sprang across the rails in front of its *tramp-tramp-tramp*, then raced away from the cars grinding past.

The raid was over. The planes were circling to the northwest. He saw the formation of wings, dark against the mother-of-pearl twilight, and the puffs from the flak bursts. Black smoke billowed from the docks into the stratosphere, and many smaller fires burned in the rail yard. Behind him, the train that had been moving stopped.

In the compound beyond the tracks he blundered into a dead end. The blood was blocked up behind his heart, his lungs could no longer process enough oxygen, and sweat poured off his face. On either side of the lane the roofs made an unbroken line against the sky. A few defiles between warehouses and packing sheds ran nowhere. He knew Balov must be close behind. He rattled the door of a net repair shop. *Latched from inside*. He stripped off his coat, wrapped it around his fist, and smashed out a pane.

The shop was dark. Shadows reached to the rafters. A loft ran out over the main floor. The swinging doors in the rear were chained. He thought there must be a way out over the roofs and mounted the ladder to the loft.

Nets were slung over rope lines stretched beneath the ceiling beams. They were the heavy nets used by fishing trawlers in deep water, and the ropes sagged under the weight.

From the front of the shop came the crunch of broken glass. Ryder froze. His eyes ransacked the dark for a weapon. He could find nothing but a small bait knife stuck, haft down, in a ceiling timber. It would only be effective at close quarters—if at all. He yanked it from the wood, anyway, and flattened back against the wall.

Below, on the shop floor, Balov's shadow slid half into view. The imprint remained stationary. Finally it advanced a little more—one, two, three steps—and Balov's head and shoulders materialized past the edge of the loft. The pistol made a dull gleam in his hand.

Ryder groped overhead in the dark for the rope supporting the big trawler nets. He sawed at the braided thickness with the bait knife. He could feel the hemp strands splitting, one by one, under the blade.

Suddenly Balov withdrew. The knife froze in place on the rope. The loft ladder shook. Balov was climbing up.

Ryder slashed a cork float from the nearest net and tossed it toward the shadowy clutter at the rear of the workshop. The soft *thunk* arrested the jerking of the ladder.

Once more the head and shoulders glided into view on the shop floor.

"Come out," Balov said.

Ryder stared down at the broad back and could remember the ease with which Balov had lifted a fifty-gallon drum of cement outside the Komsomol gymnasium in Stalingrad. He thought, *I can't take a chance with him.*

"Anton Stepanovich," Balov called out to the shadows, "there's no more time for our game."

No more time, Ryder thought, and drew the blade sharply across the last straining fibers of rope. He had a glimpse of Balov whirling and lifting an arm as the falling nets crashed down on him, knocking him flat.

Ryder dropped into the mountainous heap of meshed cord. In the next instant he had a hand clamped into the back of Balov's collar and the knife blade under his chin. But there was no need. Balov's head had hit hard against the cement and he was unconscious. A patch of blood gleamed in his scalp. His breathing was shallow but steady, and a pulse still throbbed at the big artery in his neck where the blade remained poised to slash.

Some of the tension in Ryder unlocked, and he relaxed his grip on the limp figure. He didn't want to kill Valery Vasilyevich—not if he could substitute a less lethal form of discouragement.

A thin darkness hung over Archangel. In the rail yard work crews were already taking up damaged track and sifting through debris. The dull scrape of shovels against cinder beds rose on the evening. In the confusion of hectic activity Ryder slipped back to the sawmill.

The blast had taken out the upper floor of the offices. Only the shell of the outer walls remained. He climbed the slanting heap of wreckage and squinted into the shadows.

He found Serova first and struggled to lift the beam pinning her in the debris. Then he realized it made no difference. Her neck had snapped, and the hemorrhage from her lungs left a shining clot of blood in her open mouth. Her eyes were wide, and the grey distances that he had seen the first time in them were now dilated and fixed where no one could follow.

He heard a sound, a whimper, from the rubble.

"*Nadia!*" he called out, and tore at the debris. A section of tin from the roof came loose, and he flung it away. Farther back in the shadowy pocket a white arm moved and the pale outline of a face took shape.

Ryder squirmed through the opening and crawled back to her. The same timber that had crushed Serova had saved Natasha. His fingers struggled clumsily with the knot holding the gag in place.

"Don't try to move. I'll get you out."

He dug away the jam of rubble until she was no longer trapped. But when he put an arm under her, she cried out in pain.

"It's no use, *Tosha*, I can't move."

"You've got to!"

She drew in a breath and winced, shutting her eyes tightly against another spasm. Her fingers on his arm squeezed with a gentle pressure.

"Just leave me," she pleaded in a whisper, "before someone comes."

Her skin felt clammy and cold, and he was sure she must be going into shock. The sudden possibility that he might lose her, after all, was like something black and heavy descending on his spirit. But no, he couldn't believe it would happen. It was altogether beyond comprehension. Not twice—with German bombs.

"Put your arms around my neck, *Nadia*. I can pull you out."

"I can't move my left shoulder at all."

"Then use your right arm."

"It's numb all the way down. I can't feel anything except a burning kind of pain."

"Probably just a pinched nerve," he said. His own voice now had a desperate urgency, as if it were joined to some intravenous flow of alarm that mounted a little all the time and could not be disconnected.

"*Tosha*," she whimpered, "listen..."

"We don't have far to go. You'll have to stand the pain, *Nadia*. There's no other way."

"But if they see you carrying me..."

"They'll think you were hurt in the air raid. We can get by in the confusion."

The perspiration stood out in heavy, cold drops on her face, and the intensity of the pain drove her to cry. The tears fell silently, involuntarily.

"*Tosha*...please...go without me..."

The alarm was gone from his nerves. Or perhaps it had turned to despair. If he were caught again... But that consideration needn't apply. He had Balov's pistol. If he couldn't get her out, it would only take one bullet in his own temple to close the file on Grey Wolf.

Ryder touched her face. For all the thoughts of death racing through his mind, his fingers on her cheek were full of gentleness. He smiled at her and said, "Remember that little girl you told me about? The one who went down the hill on the sled with her father? The one who laughed when they overturned in the snow? Well, I fell in love with her, too, and I can't go away and leave her." His other hand slipped into his coat pocket. The fingers closed briefly on the pistol, like a promise on an unwitnessed contract.

Chapter
46

B ALOV came to consciousness slowly, like a patient coming out of chloroform. Sensations of sound and touch returned first. He couldn't move his hands. They were bound behind him. Electrical tape held a gag in place. He opened his eyes to find himself dangling above the floor in a fishing net. The slugging pain inside his skull reached all the way into the socket of one eye.

The first thought to get past the hammering ache was that the Canadian must even now be trying to board a British ship. But how?

Balov strained at the cords binding his wrists until rope burns formed on the skin. Finally he gave up. It only sapped his strength and made his head worse.

The rope from which the net was slung went up into the dark. It looped over a rafter and slanted down again at a forty-five-degree angle and was tied fast to a post beneath the loft.

The night slipped by—impossibly slow for the man in the net. It seemed an eternity before the first grey light seeped into the workshop. Objects took shape. Toward the rear the shadows melted from an overturned boat resting on blocks. The hull was smashed in. The damage appeared to have been done some time ago. The nets looked old too. Perhaps the place was deserted, after all.

Later a dusty vane of daylight beamed down toward a pair of whaling harpoons. They stood on end, the iron barbs resting high up on the wall. If he could reach them...

Balov used the weight of his body to put the net into motion. The floor rocked back and forth beneath him. Each time, as he picked up momentum, the wall flew closer. It spun back, flew close, spun back....

The harpoons were behind him. Neck craned, he could see the barbed points sweeping into view. They were less than a meter off, and he shoved hard with his feet to alter the trajectory of the net.

Twice he came close. His fingers, outside the corded mesh, grazed the shaft. At last he managed to snatch it, but the lower end banged against a table as the rope carried back through its arc. The harpoon was torn out of his grasp.

Balov cursed. The net slowed. The muscles ached in his shoulders from holding his neck in one position.

He had to keep a calm frame of mind and address the simple physics of the problem. The weight and mass of the harpoon... the path of travel... the obstacles...

Once more the rope creaked against the rafter as he thrust the net into motion. A dozen times he swung within centimeters of the harpoon. It teased his outstretched fingers, but he deliberately held back. He couldn't risk a miss. He waited until the straining muscles in his neck were on fire, then snatched the shaft and twisted it away from the floor. This time nothing jarred it from his grasp as he waited for the rope to slow.

Both cutting edges of the barb were sharp, and he worked

them upward until they were snagged in the net. By the time he relaxed his fingers, the sweat was pouring off his face. Several minutes passed before he could begin sawing through the cords binding his wrists.

Chapter
47

DRAWN by reindeer, the cart rolled slowly from Norway House to the wharf where the destroyer HMS
Jaguar was berthed. First Lieutenant Evans, acting
for the SBNO, walked beside the four coffins.

Several crewmen waited at the gangway to bear the dead
aboard. But the Soviet marine, standing guard, motioned
them back. In the red-striped shirt and black beret, his rifle
at the ready, the marine made a picture of glowering de-
termination.

Evans drew a paper from his jacket.

"These are dead seamen from *Hartlebury* and *Empire
Byron*," the British officer said in atrociously accented Russian. "This paper gives us permission to put the bodies
aboard. It's signed by your port authorities."

"*Nyet.*" The marine shook his head.

Bloody hell, Evans swore silently. The silly Siberian bug-
ger was going to hold things up. Probably couldn't read,
either.

"You don't understand. This ship is ready to put to sea.
It's only waiting for these coffins. I can't help it if you

didn't get orders. My instructions from your port authorities are to get the bodies on board. I intend to see that it's done."

Evans hoped to bluff his way past. But the marine would not budge, his brows crimped together in an obstinate scowl. He jerked his rifle bolt to the rear, then forward, seating a round in the chamber.

"Nyet!"

Two feet away the muzzle dropped level with Evans's belly. The ugly front sight cut through the language barrier. Clearly, if the crewmen tried to lift the coffins from the dray, it was the officer who would be shot. Evans had a grisly vision of his own bloodied viscera scattered over the quay. The click of the shell driven into battery had sent a sick spasm through him. It left a bit of sour gorge in his throat.

"You are delaying a Royal Navy destroyer under combat orders. If this paper isn't authority for you, then call someone who can make a decision."

Despite the morning coolness, Evans found himself perspiring. He blamed it on the cartridge waiting to take his guts out through his liver. Turning away with the best of British nonchalance, he glanced up at *Jaguar*'s bridge. The captain and first officer stood at the rail, their figures aloof and rigid on the sky. At least they had the sense to stay out of it, knowing interference would only arouse more suspicion.

The longer the delay, Evans thought, the greater the risk of discovery. The anxiety condensed itself into moisture on his palms.

It was another twenty minutes before Boris Grigorenko from State Security appeared. A heated discussion broke out—this time in English.

"Look here." Evans thrust the permission document into the reluctant grasp of the NKVD officer. "We've had this written order for twenty-four hours. The bodies were recovered from hospital last night. They've been at Norway House, waiting for the coffins."

"Something has developed in the meantime." Grigorenko folded the paper and handed it back. "We are involved at the moment in another matter. Orders sometimes have to be changed."

"But this ship is sailing. We can't wait to obtain a new authorization. There's a war on, you know."

"We know it quite well," Grigorenko replied. "The Soviet people know it perhaps even better than the British. Better than your Mr. Churchill."

"Has it occurred to you that the chaps in these coffins were serving the Soviet Union too? In the end it cost them their lives. I should think they've paid the price for passage home. Or doesn't that count for anything?"

Grigorenko flushed. The flesh-colored warts stood out whitely in the blotched cheeks. A nerve jerked at the corner of his mouth. He said, "I will look inside the coffins. Then you can put them aboard."

'What you are saying to me," Evans replied, "is that the word of a British officer counts for nothing."

Grigorenko said to the marine, "Give me your bayonet."

"No, let me have it." Evans had a hand on the coffin that held Ryder. "I'll open it myself."

"I will open it," Grigorenko said. "They are Russian coffins."

The NKVD officer circled the dray, choosing a different box from the one Evans had touched.

Another wave of panic left Evans sick. The properties of that fear dulled his memory so that he suddenly couldn't recall the order of the coffins. Under his jacket sweat left his shirt congealed to his body.

Calloway, he thought. Where is Calloway?

Grigorenko worked the point of the bayonet under the lid and pried upward until the nails wrenched loose. The Rus-

sian lifted the top free and unzipped the body bag. The face
of the dead seaman had a waxy film, like the slick exuded
by a dead fish. The eyes were closed, the mouth wired shut.

Evans's nerves worked furiously to absorb the panic loose
in them. At fifty-fifty the odds had held. Now they were
reduced by two-thirds. The percentages no longer favored
the house.

"I think you should understand," Evans said hotly, "that
His Majesty's Government will strongly protest what is tak-
ing place here. Do you insult your Russian dead this way?
Or is it reserved for allies? I hope for your sake, Comrade
Grigorenko, you're prepared to accept full responsibility.
You'll be answering to Moscow. I can promise you there
will be a formal inquiry straightway."

The bayonet hovered over the second coffin. Evans believed it contained the girl but couldn't be sure.

"I rather think," he said, "that even our German enemies
would treat the dead less disrespectfully."

Calloway! Where was that bloody Calloway!

Grigorenko hesitated, his neck darkly flushed. The nerve
at the corner of his mouth jumped more rapidly. He inserted
the tip of the blade under the second lid.

There was a shout from the end of the wharf. A figure
ran toward them. He wore an officer's tunic and pistol belt,
and his boots pounded hollowly against the boards of the
wharf, the holster flapping against his side despite a steady-
ing hand.

The officer was a lieutenant, one of Grigorenko's people.
In rapid Russian that Evans could barely follow, he blurted
out a story, pausing only when Grigorenko interrupted with
curt questions. *A Britisher, fitting the description of the man
they were after . . . caught trying to sneak aboard the other
British destroyer in port . . . claiming to be British seaman
. . . not in uniform . . . no identification . . .*

"What name does he use?" Grigorenko snapped.

The lieutenant handed his superior a torn slip of paper on which he had scrawled the name.

The flushed anger on Grigorenko's face deepened into something like furious jubilation.

"It appears," Grigorenko struggled in English, "that the person we have been searching for has been taken into custody. He was arrested trying to get aboard the other British destroyer. He claimed to be one of the crew."

"Wasn't he carrying identification?" Evans said.

"He claims it was lost." Grigorenko smiled, holding out the scrap of paper. "He claims his name is Michael Manion."

"Well," Evans said, "I'm sure it bloody well is."

"All crews are restricted to their ships. What was he doing away from his ship?"

"Probably looking for a woman," Evans said. "What else?"

"Out of naval uniform?"

"I daresay," Evans replied, "he wouldn't have gotten very far wearing one."

Another figure, this one with the insignia of a Royal Navy sub-lieutenant, came toward them at a jog-trot. This was Niles Calloway, the officer junior to Evans on the staff at Norway House. He gave a splendid impression of vexation, not altogether a counterfeit, for he had been delayed getting to the wharf. Now he drew Evans off to one side, away from the Russians, and cupped a hand to his ear while whispering excitedly. Grigorenko watched, frowning, and the conversation he could not overhear went like this.

"Calloway, you bloody fool, you were supposed to be standing by. Did you fall into your usual damned torpid state?"

"They stopped me three times for a check."

"He's opened one of the coffins. It would have been over for us if that Russian lieutenant hadn't come round and done the job you were supposed to do."

"I'll bet my quid against your guinea that we all go out of here in a box before it's over."

"Shut up, Niles, and give it your best grave-and-guilty look."

Evans strode back to the dray while Calloway stood apart, looking grave and guilty, as charged.

"I think you will find," Grigorenko said, "that the man who calls himself Michael Manion is not an ordinary seaman missing from his ship."

"Bloody nonsense," Evans said. "What else could he be? Because a poor sod of a sailor absents himself from ship's company in civvies and turns up without ID, do you think that makes him a spy?"

"That is exactly what I think," Grigorenko said.

"This is pure flaming cock," Evans said, throwing up his hands. "I expect you believe in Father Christmas too. See here, I've got to get these coffins aboard. I would appreciate it if you would finish your search—under protest, of course."

The bayonet was still under the lid. Grigorenko glanced at his lieutenant, whose face had lost none of its excitement, and some of that tension seemed to communicate itself in a sudden contagion of impatience. The senior NKVD officer sighed and withdrew the blade.

"Take them aboard," he said to Evans. Then, with a wooden smile that seemed to serve no other purpose than to play out the game, he said, "I assume I have your word . . . a matter of honor . . ."

"How can I give my word?" Evans said with an air of acid restraint. "The coffins contain spies. Sailors who jumped ship and went off to look for a rutting time somewhere."

He watched Grigorenko and his lieutenant hurry away. The relief unlocked a spasm of shaking in his lower legs. Thank Christ. It was a prayer of gratitude, not a curse. In truth, Michael Manion *was* Michael Manion, a leading signalman from the other destroyer escort. Evans had chosen him for his physical resemblance to the Canadian, black hair, pale eyes bordering on blue, and a six-foot frame. Only the Irish dialect lacked complicity in the impersonation.

"I cannot too well disguise my speakin' voice, sir," the Irishman had said.

"If they don't identify you as the wrong man right at the start," Evans had replied, "perhaps you can play off it. With a bit of luck they might think you're faking it."

It had been far more difficult getting him off the ship after dark—half expecting the rubber dinghy to be shot out from under them—than it would be to put him back aboard once the KGB verified his cover story. They might even come to believe his balls-and-crumpet tale. The Irish were splendid liars. Evans himself would lead the search, with Grigorenko, to recover the lost billfold and ID from the place where it had been planted. Then Grigorenko would catch a rocket. Wouldn't he, though? Evans thought, Thank Christ for the Irish—the bastards!

HMS *Jaguar* had cleared the harbor by twenty minutes when Balov reached Grigorenko's headquarters. He looked at the Irishman, crimson-cheeked and sullen on a bench between two guards, and said, "That's not the man."

"But—" Grigorenko choked, then could only add a weak, "Comrade Colonel..."

"Have any allied ships left port since daybreak?"

"A destroyer," Grigorenko said. "Under combat orders from the British Admiralty."

"Nothing went aboard her?"

"Four dead bodies. Battle casualties from the last convoy. We knew about them. The ship had official permission to take the coffins aboard."

The color drained from Balov's face.

"I was there myself," Grigorenko assured him. "I checked the authorization."

"You opened the coffins?"

"I opened one," Grigorenko said, and began to stammer. "I-it contained a dead British seaman."

"And the other three?"

Once more the nerve was out of control at the corner of Grigorenko's mouth.

"I had the word of the junior British attaché. . . . Besides, he was going to open the others himself. I thought . . ."

Balov stared at the other man, not wanting to believe any of this, yet knowing it must be true.

"You're a fool," he snapped.

Chapter
48

BELOW, in the infirmary, the ship's doctor examined Natasha. Ryder translated his instructions and the girl's responses. Finally the doctor called for twenty milligrams of morphine, injecting the right deltoid muscle. For the second time tears spilled down Natasha's cheeks. But now they came with the release from pain.

"Broken pelvis. Collarbone, too, I'd say. Swelling in the left metartarsal region—could indicate a fracture. Multiple contusions, severe to moderate." The doctor paused in his charting to look at Ryder. "You say you had to carry her?"

"Yes."

"I'm only wondering how she kept quiet."

"She passed out twice."

The doctor shook his head. "Lord, they're a tough lot, these Russians."

Ryder turned back to the girl on the examination table. Perspiration beaded her face. He used a damp cloth to wipe the glaze of moisture from her skin. Under the narcotic her eyelids were already heavy.

"You won't leave me?" Her dark head moved slightly on the pillow.

"No, *Nadia*." He took her hand and smiled down at her.

In a short while sleep overtook her. The curled fingers relaxed in his hand but did not let go. The antiseptic smell of the steel cabinets reminded him of another infirmary, another bedside, a face under gauze wrappings.

But that experience seemed utterly far away. It receded across a vast distance he couldn't follow, and the fingers still gripping his hand seemed to hold him firmly in the present. It was, after all, where he now belonged.

"You'd better sleep too," the doctor said. "Give you a sedative, if you like."

"Thanks, no. But I could use a wash-up. Some clean clothes..."

Shaved and showered in the officers' wardroom, he felt duly resurrected from the dead. A brisk knock sounded at the bulkhead door, and a sub-lieutenant stepped in.

"Captain sends his compliments, sir. He'd like to see you on the bridge."

"Tell him I'll be up."

"I'll escort you, sir. First time aboard, bit dicey finding your way about."

In dungarees, bulky sweater, and sea boots, Ryder followed the officer topside. HMS *Jaguar* was steaming at twenty-four knots to the north around the Kola Peninsula. She was one of the new single-funneled destroyers of the "J" class, sleek and fast, and her armament included six 4.7-inch guns, one 4-barreled pom-pom, two quadruple machine guns, and ten 21-inch torpedo tubes.

The captain, a stocky Yorkshireman named Avery, had both elbows on the rail and his binoculars up. "I thought you ought to know," he said to Ryder, "that we have some uninvited guests."

"Coming for tea?"

The glasses came down, and Ryder observed that the blunt, humorless features were not amused.

"Have a look for yourself." The captain handed him the binoculars.

Two Soviet gunboats were bearing down on *Jaguar* from astern. Each dragged a long slash of froth behind its screws.

"Can we outrun them?"

"Doubtful," the captain said. "In any case we can't outrun that chap upstairs."

Overhead, a Stormovik bomber made a slow, wide circle against the sun.

"Number one," the captain said to the first officer. "Better sound action stations. I doubt they're after a tot of rum." He gave Ryder a resentful glance. "Or tea."

The first officer barked the order into the voice pipe. Alarm bells shrilled below. Figures spilled into view from ladders and hatchways. Reports of stations at the ready came back through the voice pipes.

The first officer reported: "Action stations closed up, sir!"

The two gunboats, *Pskov* and *Razin*, closed to within eight hundred meters. *Pskov* remained, trailing, at that distance. *Razin* pulled abreast of *Jaguar* off the starboard bow and signaled with a blinker light.

The captain spoke to his leading signalman on the bridge. "What does she say, Evans?"

Another Evans, Ryder thought, smiling. Two in one day. To Evans, the amateur magician on the quay, he would award full marks—except for allowing Grigorenko's fat posterior to cover the air hole drilled in Ryder's coffin while the NKVD officer had worked to pry the lid from the other one. What an inglorious finish it would have made—suffocating in a coffin while Grigorenko's backside served as the deus ex machina of history.

"Getting it now, sir," Leading Signalman Evans replied. "They want *Jaguar* to heave to. Asking to board her."

Ryder said to Captain Avery, "Don't let them."

The Yorkshireman scowled back at him. Clearly the prospect of a confrontation didn't please him.

"Right," he said to the signalman. "Make to her: Sorry. Can't oblige. Proceeding to sea under combat orders. Speed essential."

The signalman flashed the message on his lamp. There was no reply, but this time the gunboat sheered toward them, drawing alongside within hailing distance. Crews manned the deck guns of the Soviet craft. Ryder lifted the binoculars. The faces of the *Razin*'s bridge jumped into the glass eye-pieces. One of the group was Balov. It was Balov who raised the megaphone and shouted in thickly accented English to the *Jaguar*. "You must put your ship about—back into port. The waters ahead in the strait have been mined. Your charts don't show this. You will need a Soviet escort. You must put about for Archangel."

"He's bluffing," Ryder said.

"What makes you so bloody sure?"

Once more the megaphone from *Razin* blared across the water. "These are Soviet waters. You are under Soviet authority here. I order you to change course and put about."

"What do you propose for a reply?" the captain said.

"Tell him to get stuffed," Ryder said. "I assume there's a polite nautical term for it."

"And if they fire on us?"

"You'll have to blow them out of the water," Ryder said, "in the best tradition of Nelson."

"I believe you're serious."

"Don't I appear to be?"

"If you think they aren't capable of firing on us, you're dead wrong," the captain said. "I understand the Russian mentality."

"Do you, Captain?" Ryder said. "That's good."

"Look here," the British officer said. "I have to rely on

what you tell me. It comes down to this: I have no idea what your mission was. Is protecting it worth risking the lives of the ship's company—and possibly losing a destroyer in the bargain?"

"This one," Ryder said, "and five more like her."

"Yes." The captain nodded. "It had better be."

He switched on his loud-hailer.

"Many thanks," he shouted, "for the caution. We'll keep a sharp watch for mines. My sailing orders can only be countermanded by the British Admiralty. If there is a compelling reason for *Jaguar* to alter course back to Archangel, suggest you coordinate with Senior British Naval Officer, North Russia, in Polyarnoe. The order will have to come through channels."

Ryder heard the metallic snap of the charging handle from the heavy fifty-caliber machine gun mounted on *Razin*'s afterdeck. The gunner fired three short bursts, splitting the air with a *choom-choom-choom* as the fiery tracers licked across the bow of *Jaguar*.

Captain Avery snapped orders. The 4.7-inch guns of the destroyer traversed to target. The aft turret swung to pick up the second gunboat. *Pskov*, which had been trailing eight hundred meters astern, closed to two hundred meters. A tense silence fell over the decks of *Jaguar* and *Razin*. The Stormovik bomber still hung lazily on the sky.

Captain Avery had a Yorkshireman's bristling tenacity. He would not be pushed. Once more he switched on his loud-hailer.

"We have a war to fight," he said laconically. "I should much prefer to sink Germans."

On the bridge of the *Razin*, Balov towered over the other men. He was clearly in charge. The tanned face strained intently through some cold appraisal. He might have been studying a chess problem—the utility of sacrificing a rook for a knight. Or would they adjourn to stalemate? It was Balov's decision.

The megaphone in the oversize hand came up slowly. It seemed an interminable time before his voice cut calmly across the narrow interval where the sea ran in glinting whispers and the bomber's distant drone beat back against the silence.

"Captain," he called. "Tell your passenger . . . I'll look for that girl we once knew . . . in Stalingrad."

The captain gave Ryder another hard glance.

"Did you know him?"

"I knew him," Ryder said.

"Better hope there's nothing bigger than a gunboat between us and the Barents Sea." The captain bent to the voice pipe and barked to the wheelhouse: "Full ahead! Steer to port ten degrees."

The gunboats fell back in the creamy wake of the destroyer. Ryder lifted the glasses. He had a final glimpse of Balov staring after them. The megaphone still dangled at arm's length. His blond hair was blowing in the wind, and the smile curled into his mouth was something no one would ever decipher. Perhaps he was thinking about the lions.

Above the Kanin Peninsula the lead-colored seas pitched the mast of *Jaguar* into a gentle roll. Ryder stood alone on the fantail and stared at the receding coast of Russia. It hung on the horizon, half formed like the purple of a moon in daylight. His cupped hands raised a match to a cigarette.

Those who are truly Russian will always come back to die. . . .

He could remember Krylov's sad smile that morning in the timber below the train as they watched the sun lifting across the frozen marshes of the White Sea.

Did it change anything—anything at all? In the splendid vanity of power only Cleopatra's nose would matter. But perhaps honor would justify the delusion a little . . . and there would always be soldiers' music on another street, sometime, somewhere. . . .

Captain Avery appeared on the fantail. He gazed hard at the Canadian, but his stare had no trace of its earlier hostility. Mixed in it now were curiosity and some obscure respect. He waved a pink message form.

"Signal from Admiralty. Most Immediate. You have some exalted friends."

Ryder unfolded the cipher. Terse and cryptic, it read: "SOVIET PREMIER URGING AUGUST MEETING MOSCOW VIA TEHERAN WITH PRIME MINISTER UK. AS REGARDS OPERATION GREY WOLF, CAN YOU STATE WHETHER USSR HAS IN POSSESSION EVIDENCE WHICH COULD BE USED TO EMBARRASS OR COERCE HIS MAJESTY'S GOVERNMENT SHOULD AUGUST MEETING TAKE PLACE?"

The lettering across the pink sheet faded into an image of a frozen pond outside Leningrad, a wolf clumsily shot leaving blood in the snow, and a boy's tears.

"Downing Street," the captain said. "He'll want an answer straightway."

Ryder squinted once more at the coast streaming away in the cigarette.

"Tell him," he replied, "the grey wolf said nothing. . . ."

Historical Footnote

WESTERN sources document two attempts on the life of Josef Stalin. The first—a shooting—occurred near Adler in the Caucasus in 1930. The second involved a Soviet officer and took place in 1942 in Moscow.

But what about the undocumented attempts? The power struggles? The mass extermination of "reactionary" enemies? They can only be the basis of fascinating speculation. State Security files bulge with plots against Stalin. How many were fabricated? How many were real?

The Yezhovshchina, the great purge of 1937–38, claimed 7 million victims. Some 35,000 career officers, more than half the officer corps, were imprisoned or executed. The senior ranks were hardest hit. Three out of five marshals were shot. The general officer grades lost 90%, while 80% of the colonels met a similar fate. Was Stalin's fear of a military coup real or imagined?

In the fall of 1952 the Chief of the Kremlin Medical Directorate was removed from his post. Nine Kremlin physicians were imprisoned, accused of a conspiracy to assassinate prominent members of the Party and the Red Army. The doctors were allegedly in league with British Intelligence. State Security, under Stalin's orders, had spent a year preparing the case. Stalin's death in 1953 ended the charade. Or was it a charade? Stalin's paranoia about enemies everywhere may indeed have had some basis in fact. The world can only wonder.

In the dark days of the German advance on Moscow a curious incident has been recorded. During a session attended by Averell Harriman and Lord Beaverbrook, a preoccupied Stalin is reported to have "doodled"—drawing numberless pictures of wolves and filling in the background with red pencil.

As to the other characters in the novel . . .

A. N. Poskrebyshev, head of Stalin's personal secretariat, vanished the night of Stalin's death. There are conflicting reports surrounding his disappearance.

Lieutenant General Nikolay S. Vlasik, chief of Stalin's Guard Directorate, fell from favor in 1952. A three-man Party Commission, formed to identify and eliminate wasteful practices in State Security, eliminated Vlasik and several key department heads instead. Dismissed from the Party and assigned as deputy chief of a labor camp in Sverdlovsk, Vlasik was soon thrown into prison where he died. Lavrenty Beria headed the commission.

Lieutenant General Andrei A. Vlasov, one of the few talented officers surviving the great purge, took command of the Second Shock Army early in 1942. By June the abandoned army was encircled and starving. The trapped forces were under constant attack from ground and air. Each time Vlasov radioed for help, he was told to press the attack. Finally the general ordered his surviving men to destroy all equipment, break into small groups, and attempt to escape.

Stalin's insistence on no retreat had cost nearly 100,000 men.

A German patrol came upon Vlasov in a farmhouse near Siverskaya. At Lotzen, the German Headquarters in East Prussia, his story took a bizarre turn. Vlasov raised an army of Soviet defectors (the ranks would eventually swell to more than 100,000) and joined the Wehrmacht to liberate Russia from Stalinism. At war's end he surrendered to U.S. forces in Czechoslovakia. He was returned to the USSR, tried for treason, and shot.

Marshal Georgy K. Zhukov's immense popularity disturbed Stalin even before the war was over. In 1944 Zhukov was placed under the "protection" of the Guard Directorate. Outwardly comparable to Secret Service protection of top U.S. political figures, it had a different purpose for Zhukov. He realized belatedly that his "staff" had been installed to monitor his activities, rather than protect him.

In 1946 the Marshal was abruptly reassigned from his occupational command in Germany to a minor post in the Odessa Military District. But Odessa was too public a place. After a short period he was again transferred—this time to command the remote Ural Military District in Sverdlovsk. He remained in obscurity until Stalin's death.